THE CHARITY OF A VISCOUNT

LINDA RAE SANDE

Twisted Teacup
PUBLISHING

Early November, 1818, Stanton House, Mayfair

"I'm not a bad person. Really, I'm not," Mary Baker said as giant tears streamed down her face.

"Of course you're not. No one is saying you are," Mrs. Barstow said in hushed tones, rather dismayed the housemaid was weeping. "But you cannot keep doing this. If I catch you again, I will have to let you go," she added, attempting to be as stern as possible with the petite housemaid. In all her years as housekeeper of Stanton House, she had never had to dismiss a maid for being caught *in flagrante delicto.*

Mary's eyes widened in fear. "Oh, please no. I'll be very good, I promise," she wailed.

Mrs. Barstow rolled her eyes. "It's that being 'very good' that has you in this mess to begin with," she countered, not exactly sure if that was really the case. But the enthusiasm the girl exuded as the household's tallest footman tupped her in one of the guest bedchambers suggested she was quite experienced in carnal matters. "I know you are not the one to blame, but you also know as well as I do that *you* will be the one let go before Harrison dismisses any of the footmen," she warned, referring to the butler.

How could he? The footmen of Stanton House were the envy of every other house in Park Lane. The late Mrs. Batey had seen to that before dying in the childbed after having given birth to her third babe. Since she never expected to be a viscountess—and she never was—she had thought to at least have something about which to be proud.

Handsome footmen filled the bill.

Her head dipping, Mary sighed and then sniffled. "It's not fair," she whispered. All the footmen in Stanton House were tall and handsome. Virile. Friendly, too, and ever so willing to oblige her when she needed assistance. "I just needed help with the coal buckets."

The housekeeper blinked. "Coal buckets?" she repeated. "Whatever do *coal buckets* have to do with this?"

"Well, everything," Mary replied as one of her hands swept the air. "They're the reason I've been having to service the footmen."

Mrs. Barstow closed her eyes and silently prayed for guidance. "I am going regret asking this, I am quite sure, but can you please explain yourself?"

Mary sighed. "When they're full, the coal buckets are too heavy for me to lift and carry up the stairs," she explained.

"You can take them up half-full and merely return for more," the housekeeper argued.

"Oh, I used to do that," Mary replied with a nod. "But then one of the other maids accused me of taking too much time in transporting the coal buckets up the stairs, seeing as how I had to make two trips instead of just the one, and then Rodney—he's one of the footmen—"

"Yes, I'm well aware of Rodney," Mrs. Barstow murmured with a roll of her eyes. The very tall footman was far too handsome, what with his ginger-colored hair and bright blue eyes, and he knew it.

So did every other female under the roof.

And in Park Lane.

"—He saw me struggling with the full bucket, and he offered to carry it up for me."

Frowning, Mrs. Barstow was about to comment on how considerate it was he would make such an offer, but then she soon realized what was about to come.

The bargain.

"In exchange for something, no doubt," the house-keeper said on a sigh.

"How did you know?" Mary asked in awe.

Mrs. Barstow gave her a quelling glance. "Because I'm *old*, and because I see what these footmen get away with just because they're too good looking for their own good," she replied in disgust. "So... just the one tumble then?" she asked, attempting to clarify whatever arrangement the two servants might have made with one another.

"One for every day he—or whichever footman—helps me. It's the least I can do," Mary replied with a shrug. "I don't mind a bit, especially since it seems to make them happy. And me, as well."

"You do realize you're... prostituting yourself?" Mrs. Barstow asked in shock.

Mary shook her head. "Oh, no. Haven't done that since my days as a harlot over at Mrs. Gibbons' brothel in Covent Garden," she replied, just before her eyes rounded. "I probably shouldn't have mentioned that. It was my first position. Well, not *that* one, but as a housemaid," she went on, despite how Mrs. Barstow's hands had lifted to her ears and covered them while her face took on an expression of pain.

Mary sighed again as her shoulders slumped. When the housekeeper dropped her hands, she added, "I'm not taking any blunt from the footmen," she whispered. "I'm just thanking them for their help, is all."

"They're helping because they have an expectation of recompense!" Mrs. Barstow countered. Fighting to keep her patience, she asked, "What happens when you find yourself with child?"

The housemaid's lips formed an 'o' as she shook her head. "I wouldn't let that happen. I saw to it the footmen all have French letters," she argued.

Thinking she should feign a fainting spell, Mrs. Barstow decided instead to learn how this was possible. Rumor had it French letters were expensive. Illegal. And rare. "I rather doubt that," she challenged.

"I had some from the brothel. The girls there don't like gettin' diseases, and neither do the men, so they make the customers wear—"

"Yes, well, that's to be commended," the housekeeper interrupted, deciding this conversation had gone on long enough. She had menus to plan and arrangements to make on behalf of her employer, Marcus Batey, Viscount Lancaster.

"Please don't dismiss me."

Allowing a rather long sigh, Mrs. Barstow realized a discussion with Harrison, the butler, would be required. "Then don't do it again," she warned. "Why, when Mr. Harrison learns of this, he might require you to *marry* the man."

Mary frowned, wondering why the housekeeper made that option sound so bad. Well, depending on just which footman she would be required to marry, she supposed. She wouldn't mind being married. Then she could engage in sexual congress as often as her husband was willing.

"I won't say anything to his lordship," the housekeeper continued, "but if it happens again, I will have to."

Mary Baker lowered her eyes and allowed a nod. "Thank you, Mrs. Barstow." The housemaid finally stood and gave a curtsy before taking her leave of the housekeeper's small office, her shoulders slumped and her eyes once again filled with tears.

"*D*id she fire ya?"

Mary lifted her head to find Rodney looming over her. The Irish-born footman had probably been standing outside the housekeeper's office the entire time she was with Mrs. Barstow. How much had he overheard?

Mary shook her head, which had the collected tears streaming down her cheeks. "Not this time, but she will if she catches us again," she whispered, deciding not to mention that she was in danger of being caught with any one of the four footmen under employ at Stanton House. She had engaged all of them in sexual congress in exchange for their help on any number of occasions.

And not just for carrying buckets of coal.

Rodney dared a glance at the housekeeper's office door and pulled Mary down the hall a ways before saying, "I am sorry," he murmured. "Not sorry about what we was doin', but sorry about gettin' caught, I mean," he whispered.

"From now on, I have to carry my own coal buckets," Mary said, just before she sniffled, ignoring his apology.

Screwing up his face in disgust, the footman shook his head. "No, you don't."

"If you do it for me, you'll have to do it for all the other housemaids," she countered, the back of a hand wiping away tears. "Without expectation of recompense," she added, careful with how she pronounced the words, especially since she wasn't completely sure what they meant. "Mrs. Barstow said she was going to speak with Harrison. He'll be watching you." He would be watching the other footmen, as well, which meant she couldn't carry on as she had been with any of them.

Rodney considered her comment. "Or the four of us can carry all of your buckets every day," he offered.

Mary's eyes rounded, her suspicion evident. "They'll be expecting something in return," she replied with a shake of her head. "And the other maids aren't like me."

"Fast, you mean?" Rodney teased.

Mary gave him a quelling glance. "See if I ever let you tup me again," she said on a huff. "Pity, too, because I rather like your tumbles," she added.

"Me, too," Rodney replied. Disappointed, he gave a shrug and left her pressed against the hall wall.

Mary watched him go before she allowed her tears to flow freely. "Bastard," she whispered.

Chapter 1

AN EVENING AT WHITE'S PROVES ENLIGHTENING

Later that night

Three viscounts and a bank clerk sat regarding their glasses of brandy, each one deep in thought.

"I believe I would like to take another wife," Marcus Batey, Viscount Lancaster, said just before he drained his rummer. "I miss being married."

The bank clerk nodded his agreement. "Until a few months ago, I didn't realize how much I needed a wife," Theodore Streater said. "I adore my new wife. In fact, I am wondering why it is I am here instead of at home with her."

The man to his left boggled. "Because you agreed to join me for a drink," George Bennett-Jones, Viscount Bostwick, replied with a hint of offense. "I, too, adore my wife, but I thought I should remind the others here at White's that I am still a member and make an appearance for propriety's sake." He paused and then furrowed a brow. "And you've been a member for several months. 'Bout time you made another appearance."

The youngest viscount regarded the other gentlemen and gave a shake of his head. "I am not married. I have no desire to *be* married. And I am not missing anyone on this fine evening," Luke Merriweather, Viscount Wessex, announced proudly. He regarded his brandy with a frown, though, and set it on the nearest side table.

The other three gazed at him in disbelief. "You have no idea what you're missing," George replied, his head shaking in disbelief.

"No idea," the bank clerk chimed in.

"I miss my wife," Marcus agreed. "So much so, I have decided this is the year I shall find a new bride."

The other three regarded him with raised eyebrows, wondering if the man realized that 'this year' was just about over.

"Spoken as if you might already have one in mind," Luke accused.

Marcus angled his head first to one side and then the other. "Perhaps," he teased. "I have held a particular woman in high esteem for... for a very long time," he admitted on a sigh.

Too long, in fact. He would have taken her to wife twenty years ago if she hadn't already been betrothed to another. Betrothed to a man who only wanted her because Marcus wanted her first. Well, that spiteful earl was dead now, and his widow was surely done with mourning.

"A particular woman?" George repeated. "Do you wish to share her name so that we might help you in this endeavor?" He knew Viscount Lancaster had been a widower for two years, his wife having died in the childbed. At least his spare heir had been born alive and was nearly two years of age. A nurse was seeing to the tyke's welfare as Lancaster's heir attended university. His daughter, Analise, had completed two years of finishing school and was old enough to make her come-out. She would do so at Lord Attenborough's ball later this week.

"I do not, as I do not yet know if she is even here in the capital," Marcus replied, his words a bit of a white lie. Actually, he knew she was in London, but he didn't want these other gentlemen to know the target of his secret admiration.

At least, not yet.

George regarded him with a dubious expression. "Spoken as if you really *do* know her whereabouts," he murmured, loud enough for only the older viscount to hear.

Marcus dipped his head and angled it in George's direction. "Perhaps," he hedged.

"Then let us hope she has an invitation to the Attenborough's ball," George replied.

Furrowing a brow, Marcus gave a visible shudder. "The very ball where Analise will be making her come-out," he said on a sigh.

This bit of information seemed to interest Viscount Wessex. "I shall be sure to ask her to dance," Luke offered. "That is, if her dance card isn't already full."

His eyes widening in alarm, Marcus seemed tongue-tied for a moment. "Perhaps I should be considering a convent for her," he murmured.

George was about to laugh at the older viscount, but thought better of it. He had a daughter that would one day make her come-out, too. Sixteen years was a long time into the future at least. He hoped he still might possess enough skills with a sword to defend her honor should it become necessary. "If she's like most young ladies, she won't accept a marriage proposal her first Season out," he said, hoping to assuage Marcus's fears.

"There's that," Marcus agreed, relaxing for the first time in several minutes. He noted the stricken expression on Teddy Streater's face and straightened. "You look as if you..." He was about to say "might faint," but thought better of it. "Are you feeling poorly?"

Teddy shook his head. "All this talk of daughters has me hoping it's a boy."

Three pairs of eyes blinked at the bank clerk.

Then George's eyes widened, as did those of the other two viscounts. "It?" George repeated in alarm.

Nodding, Teddy lifted his brandy and drained it. "Daisy is with child," he announced. Saying the words aloud had his shoulders rising, as if a giant weight had been lifted from them.

A chorus of "huzzah" replied to the announcement, drawing the attention of several nearby card players.

"I was going to tell you on the piste this afternoon, but I couldn't decide just how," Teddy said apologetically, his comment aimed at George.

"If I had learned it from someone else, you might have found yourself skewered," the viscount accused, although he did so with a wide grin. "At least I know how you'll be spending your evenings."

All three of the men regarded George with interest. "Oh?" It was Marcus who responded, but Teddy leaned forward in his chair.

"Do tell," the future father insisted.

"Foot rubs, of course," George replied with a shrug, as if they all should have known the answer. "And they can be done one-handed," he added with a nod to Teddy. The man might have been missing most of his right arm, but that wouldn't preclude him from seeing to his wife's swollen feet for the rest of her pregnancy.

Luke and Marcus exchanged glances. "I knew that," Marcus said in his own defense.

"And now I suppose I know, too, although I rather doubt I'll have use of the information any time soon," Luke said with a shrug. "Maybe mention it to my brother by marriage." His younger sister, Eleanor, was married to Charles, Earl of Wakefield, and she was expecting a child next spring.

The word of a certain young woman's come-out at the next ball had Luke's interest piqued, though. He may not be in the market for a wife just yet, but he could certainly window shop.

When the glasses were empty, the four gentlemen took their leave one by one until only Marcus was left. He might have gone at the same time as Lord Wessex, but he was lost in thought, and the younger viscount decided to simply leave him to ruminate.

*T*he comment about foot rubs had Marcus thinking of his younger son, the two-year-old probably asleep in the nursery at Stanton House. A twinge seemed to grip his heart just then at the thought that he wouldn't have another opportunity to perform such a simple task for a wife.

Unless he did find a new wife.

And got a child on her.

When Marcus Batey considered taking his leave of White's, he knew exactly who he wanted to fill that role, even if he hadn't given a thought to her feet.

Now that's all he could think about.

Spotting Lord Attenborough among those who were playing whist, he decided he would wait until the gentleman had completed his game and have a word with him. Mention that a certain widow had recently returned to London. Suggest she might have been left off the guest list. Ensure an invitation was sent.

Then he would see to it she danced with him—at least one waltz.

And he would do his very best to see to it he didn't step on either one of her feet.

Chapter 2

A POSITION IS ONCE AGAIN OPEN

The following afternoon, at Bostwick House, Mayfair

Ever the attentive husband, George Bennett-Jones, Viscount Bostwick, knew something was amiss when his wife returned from an afternoon spent at her charity's office. Elizabeth usually shot through the vestibule and hurried up the steps to the nursery, anxious to greet their young son, David, and daughter, Christina. After a few minutes in their company, she would seek him out and bestow a kiss on his cheek and perhaps his lips if he managed to keep her in his company longer than a few seconds.

On this day, she made her way to his study and leaned against the door jamb in a manner suggesting she needed the solid wood to remain upright. The expression on her face made it apparent tears were imminent.

"Whatever has happened?" George asked as he stood and rushed to pull her into his arms. She smelled of jasmine and wet wool, and her small stylish hat was dotted with drops of water as was her hair. That was the moment he realized it was raining. At least outdoors.

Her tears hadn't yet started falling.

"Mrs. Burton has given her notice," she replied on a sigh. "Her last day is Friday." Elizabeth's eyes brightened even more.

"Did she give a reason?"

Elizabeth nodded. "Because she's marrying on Saturday." A tear escaped the corner of her eye and left a wet trail down the side of her cheek before George could reach up with a thumb to gently brush it way.

"Isn't she already married?"

Elizabeth gave him a quelling glance. "Widowed." She sighed again. "This is the fourth matchmaker to leave my employ since I started 'Finding Wives'," she complained, her shoulders slumping beneath his hold.

"But is she marrying one of your clients?" George asked gently.

"Well, yes," she acknowledged with a nod. "There is that."

George closed his eyes, not exactly surprised another of a long line of matchmakers had quit his wife's charity, 'Finding Wives for the Wounded.' The three before Mrs. Burton had all ended up married to old fogies for whom they had been contracted to find suitable wives.

He often wondered if they took the position for the sole purpose of finding a suitable husband for themselves. Being a matchmaker allowed them to discover nearly everything there was to know about a man, after all. Class and economic status, close relatives, maladies. "So, your charity is a success. You cannot be too disappointed."

"If I wasn't feeling so very tired, I might actually feel gladness for Mrs. Burton," Elizabeth murmured.

George took that opportunity to kiss his wife, capturing her lips with his own to see to it her mind might move to more pleasant thoughts, such as *why* she was feeling so tired. He knew why—the first two babes who had managed to exhaust his perpetually active wife were upstairs in the nursery. Since she hadn't shared news of another babe on the way, George wondered if *he* would have to be the one to tell her she was expecting their third child.

Better he do so when she wasn't quite so melancholy.

"Would you like me to place an advertisement for a matchmaker in *The Times?*" he asked gently, when he finally pulled away.

"Advertisement?" she repeated, her eyes glazed over as if all thoughts of her charity had left her head.

George grinned. "I'll see to it straight away. In the meantime, perhaps you'll want to pay a call on the nursery," he suggested. A grin split his face just then, happy to know his kiss seemed to have cleared up any sadness she was feeling. "Maybe tell those two hellions there is another devil on the way?"

Elizabeth blinked twice, her head seeming to waver a bit before he reached out a hand to her cheek to steady her. "On the way from where?" she asked in confusion.

Chuckling, George placed the flat of the same hand against her belly and then leaned down to nibble on an earlobe. "From the same heavenly place from whence *they* came," he whispered.

Her eyes widening in understanding, Elizabeth stared at her husband. "How did I not know?"

George allowed a shrug. "And here I thought you were keeping secrets from me," he replied as he arched a brow.

Shaking her head from side to side, Elizabeth finally allowed a grin. "How long have *you* known?"

Angling his head first left and then right, George wondered if he should tell her the truth. And if so, what timeline he should mention. It had been at least a month. Maybe two.

He didn't have to say anything, though, when Elizabeth's eyes widened even more. "That long?" she cried out. She frowned before she blinked a few more times. "Does father know?"

"Oh, he knows," George said with a nod, remembering how David Carlington, Marquess of Morganfield, regarded his daughter when she nearly fell asleep during the soup course the last time they had been to Carlington House for dinner.

"And mother?" Elizabeth whispered in dismay.

George frowned. "Not sure about her," he replied with a shake of his head. "But I doubt it. She was too excited about your brother's return to London the last time we had dinner there," he added.

Indeed, Adeline, Marchioness of Morganfield, could barely contain her excitement at learning Christopher Carlington, Earl of Haddon and heir to the Morganfield marquessate, would be back in London after having finished his studies at university. The missive containing the news had been delivered mere moments before dinner commenced that evening.

Which meant there would be another young buck in attendance at the next *ton* ball.

"Do you think my brother knows?" Elizabeth asked, allowing George to keep her propped up.

"I rather doubt it." He reached down and captured the

back of her knees against one arm and lifted as he leaned her shoulders against the other arm.

"What are you doing?" she asked, her arms quickly wrapping around his neck.

"Taking you to the nursery. I think it's time you took a nap, and who better to take it with than your children?"

Elizabeth sighed. "A nap sounds perfect," she agreed.

She was asleep even before he reached the top of the stairs.

*B*ack in his study a few minutes later, George pulled a sheet of parchment from his desk and put pen to paper.

Position for the perfect matchmaker. Busy office seeks a woman to match eligible bachelors with women seeking husbands. Experience preferred, but not required. Hours negotiable. Apply at 30 Oxford Street.

George wondered if he should include a mention that the eligible bachelors were still unmarried because they had been wounded in the wars and weren't of a mind to attempt courting of their own accord. He thought better of it, though, before addressing and folding the advertisement. A good matchmaker would know to make a man think it was *his* choice to court a woman. To make him believe he was doing the chasing until the woman caught him.

Or perhaps it was the *woman* who was doing the chasing and the *man* who caught her.

George blinked, deciding he would leave thoughts like

that to a matchmaker. And for whomever she made matches.

Dripping melted wax and then pressing his seal into the dark red puddle, he regarded the advertisement a moment before calling for a footman to deliver it to the newspaper offices.

With any luck, it would run in the following day's paper. With even more luck, a matchmaker of some skill would see it and appear at the charity's office in a day or two.

Although he had some experience in matchmaking—George had seen to it his best friend ended up with a duke's daughter as his wife—George didn't want the responsibility for anyone else.

He knew first-hand matchmaking was hard work.

But then again, if circumstances required it, he might be available for just one more match.

Chapter 3

NEWS OVER BREAKFAST
IN BED

The following morning, Wadsworth Hall, Westminster

"Do you think you'll ever wear this again?" Thompkins asked as she held a black bombazine dinner gown over her arms. Decorated with tiny jet beads at the edge of the high neckline and around the deep cuffs of the long sleeves, the gown's style was still current with respect to fashion.

Charity, Dowager Countess of Wadsworth, looked up from the latest issue of *La Belle Assemblée* and regarded her lady's maid before her attention went to the gown in question. She shuddered. "Never," she replied. "Put it with the others," she instructed, furrowing a brow when she noticed how large the pile of widow's weeds at the end of the bed had grown.

Why she hadn't seen to cleaning out her dressing room the Season before when her year-long mourning period had ended—or before she had made the move from Suffolk to London last June—Charity wasn't sure. But now that her aunt was newly widowed and had discovered her funds were limited—Uncle Robert had apparently been a poor gambler—Charity thought it the perfect time to do so.

Thompkins added the gown to the black fabric mountain at the end of the bed. "Would you like to dress now, my lady? There are a few gowns left in your wardrobe."

Although she had finished a cup of chocolate, Charity hadn't yet made a move to get out of bed. As diverting as she expected London to be after all those years in Suffolk, she had no place to go and no plans to pay calls on anyone that day. "I think not. In fact, I believe I shall take my breakfast in bed," she said, setting aside the journal. "Give us a chance to finish clearing out every bit of black and see to it the trunk is packed and delivered to Aunt Lydia before this day is done."

Thompkins allowed a nod. "I'll see to it right away, my lady," she said as she made her way to the bedchamber door.

"Oh, and have *The Times* brought up when it arrives," Charity ordered, "And any posts that might have come this morning."

Blinking at her mistress's unusual request, Thompkins dipped a curtsy and hurried out of the bedchamber.

Left alone for at least fifteen minutes, Charity settled back into the mountain of pillows at the head of the bed.

She could just imagine what the few servants of Wadsworth Hall might be saying about her. After nearly two years of living the quiet, predictable life of a widow of the aristocracy, Charity had decided it was time she do something unpredictable.

Breakfast in bed.

What other activity could she pursue that would have their tongues wagging? A ride in the park perhaps—on a horse rather than in her barouche? A glance at the issue of *La Belle Assemblée* had her cringing when she remembered her riding habit was probably five years of out of date.

Perhaps she could host a card party. Invite the ladies who paid calls on her back before her husband's death. Except she really didn't enjoy whist all that much, and card parties tended to result in disparate conversations and whispered gossip that didn't always favor the hostess.

The fingers of one hand absently traced the outline of a collarbone and she winced. Although her son was doing his best to seeing to the expenses of Wadsworth Hall, keeping the pantry stocked was becoming a challenge. She had been opting to forego formal dinners in favor of simpler fare so that there would be enough food for the servants, and breakfasts had been reduced to toast and an occasional egg.

She was considering a trip to the British Museum when Thompkins returned to her bedchamber with a breakfast tray, the newspaper, and three posts.

"A footman just delivered this one, my lady," Thompkins said as she held out what appeared to be an invitation. "Wore the Attenborough livery, he did," she added, an eyebrow arching in approval.

Impressed Thompkins would even know the colors of the Attenborough livery, Charity realized her lady's maid was probably seeing one of the Attenborough footmen on her day off. "Should I open it first, do you suppose?" she asked as she glanced at the other posts.

In the middle of folding one of the black gowns, Thompkins paused. "It's an invitation to their ball."

Charity blinked and then realized the footman must have mentioned the nature of what he delivered. She broke the wax seal and read the engraved card, wondering how the Attenboroughs had even known she had returned to the capital. "Rather thoughtful of them," she murmured, noting the date was just a few days away.

The Attenboroughs had obviously just learned of her return.

"Will you go?"

"I will," Charity replied, hoping one of her ballgowns wasn't too terribly out of fashion. She opened the other posts, pleased to discover the Attenboroughs weren't the only ones who knew she had returned to London.

She, of course, would write to accept the invitations to Lord Attenborough's ball and Lady Morganfield's *soirée* in honor of her son's return from university, but she decided to decline the opportunity to ride in the park with a viscount.

This last invitation had her experiencing a brief moment of feeling flattered, but then she noted the name at the bottom and felt only confusion.

Viscount Lancaster?

She wasn't even sure if she knew the current 'Viscount Lancaster'. He was probably some randy, ne'er-do-well young buck who had no idea she was...

Charity blinked and glanced up from the invitation to ride.

There wasn't a randy, ne'er-do-well young buck in the family because Charles Batey, Viscount Lancaster, had never fathered an heir. His dowager viscountess, Elise, had been left in London whilst Charles spent his days and nights at his hunting lodge with a string of mistresses.

Or, at least, that's what *The Tattler* implied with its frequent articles on the matter.

Poor Elise.

Or not. She was a Burroughs, after all. Even if Elise

had never remarried, her brother, James, Duke of Ariley, would have seen to her protection. He adored his youngest sister.

Charity gave her head a shake, finally remembering that Charles Batey, the former viscount, had died the year before. His younger *brother* had inherited the viscountcy.

She struggled a moment before finally pulling the brother's name from memory.

Marcus.

Well, at least Marcus wasn't a randy, ne'er-do-well buck, either. He was married. Father to two sons as well as a daughter who was probably on the verge of her come-out.

Charity blinked.

Why would a married father of three invite me to go for a ride in Hyde Park?

There was that moment of confusion followed by real-ization, then alarm, and finally disbelief.

He intends to offer carte blanche!

Charity seethed with anger, incensed anyone would expect her to warm their bed now that she was a widow and done with her mourning.

How dare he!

Was this Lord Lancaster like his older brother? Having *affaires* with other widows? Carrying on with a string of mistresses?

There was one way to find out. The gossip rags kept track of such information.

Thinking she might be in possession of the latest copy of *The Tattler*, Charity reached over to the nightstand and rifled through the precariously-stacked journals. While searching several of the weekly news sheets for any mention of a Lancaster, she found an article confirming

Elise, widow of Charles Batey, had married Godfrey Thorncastle, Viscount Thorncastle. Everyone in the *ton* knew Godfrey had held a candle for Elise Burroughs Batey almost his entire life, so this was good news.

Checking the date on the issue of *The Tattler* she held, she rolled her eyes. It was from last May!

Well, so much for old gossip.

She perused several more issues in search of any news of a Lancaster. She finally located a brief obituary of Mrs. Marcus Batey. *Joan Harrington Batey.* The daughter of an earl, Joan had died giving birth to a son. Besides her husband, she left behind a son, Andrew, a daughter, Analise, and the baby, John.

Charity checked the publication date and rolled her eyes. The issue was nearly two years old!

Besides cleaning out widows weeds, it seemed it was time to weed out old gossip rags as well.

Charity swallowed and dared another glance at the invitation for a ride in the park, determining from the simple signature that it was from Marcus Batey. Her earlier anger dissipated. He was a widower, and he had been for nearly two years.

She wondered if the younger son was still alive. He would be about two now. The age at which he would test his nurse and his lungs, display his stubbornness, and attempt to create pall mall in every room of the house. Charity knew because she had given birth to two of them. Thank the gods they were grown.

Despite his youth—he was barely eighteen—the Wadsworth heir, Benedict, had taken his seat in Parliament with the session that had just begun. In the meantime, he had been seeing to the business side of the earldom and apparently ruffling some feathers as he did so.

He expressed a desire to be more hands-on in the running of the earldom, eschewing the advice of his late father's man of business with the claim that said man had nearly bankrupted the earldom.

Benedict had not asked for advice from his mother, and she didn't expect he would. She offered her assistance and took relief in learning he would call on her if he was in need of anything. He assured her she could live in Wadsworth Hall as long as she wished while he lived in one of the earldom's small townhouses close to Parliament.

Her youngest son, Benjamin, had just started university in Oxford. His fascination with the heavens above had him spending his nights staring through the long tube of a telescope. She supported his hobby, hoping his evening pursuits wouldn't be redirected to something more earth-bound, like a harlot. Apparently Benedict was satisfied with his brother's choice of education, since he was seeing to his housing and allowance.

One of the late earl's mistresses was not treated so kindly. She was summarily dismissed without so much as a bauble and informed she was to vacate her leased town-house at the end of the contract

Of the other, she hadn't heard a word.

Charity wondered from where her son's opinion of the two women had been formed. She had never said one word of her husband's infidelities to anyone. However, she remembered quite clearly how Benedict had stared at her when he paid a call in Suffolk last May. *When was the last time you ate anything?* he had asked, his brows furrowed in worry.

She had been stunned to realize her weight loss was noticeable, an unfortunate side effect of having lived on meager rations the past few years. The Wadsworth earldom, at one time a thriving business concern, had suffered under her husband's lack of attention—his man of business had probably been embezzling—and his tendency to spend too much on his mistresses. With the coffers nearly empty, her allowance had been slashed, most of the servants had been let go, and Charity simply adapted to a life of less.

Your collar bones are showing, Mother.

The reminder of that particular comment had Charity wincing, her fingertips moving to trace the line of those bones through the fabric of her night rail. Despite there being a bit more in the pantry these days, she was still forced to be careful with expenses and had only a skeleton staff for Wadsworth Hall. Although the house might have one day been a fashionable abode—perhaps the century prior—it was no longer.

Turning her attention to *The Times*, Charity was considering just what unpredictable something she might do that day when she found her gaze perusing the postings at the back of that day's newspaper.

Position for the perfect matchmaker. Busy office seeks a woman to match eligible bachelors with women seeking husbands. Experience preferred, but not required. Hours negotiable. Apply at 30 Oxford Street.

Leaning back in the pillows, Charity considered the sentences in reverse. *30 Oxford Street* was a familiar address. That's where Lady Bostwick housed her charity, 'Finding Work for the Wounded'—and her other charity, 'Finding Wives for the Wounded'. Charity knew this because her solicitor, Andrew S. Barton, Esquire, had his office right next door.

Her eyes rounding, Charity realized two things at once. First, the latest matchmaker for 'Finding Wives for the Wounded' had obviously found a husband for herself and then given notice. Probably one from among the wounded men for whom she was supposed to find a mate.

And second, the position didn't require experience.

How hard could it be? Charity wondered. Matching women to men? What did it matter if those men had scars from the wars? From Charity's experience, if a woman was in the market for a husband and couldn't find a suitor from among her contemporaries, she would take what she could get.

Tearing the advertisement from the paper before quickly finishing her breakfast, Charity had her plan in place for the day.

Get dressed, which might take an hour depending on how long Thompkins fussed over her hair. Take a ride to 30 Oxford Street, which might take an hour, depending on traffic. Apply for the matchmaker position, which might take ten minutes. Or more if she caught Lady Bostwick in her office.

"Thompkins, I need a carriage gown," Charity announced as she stepped out of the bed and stripped her nightrail from her body. "And the town coach. I'm paying a call on a charity."

Her lady's maid blinked as she added yet another black gown to the pile at the end of the bed. "Yes, my lady," she replied, her eyes darting to one side. "I believe there are two or three left in the dressing room."

Charity sucked a breath between her teeth, her gaze going once again to the pile of black at the end of the bed. Perhaps she wouldn't give up *every* black gown. It wasn't as if she could afford a modiste to replace them.

She could get rid of old journals, however.

"And you can throw out every issue of *The Tattler* that is older than last week," she added, pointing to the pile on her nightstand.

Thompkins regarded the stack of news sheets before turning an expression of surprise on her mistress. "Yes, my lady." Never mind that she could barely read.

Wait until the other servants hear about this!

Chapter 4

A FATHER BOGGLES

eanwhile, at Stanton House

"Can you please repeat what you just said?" Marcus Batey, Viscount Lancaster, said to the dark-haired woman who had arrived at Stanton House with a phalanx of other women equipped with sewing baskets. They had made their way to Analise's bedchamber and disappeared behind the carved wood door more than an hour ago. The viscount's curiosity had him knocking on that same door in an effort to ensure Analise hadn't fainted.

Or climbed out the window.

Madame Suzanne's eyes widened. "Your daughter will require no fewer than three ballgowns, two dinner gowns, two riding habits, a carriage gown, and five morning gowns with matching pelisses or spencers, a mantle, and a redingote," the modiste said, sounding ever so patient. She had no doubt had to do the same for others who employed her to outfit their daughters for a Season and couldn't believe her list of supposedly required clothing.

Even though he was impressed the modiste had

managed to repeat exactly the same words she had said when he asked as to what she was doing with so many gowns and what-not scattered about his daughter's bed, Marcus frowned. He was, truth be told, impressed that she managed to provide *exactly* the same list the second time. "It sounds like the same clothes my late wife was told she needed when she married me," he replied on a sigh.

His gaze went to the gown his daughter was wearing, a cream muslin confection with purple pansies and ribbons trimming the neckline and bottom ruffle. A memory of her mother wearing a nearly identical gown had a lump forming in his throat.

"Oh, that cannot be," Suzanne argued, a slight French accent evident in her words. "A new bride would have required at least three carriage gowns and five dinner gowns."

Screwing his face so it displayed his annoyance, Marcus was about to admit the modiste was right—Joan always had five dinner gowns, replacing them one at a time as the dictates of fashion changed—when Analise tugged on his sleeve. He turned his attention to her and allowed a lopsided grin. "Let us hope you receive an offer of marriage at your first ball of the Little Season," he teased. "I cannot imagine having to do this again next spring."

Analise's eyes rounded. "But—"

"I'm teasing, darling," he interrupted, rather glad to see that the thought of receiving a proposal so soon after her come-out had her shocked, and not in a good way.

"I don't really require two riding habits and five morning gowns," she said in a quiet voice, as if she didn't want the modiste to overhear her words.

"But you shall have them," her father countered.

"You're my only daughter. It's not as if I'll ever have to do this again."

"You will if I don't get married this year," Analise replied, dimpling with her tease.

"That's it!" he called out in a loud voice. "I'm sending you to a nunnery." A huge grin gave away his mirth.

Madame Suzanne couldn't seem to decide if she should smile or frown at her client's antics. One moment, the viscount seemed dismayed at learning what would be required for his daughter's come-out, and the next, he seemed as happy as a lark. "Do you wish me to continue with the fittings, my lord?"

Marcus nodded. "Yes, yes, of course," he replied as he regarded Analise. The familiar cream frock with purple pansies and green ribbons had him imagining his late wife, but he shook away the thought as quickly as it appeared in his mind's eye. "And do be sure her favorite ballgown is ready for Lord Attenborough's ball."

Madame Suzanne dipped a curtsy. "Of course, my lord." With a signal to her seamstresses, the team continued their work on the hem of the cream gown as the viscount took his leave of the bedchamber.

Just outside the door, Marcus leaned against the hall wall and closed his eyes. Before today, he hadn't realized how much Analise looked like her mother. Standing on a box in the middle of the three kneeling seamstresses who were busy hemming the gown, Analise looked exactly the same as Joan had looked on a day they had taken a picnic. He was sure Joan had been wearing that very same gown.

And before his evening at White's with the Lords Bostwick and Merriweather and Mr. Streater, he hadn't realized just how much he *missed* her mother.

Another moment, and he was imagining an afternoon

spent in Joan's company, an afternoon in the park, with a blanket spread out on the clipped lawn in the shade of a maple tree. He had carried a basket filled with their luncheon and a bottle of wine. He was leaning on an elbow, watching as Joan took each item out of the basket and placed it within easy reach.

"Whatever possessed you to suggest a picnic?" she asked as she handed him two glasses and the bottle of wine. A footman had seen to opening the bottle before they took their leave of their small townhouse in Marylebone.

Marcus considered the question, hoping she would tell him the news he was sure she meant to tell him the night before but couldn't when they were interrupted by his damnable brother, Charles. "The weather is fine, and I thought to continue where we left off last night."

Joan nodded. "Before your brother arrived. Was he...?"

"Drunk, yes," Marcus replied in disgust. "But I didn't have the heart to send him home to Elise." He gave a shake of his head. "What I mean to say is that I didn't wish to force his company on her. As you know, I like my sister-in-law very much, and I dislike my brother immensely."

Joan might have felt a pang of jealousy just then, but she knew what he meant. Elise was a duke's youngest daughter, forced to marry Viscount Lancaster because, rumor had it, her father couldn't afford a dowry for her, and Lancaster had agreed to forgo a dowry in exchange for gaining her as his wife.

Her eyes darting to the side, Joan finally nodded her understanding. "Promise me you'll never behave as he does."

Marcus straightened on the blanket until he was

sitting up. "That's an easy promise for me to make," he replied. "I promise I shall never behave like Charles."

Allowing a prim smile, Joan nodded. "Good. Because you're going to be a father before Christmastime, and I shan't..."

Joan's words were interrupted when Marcus reached out and pulled her into his arms. "I knew it. I was sure you were going to tell me last night," he said before he kissed her thoroughly. "I adore you," he added before he kissed her again, oblivious to the nurse and two small children who passed by on the nearby crushed granite path. The poor young woman was attempting to shield the tykes' eyes from the scandalous activities happening beneath the maple tree.

"Marcus!" Joan scolded, when she was finally allowed to come up for air. They had been friends since childhood, but at no point had there been this kind of passion in their union.

But the viscount was digging into a waistcoat pocket, his grin widening as he extracted a small pasteboard box. "Thank you," he said as he gave her the box. "I know it's not much, but I shall acquire the entire demi-parure for you. Eventually. I promise."

Joan regarded him in surprise before lifting the lid from the slim, square box. A gold bracelet festooned with amethysts lay in a perfect circle at the bottom. "Oh!" she managed before she reached out and bussed him on the cheek. "Purple gemstones are my favorite," she whispered as she pulled the jewelry from the box.

"Here. I'll help you with the clasp," Marcus said as he took the bracelet from her, opened it, and wrapped it about her wrist. He secured the fastening and then straightened. "It's perfect with that gown," he murmured, noticing the purple pansies scattered about the creamy muslin fabric.

"Oh, indeed," Joan whispered before she leaned over and kissed him on the lips.

Marcus was in the middle of returning his wife's kiss when his daughter appeared in front of him.

And not as he would have expected just then, all tiny and wrapped in a soft blanket, smelling like a baby and making baby sounds that would have him visiting the nursery more often than he admitted to his wife. But rather as a young lady, her eyes rounded in disbelief.

"Father, you're doing it again," she whispered hoarsely.

Marcus blinked several times, unsure for a moment if he was staring at his late wife or his grown daughter. Analise was wearing the gown with the pansies and green ribbons. "Doing what?"

Rolling her eyes, Analise said, "Daydreaming. You're doing it more and more these days."

Alarmed at her comment, Marcus gave his head a shake. "I am not," he countered.

"Last night, during dinner, you were lost in thought for three entire courses," she accused, her hands balled into fists at her sides.

About to argue, Marcus held his comment when one of her forefingers came up in the very same way Joan's might have to stave off an argument.

"I know because I threw a potato at you during the meat course, and you didn't even notice."

His brows furrowing in disbelief, he was about to say that there had been no potatoes anywhere but on his plate when she added, "It bounced off your arm and landed on the floor. Horace ate it."

His eyes widening, Marcus sighed. "No wonder that

dog was so flatulent this morning. I nearly had to vacate my study," he claimed in disgust.

Analise's eyes darted to the side just then. She wasn't about to admit she had fed Horace her Brussels sprouts. Since her father had been oblivious to the tossed potato, she sorted he wouldn't notice that any other vegetables had disappeared from her plate—other than in the usual manner. "You also ignored my comment about the footman riding the housemaid I saw in the library."

She didn't want to tattle on the servants—the two resumed their work quite quickly after their tumble ended —because they were completely unaware of her presence behind a bookshelf. And seeing how happy they seemed as they engaged in their activity had her hoping she might find such joy in the marriage bed.

"What about the housemaid and the footman?" her father asked, a brow furrowing. Why, just the day before, Harrison had mentioned something about a randy maid, as if it was the young woman's fault that she'd been caught with a footman in the middle of a quick tumble.

Analise swallowed. "It was nothing, really. They didn't know I was in the library, or I'm quite sure they would have chosen a different room in which to... ride one another," she stammered.

Deciding he didn't want to know which housemaid or which footman had been engaged in improper behavior— in the library of all places—Marcus closed his eyes. "I'll have a word with the butler," he said, opening his eyes to regard her for a moment. His gaze went down the front of her frock. "Was that your mother's gown?" he asked, deciding to deflect her attention from his frequent bouts of daydreaming and the servants' amorous activities.

Analise glanced down. "It was," she admitted with

some hesitancy. "I apologize for not having asked, but mother rarely wore it, and Miss Suzanne said it only needed to be shortened—"

"It's quite all right," her father assured her, holding up a staying hand. He had half a mind to ask if there might be others in his late wife's wardrobe that could be reworked for Analise. "Could you just stay there a moment?" he asked as he held up a finger before he suddenly rushed off down the hall.

Analise sighed as she watched her father head to her mother's bedchamber and disappear for a moment. Her eyes widened when he emerged carrying something in the palm of his hand. "What is that?" she asked, meeting him halfway.

"Hold out your arm," he ordered, taking a moment to undo the clasp of the gold bracelet with the amethysts he had given Joan during that picnic long ago. He wrapped it about Analise's wrist and secured it, all the while fighting a lump in the back of his throat. "There," he said as he leaned down and bussed her on the cheek.

Analise stared at the bracelet before turning her gaze back onto her father. "It's beautiful," she whispered. "Was it mother's?" She couldn't remember ever having seen her mother wear it.

Marcus nodded. "A gift to her when she told me she was expecting your older brother. I bought the demi-parure and gave her the matching necklace when she told me she was expecting you." He had intended to give her the earrings when his son was born, but she died before he had a chance.

"Thank you, Father," Analise murmured, her eyes brightening. She was about to ask about the necklace, but thought perhaps it had been buried with her mother. "I shall wear it every time I wear this gown," she added.

"She would like that," Marcus replied, almost wishing he had given her the necklace as well. But he could do that another day. The day she announced her betrothal. Or the day she married. Or the day she bestowed him with a grandchild...

Marcus blinked. And blinked again. Perhaps a nunnery was in his daughter's future. Although seeing her in this gown had him realizing it would be very unfair not to at least allow her the Little Season.

First, the Little Season. Then the nunnery.

Chapter 5

A NEW MATCHMAKER
MAKES HER DEBUT

*eanwhile, at Finding Wives for the Wounded,
30 Oxford Street, London*
Dressed in her very best carriage gown, Charity,
Countess of Wadsworth, regarded the two shingles that
hung above the door to Lady Bostwick's charities.
Although she hadn't lived in London when the first charity
was started, word of its success had reached Suffolk by way
of an article in *The Times*.

Now that the wars had been over for a few years, she
supposed there were fewer applicants seeking employment
and more seeking companionship. If the line of men just
inside the door was any indication, Elizabeth Bennett-
Jones, Viscountess Bostwick, had created another
successful charity.

Winding her way past the former soldiers, Charity
looked in vain for the proprietress. A rather large man
spotted her, though, and his eyes widened. He made his
way in her direction.

"Thank you for coming. We thought perhaps you had
changed your mind," he said as he cleared a path for her

and led her to a desk in the far corner. "Oh, where are my manners? Nicholas Barnaby, at your service," he said with a bow. "And that man over there—" he indicated a shorter man at a desk on the opposite side of the room—"That's Augustus Overby. He sees to taking the initial information so there's not so much for you to have to record. You probably have your own questions you want the men to answer."

Charity stared at the man, realizing two things at once. He thought she was someone else, and that meant the position had already been filled. "I believe you must have me confused with someone else," she said, about to turn and take her leave.

"You're the new matchmaker, aren't you?" Nicholas countered. "Lady B said you would be here today." He leaned over and added, "Actually, she said she *hoped* someone would show up and simply fill the position. You are here, so it's yours if you want it." He straightened and allowed a shrug.

Charity blinked several times. "I thought there might be some *competition* for the position," she replied, her attention going back to the line of men—there had to be at least ten—waiting to speak with Mr. Overby. Three more were in chairs near the desk he had indicated would be hers.

She was about to give her name as Lady Wadsworth, but thought better of it. "I am... Mrs. Seward," she said, deciding the use of her maiden name would keep her from being remembered as the widow of an earl. "So good to make your acquaintance," she said then, offering her hand. "May I ask why it is the position is available?"

Instead of lifting the gloved hand to his lips, Nicholas gave it a firm shake. "We've been through four matchmakers since this charity started," he said on a sigh. "All of them found their new husbands whilst they worked here." This last was said with a hint of pride, as if a marriage made up of a matchmaker and former soldier or sailor was something about which to be proud.

"Am I the only applicant?" Charity asked, once she had determined she was the only female in the place.

"Indeed. And seeing as how you're here and ready to get started..." He lifted his hand and waved toward the desk. "The position is yours."

Charity had half a mind to rush out of the small office and return to her townhouse, climb into bed, and never venture out again. But the expression on one of the men's faces had her reconsidering. Despite the apparent loss of a hand, he looked hopeful. Dressed in a suit of clothes suggesting he was a clerk, he looked like any other young man one might find in an office. In fact, as her gaze swept the others in line, she was surprised to find only two who appeared downtrodden. Poor. Unemployed.

Perhaps they were in line for the other charity.

"Where are the women?" she asked, thinking there should be some in search of husbands.

Nicholas allowed a shrug. "Some days, we see one or two," he replied. "That's the hardest part of this operation. Finding the potential wives."

Furrowing a brow, Charity took another glance at the line of men before she pulled back her shoulders and considered her options. How hard could it be? A few advertisements in newspapers...

She blinked, just then remembering she shouldn't expect all women to be capable of reading, let alone having access to newspapers. She would have to devise a different way to get the word out to unmarried women.

"I'll need a pen and a bottle of ink," she said as she turned her attention back to Nicholas.

"They're on the desk," he replied. "May I take your coat?"

Charity removed her gloves and allowed the tall man to see to her mantle. A moment later, she was seated and introducing herself to the man closest to the desk.

"Roger Weatherby. I am honored to make your acquaintance, my lady," the former soldier said as his hands moved to rest atop his ball-topped cane.

"Likewise. Are you employed, Mr. Weatherby?"

"I am. Valet to Viscount Merriweather. I have a room in his townhouse in South Audley Street."

Charity arched an eyebrow, impressed by the young man's credentials. "Tell me, Mr. Weatherby. What characteristics might you be seeking in a wife?"

The valet took a deep breath. "I was shot over in Belgium. As a result, I have a terrible limp, so she'll have to abide it," he replied. "But otherwise, I am fit. Everything else works as it's supposed to."

Heat colored Charity's face as she considered the young man's words. Was he referring to...? She gave her head a shake. "Tell me about your idea of a perfect wife," she urged.

Roger inhaled and then said, "She would be comely and not too thin. Her hair color should be dark—black, if possible—but I like it long when it's not up in a bun."

"Go on," Charity urged, thinking he was describing just about every unmarried girl in London.

"No older than me. I'm five-and-twenty. And..." He stopped and allowed a sigh.

"And?"

"She should be... *willing*, if you understand my meaning."

Charity blinked. "Oh. In... in the marriage bed, you mean?" she whispered.

"Is that too much to ask?" he queried, doubt in his voice. "I'm not blessed with a good deal of coin, so I don't plan to visit brothels after I take a wife."

Giving her head a shake, Charity realized she might have to amend the questions she had been thinking of asking the women. "Not at all, Mr. Weatherby. Wives should be amenable to the marriage bed. Is there anything else?"

Roger allowed another sigh. "It's all right if she's in service, seeing as how I am."

A spark of hope erupted in Charity. "So, a housemaid or lady's maid?" she asked.

"And not too far away. Wouldn't want her to be employed over in Cheapside or down in Chiswick."

"Of course not," Charity agreed. "Someone in Mayfair." She wrote a few notes on his sheet and then gave him an encouraging smile. "Should anyone match your criteria, I shall send you a note to arrange a meeting," she said, glancing at his form to be sure an address was listed.

The valet finally nodded. "Thank you, my lady," he said before he used his cane to help lift himself from the chair.

"You're welcome, Mr. Weatherby. You'll be hearing from me."

Charity watched the valet as he limped his way to the door, realizing just then that if he hadn't been shot, he would probably already be married and the father of several children.

Another gentleman sat down before her, and soon she was asking him the same sorts of questions.

*F*our hours later, the fingers of her right hand stained with ink, Charity leaned back in her chair and regarded the papers scattered about her desk. Applications, all of them for men seeking wives.

One thing was certain. She would have to send Lord Lancaster a note declining his invitation for a ride in the park on the morrow. Her afternoons would be spent finding wives for the wounded.

She had a thought of where to start the search—many a modiste employed unmarried seamstresses, and nearly every household employed single maids—but she needed a way to reach them.

Word of mouth, she thought just then.

Daring a glance at her chronometer, she thought of the parade of aristocrats that would be descending on Hyde Park in another hour. A parade that would include any number of grooms and other servants.

And weren't they the very best gossips?

Helping herself to a stack of calling cards bearing the charity's name and address, Charity allowed Mr. Barnaby to help her with her mantle before she took her leave of the office.

"Will you be back?" he asked, worry evident in his features.

"I will," she promised, affording him a smile. "I'm off to..." She frowned, realizing she really should pay a call on the charity's founder before pursuing some potential wives. Lady Bostwick deserved to know the position had been filled. "To pay calls." She paused. "Where do you suppose I will find Lady Bostwick?"

Mr. Barnaby checked his pocket watch and grinned. "At Bostwick House, I expect. Probably in the nursery. She's got two bairns, you see."

Remembering what life had been like for her when she'd had two small boys, Charity allowed a nod. "Of course," she replied, deciding it wasn't too late to pay a call in Mayfair.

Chapter 6

MEETING AN EMPLOYER

A half-hour later at Bostwick House

Sitting in a rather indecorous manner on the floor of the nursery, Elizabeth regarded her son's tower of blocks and held her breath. This latest construct was his tallest yet—nearly as tall as he was—his wooden blocks stacked in a haphazard fashion that would result in a wreck of monumental proportions should she so much as breathe on it.

"All done," he announced proudly, his chubby arms rising into the air in celebration.

"It's wonderful, David," she replied with as much enthusiasm as she could muster.

Christina, old enough to sit and watch as her brother built his tower, followed suit with her own arms, her tenuous grip on a stuffed doll giving way as she happily imitated her brother.

The soft doll struck the side of the tower. For a moment, Elizabeth held her breath as the stack of blocks leaned first one way and then another. Just when she thought it would right itself and come to rest in a mostly

45

vertical aspect, Christina giggled, leaned over, and poked her finger against one of the blocks in the middle.

She continued to giggle as the entire tower crumpled to the carpet below. Once again, her arms went into the air in triumph as both Elizabeth and David let out cries of disbelief.

"'Tina!" David complained at the same moment Elkins, the butler, appeared in the doorway.

Elizabeth was sure he was suppressing a grin. How could he not find the scene amusing? Her on the floor with her children, playing with wooden blocks.

"It wouldn't hurt for you to allow just a hint of a smile, Elkins," she chided him.

"Very well, my lady," he replied, a barely-there look of amusement appearing on his potato-like face. "Lady Wadsworth has paid a call. Should I tell her you are out?"

Elizabeth blinked. "Lady Wadsworth?" she repeated in surprise. She knew of the widowed countess, although she had never been introduced to her. "I will see her, of course," she replied. "In the upstairs parlor. Please have a tea tray brought up."

She glanced over at her children. "Mother must see to a caller. You," she reached out to grasp one of Christina's chubby fists. "No more pushing down your brother's blocks. And you..." She gave her son her very best smile. "You must build another tower just as tall," she encouraged. "Perhaps with a larger bottom."

She regarded her position on the floor and felt a hint of relief when she realized Elkins had already made his way to the stairs. He wouldn't be paying witness to her trying to get up from the floor. "But first, you must help me up so I can find Mrs. Foster."

Having helped his mother rise from the nursery floor on a number of occasions, a tricky endeavor when she was round with Christina, David was quick to lend a shoulder. She leveraged herself up from the floor, the pins-and-needles of a leg having gone to sleep causing her to limp for a few steps before she could walk somewhat normally. At hearing her name mentioned, Mrs. Foster, the nurse, was quick to move into the playroom. "Do you need help, my lady?" she asked in alarm.

Elizabeth shook her head. "I'll be fine. These two will be ready for some refreshments soon, I expect."

"I will see to their tea, Lady Bostwick," Mrs. Foster said as she curtsied.

"I will return when it's their bedtime," Elizabeth promised as she leaned over and kissed the tops of her two children's heads. About to take her leave, she couldn't help but notice that the nurse elected to sit in the rocking chair rather than on the floor.

Wise woman.

By the time Elizabeth made it to the parlor—she had stopped in the mistress suite to shake out her skirts and dare a quick glance in the cheval mirror—her leg no longer felt as if it were a dead limb she was dragging about. She paused on the parlor's threshold, gratified to find a tea tray had already been delivered. One of the maids was seeing to a cup of tea for Lady Wadsworth while another delivered a plate of biscuits. The servants both curtsied and quickly took their leave of the parlor. Elizabeth was left to wonder by herself why the countess had paid a call.

"Lady Wadsworth, so good of you to call," Elizabeth said as she breezed into the parlor.

Charity stood up from the settee and moved to join

her by the door. She dipped a curtsy to match Elizabeth's. "Call me Charity, please."

Elizabeth's eyes widened. "Then I am Elizabeth Bennet-Jones. I don't believe we've ever met." The two shook hands.

"I apologize for arriving so late in the afternoon," Charity said as they made their way to the upholstered furnishings set up around the low table on which the tea tray sat. "I've arrived without so much as an appointment," she added as she regarded the younger woman. She knew Elizabeth couldn't be older than five-and-twenty, and she displayed a glow that suggested she was enjoying her role as a viscountess—and a mother.

"Your arrival is most fortuitous. Would you believe me if I told you I've been sitting on the floor of the nursery playing with my babes for the past hour?" Elizabeth asked, shaking out her skirts as if to reinforce her claim.

"I would, if only because Mr. Barnaby made mention of you spending this time of the day with your children," she said. "I admit to a bit of jealousy at learning you have a daughter. I only ever had sons."

Elizabeth's eyebrows arched. "Did he now? Well, I'll have you know my daughter just managed to destroy a most impressive tower of wooden blocks—built by my son —with a single push of one of her little fingers," she replied. "All while taking delight in the destruction. I fear she might be a hoyden." Then her eyes widened when she realized what Lady Wadsworth had said about Mr. Barnaby. "You've been to the office," she added in awe.

Nodding as she allowed a smile at imagining the scene the viscountess described, Charity replied, "I have. I thought I should let you know that I am the new matchmaker, made so without so much as an interview or the need to provide a character. I do hope you're amenable," she said as she retook her seat in the floral upholstered settee.

"Amenable?" Elizabeth repeated in surprise. "I am ecstatic! But however did you know I was in need of a matchmaker?" she asked as she moved to the chair across from Lady Wadsworth. She lifted the tray of biscuits and held it as Charity helped herself to a lemon biscuit.

Furrowing a brow at hearing the query, Charity regarded Elizabeth a moment before she said, "Why, I read the posting in this morning's *The Times*," she replied.

Elizabeth blinked. She had been on the verge of saying something along the lines of "What posting?" when she realized what had to have happened.

"I love my husband," Elizabeth blurted.

It was Charity's turn to blink. "I don't know that he was involved in my hiring," she hedged. A hint of jealousy once again had her wishing for an entirely different life.

One apparently exactly like that of Lady Bostwick.

"I only met Mr. Barnaby, you see," she went on. "He claimed I had the position because I was the first to appear and claim it."

Elizabeth formed a mental picture of what that had to have looked like. Mr. Barnaby was probably feeling overwhelmed by the number of applicants that had been appearing in the small office on a daily basis, ever since the shingle for the new charity had been hung. "Oh, but my George *was* involved," Elizabeth insisted, her attention on the biscuit tray. "The latest matchmaker, Mrs. Burton, informed me only yesterday that she was vacating the position. She's getting married in a few days, you see. To one of the charity's applicants. Bostwick must have seen to it the position was listed in the newspaper. Just as he promised he would. Only last night, in fact."

Charity allowed a wan smile. "It must be such a treat to have a husband who is so... so supportive of your charitable efforts."

"Oh, it is," Elizabeth agreed with a nod. "He was a patron of my charity even before I met him," she claimed. "Because I helped his best friend gain a position at a bank." She took a sip of tea and allowed a huge smile. "Tell me then. When can you start?"

Her eyes darting to the clock on the fireplace mantle, Charity finally replied, "Five hours ago." At Elizabeth's look of shock, she added, "Since there were so many men in line, I thought it best to simply get started."

"Oh, bless you," Elizabeth said. "Which means I must bring up a rather delicate matter."

Charity stiffened. "Oh?"

"It's about your salary," Elizabeth replied. "The charity pays its employees monthly—"

"But, I wasn't expecting to be *paid*," Charity countered, although she felt a hint of relief to learn there would be some compensation. She had learned from Mr. Barnaby that every match resulted in an agreed-upon donation to the charity, based on a man's ability to pay.

Elizabeth gave her a quelling glance. "Given how much time you'll have to spend at the office, I really must insist you be compensated. Think of it as... as extra pin money."

Pin money.

Charity hadn't had much in the way of pin money over the years. Wadsworth had been such an extravagant spender when it came to his past-times, there was rarely money left to pay servants or the bills associated with his estates.

The thought of having money to spend on fripperies was rather pleasant. Buying a new gown or a new pair of slippers had her brightening. "I suppose I could use a new ballgown," she murmured. "I've been invited to Lord Attenborough's ball," she added with an arched brow. "My first evening event since returning to London."

"Oh, the Attenborough ball is always so entertaining," Elizabeth agreed. "One of my friends accepted a marriage proposal there a few years ago. In his gardens, I think it was."

Charity allowed a wan smile. "I rather doubt I shall be visiting his lordship's gardens."

"Oh, but you must," Elizabeth insisted. "At least to see his flowers. And the statuary, of course." Her face took on a dreamy expression. "Enjoy the kisses."

Her face taking on a pinkish cast, Charity blinked as she watched the viscountess imagine whatever it was that had been done to Elizabeth the last time she was in Lord Attenborough's gardens. Something pleasant, obviously. Something pleasurable. Something entirely scandalous.

Charity cleared her throat. "To enjoy kisses would require someone to bestow them on me," she murmured with a shrug. "I rather doubt I have that to look forward to."

Elizabeth leaned forward and said, "I experienced my first kiss at a ball." Her face displayed a grimace. "It was *awful,*" she whispered, remembering how the wet and slobbery kiss planted on her by Lord Trenton reminded her of being kissed by her best friend's dog. "But the second one was... well, it was George who kissed me then." She inhaled and sighed at remembering that particular kiss. How it had started after a sip of champagne, and how her knees had felt weak and her head spun from the sensations the viscount created with his lips. Her shoulders rose and fell in a quick shrug. "And now we're married with two babes and another on the way."

"Another?" Charity repeated. "Congratulations are in order then." The pang of jealousy once again passed through Charity as she listened to the viscountess describe her life. The woman was so happy! Allowing a sigh, she added, "I should take my leave. I wish to prepare for the morrow. I have some ideas of how I might find some eligible women for all these men who are in search of wives," she explained.

Elizabeth's eyes widened at hearing this. "Not even a day into it, and you're already plotting," she accused lightly. Then she furrowed a brow. "I do hope Mrs. Burton left some notes."

Charity nodded. "I found a rather detailed accounting of her work," she replied, recalling how the notes about each gentleman made it clear Mrs. Burton was after a match for herself. In her short tenure, she had at least managed to match nine couples—ten including her and the man she was to marry.

"She is the fourth matchmaker to find a match for herself since I started this endeavor," Elizabeth groused. "At least I can be assured *you* won't be marrying any of the applicants."

About to ask why the viscountess would say such a thing, Charity realized that all the applicants at 'Finding Wives for the Wounded' would be of a lower class than she. None of the men she had spoken with that day had been officers in the British Army or in the navy, for that matter, and certainly none had been aristocrats.

Should an aristocrat require the services of a matchmaker, they could afford to hire one directly. "You are right, of course. Especially since I have no intention of remarrying," Charity finally replied.

Elizabeth had watched the countess as she pondered her comment, wondering at the woman's wistful expression. The claim that she wasn't expecting to take another husband wasn't a surprise given her first marriage was such an unhappy one. Everyone in the *ton* knew the late Lord Wadsworth had been a cur. "Do let me know if I can be of assistance," she offered. "And the men in the office are there to help. Use them," she added.

Charity wasn't sure how she could employ Mr. Barnaby or Mr. Overby, but she knew she had much to learn about her position. "I'll see what kind of trouble I can get myself into," she replied with an elegantly arched brow. She stood up and regarded Elizabeth for a moment. "This may seem an unusual request, but might I pay a call on your nursery? My boys are both grown and out of the house now, but you mentioned having a daughter."

Allowing an impish grin, Elizabeth stood up and said, "I'll take you there. They may be in the middle of their dinner, but they adore visitors."

On their way up to the second floor, Charity said, "You might let the viscount know his post in the newspaper was a success. And that it can be removed from future issues of *The Times*. I shouldn't wish to have anyone else show up to take the position, or Mr. Barnaby might hire them, too."

Elizabeth rolled her eyes. "I'll remember you said that when you inform me you're leaving the position because you've landed a new husband," she teased.

A look of shock appeared on Charity's face. "My mind is made up on the matter, so that will never happen."

Leading the way into the nursery, Elizabeth beamed when her children both greeted her with cries of "Mama!" From the number of blocks on the floor versus those that stood in a stunted tower, it appeared Christina might have employed her destructive tendencies once more.

David struggled to his feet, hurried to stand before the two ladies. He gave a bow, nearly toppling over as he did so.

"Lady Wadsworth, may I have the pleasure of introducing you to my daughter, Miss Christina, and to Master David, the heir to the Bostwick viscountcy?"

"It's very good to meet you, Master David," Charity said, reaching out with a hand. She intended to pat David on the shoulder, but the tyke intercepted her gloved hand with one of his own small hands and pretended to kiss the back of it.

Surprised by the gesture, Charity dared a quick glance in Elizabeth's direction. "Why, I think my boys were nearly five before they learned such a courtesy," she murmured before turning her attention back to the boy, giving him a nod.

Elizabeth dimpled. "My husband has been seeing to his education," she whispered, but even as she said the words, she noted how Charity's attention had turned to Christina.

The five-month old, sitting on the carpeted floor with the skirt of her short gown splayed around her, held a doll and squealed in delight at the attention. The evidence of two lower teeth clearly showed.

"May I hold her, do you think?" Charity asked in a whisper.

Elizabeth allowed an expression of surprise. "I suppose. Although let me be sure her nappy is dry." She hurried over to her daughter, who had already held out her arms in anticipation of being lifted from the floor.

"Oof," Elizabeth said as she hefted the girl into her arms. "Lady Wadsworth is going to hold you," she said just before she kissed Christina on the cheek.

A string of unintelligible words followed until Christina was securely in the crook of the countess's arm.

"She is adorable," Charity commented as she regarded the babe up close, one of her fingers stroking Christina's cheek.

Christina still held her small doll, but her attention had gone to the fur collar of Charity's pelisse. She pressed her face into it and then turned her head so her cheek rested against it.

"Oh!" Charity mouthed as she watched the babe's long lashes close. "Well aren't you just the most precious little girl?"

Elizabeth watched as her daughter fell asleep in the countess's arms. "Would you like to put her down? I know how heavy she gets after a time." She indicated the bassinet in one corner of the room.

"I suppose I must," Charity murmured quietly, finally moving to put the girl down. She stood over the bassinet a moment before allowing a sigh. "She looks like an angel," she whispered.

Not about to argue, Elizabeth joined the countess at the bassinet and sighed. "I fear she will be spoiled rotten."

Charity shook her head. "If you keep running your charity, she will grow up understanding the importance of helping others," she said in a quiet voice.

Furrowing a brow, Elizabeth considered the comment

for a moment. "You're right, of course." She hadn't given a thought to ever closing the charity, but changing times and circumstances might have her altering its mission.

"I must take my leave," Charity said when Mrs. Foster escorted David to the small table and chair for his refreshments.

"I'll see you to the door," Elizabeth offered, and the two took their leave of the nursery.

As they made their way down the stairs and to the front door of Bostwick House, stepping around a doll and a rubber ball, they chatted amiably about the upcoming ball.

"I am going only to observe," Charity murmured as she reached the front door. "I certainly hold no expectation of dancing."

"You will dance if you are asked, though?" Elizabeth half-asked.

Charity raised an eyebrow. "I suppose I will then," she hedged. She exchanged curtsies with Elizabeth. "Have a good evening, and thank you for the tea."

Elizabeth watched Charity take her leave of Bostwick House and climb into her town coach, not sure if she wanted to believe the countess or not.

On the one hand, she wanted the matchmaker position occupied as long as possible.

On the other, she couldn't help but think Charity could benefit from a match of her own, for Elizabeth had the distinct impression the countess yearned for another child.

A daughter.

Chapter 7
MEDDLING

*L*ater that evening

George sipped his cup of coffee and regarded the clock on the mantle in the library. At any moment, he expected Elkins would announce dinner was served, but he had hoped Elizabeth might join him before that happened.

Having spent the night before last with colleagues at White's, he had news to share. He had intended to do so over breakfast yesterday morning and again this morning, but Elizabeth was still sound asleep when he made his way downstairs, and he didn't have the heart to awaken her.

When Elizabeth appeared, she did so as if she'd been blown into the room. "I apologize, George," she said, her skirts barely catching up to her as she moved to join him on the settee.

He quickly set his coffee on the side table, well aware Elizabeth wouldn't wait for him to stand up. She, in fact, nearly fell onto him as she leaned over to kiss him.

He gathered her onto his lap and returned the kiss, rather stunned at how amorous she was for so early in the evening. When she came up for air, he said, "I have looked forward to that all day."

Elizabeth dimpled. "You knew?" she countered.

George was about to respond in the affirmative, but then realized she might be referring to something else. "Maybe," he answered carefully.

"Your post. In *The Times*. It worked," she said happily. Then she sobered. "Which means you have to cancel it."

Taken aback by this bit of news, George arched a brow. "You've already hired another matchmaker?" he asked in surprise. "That didn't take long."

"I didn't do the hiring," she replied as she shook her head. "Mr. Barnaby did."

A look of alarm appeared on the viscount's face. "Oh, no," he whispered, imagining yet another husband-hunting widow in the position. Mr. Barnaby might have been married to one of the teachers at Warwick's Grammar and Finishing School, but he wasn't the best judge of those who arranged marriages.

"Oh, it's all right," Elizabeth assured him. "Lady Wadsworth is perfect for the position. She paid a call this afternoon after spending several hours at the office."

This bit of news had George even more shocked. "Wadsworth's poor widow?" he asked in disbelief.

Elizabeth furrowed a brow at hearing his reaction. "*Poor*, as in you feel sorry for her? Or *poor* because...?"

George's eyes darted to one side. "Both?" he finally responded.

Inhaling sharply, Elizabeth regarded him for a moment. "The gossip was true then?" she asked, moving off her husband's lap so she could sit next to him on the settee. She knew if she stayed on his legs too long, they would fall asleep, and having experienced the pins-and-needles sensation herself earlier that day, she didn't want him suffering the same fate.

"If the gossip implied she inherited little because Wadsworth spent most of it, then yes," he replied.

Elizabeth screwed up her face. "I was referring to his lack of... *fidelity*," she said, whispering the last word.

"That, too," George agreed, grateful he had married a woman who would never take a lover. He wouldn't abide sharing Elizabeth with anyone—couldn't—nor would she abide him with another woman.

"I told her she would be paid," Elizabeth said.

"She no doubt denied needing the money," he guessed.

"How did you know?"

"But she graciously agreed when you pressed the issue," he continued, ignoring the query.

"Indeed," she replied with a nod. "I told her to consider it pin money."

George allowed a nod of his own. "A perfect response." When her brows furrowed in confusion, he added, "You allowed her to keep a modicum of pride, my sweet. *Brava*."

Elizabeth regarded him a moment before she allowed a wan smile. "Thank you," she said, although there was a hint of hesitation in how she said it.

George kissed her temple. "So... shall we wager on how long she stays in the position?" he asked, his lips quirked in a teasing manner.

Her shoulders slumping at the question, Elizabeth said, "It's not as if she will find a suitable husband from among the men who have been applying," she argued. "We don't get many officers, and we certainly don't have any wounded aristocrats—or *any* aristocrats, for that matter—coming into the office."

About to counter her claim—George had spent many an hour in the small office, although he had never done more than read applications in an attempt to locate someone—he decided instead to say, "One month until she's accepted an offer."

Blinking, Elizabeth stared at her husband for a moment. "But, Charity assured me she has no intention of remarrying," she argued. Then she remembered how Charity behaved with Christina. "Although I think she would love having a daughter of her own. She's quite smitten with Christina."

"Everyone is smitten with my daughter," George replied proudly, the comment about the countess no surprise. Playing wife to a libertine such as Wadsworth would put any woman off of remarriage. "I'll be defending Christina with my foil for years to come," he added as he pantomimed swinging a fencing foil. "*En guard!*"

About to giggle at his antics, Elizabeth suddenly sobered. "You may not have to if she's the hoyden I'm afraid she's turning into."

George blinked. "What has she done now?" She wasn't yet a year old!

Elizabeth held up her index finger and poked it in his chest. "Took down the entire wooden Tower of David in one little push. Twice, I think."

Grinning, George lifted her finger to his lips and moved to suckle it.

"Dinner is served, my lord, my lady," Elkins announced from the threshold.

"Thank the gods. I'm starving," George said as he gave up his hold on Elizabeth's finger.

Finally allowing the giggle she had suppressed a moment ago, Elizabeth allowed George to help her up from the settee. "Did you fence with Mr. Streater this afternoon?" she asked as they made their way to the dining room.

"I did indeed."

"And?" she prompted.

"And... what?"

She let out a sound of impatience. "How is married life for him?"

A widower, Teddy Streater had married Daisy Albright at the end of July. He had hired the former spy to be the headmistress of his late mother's concern, Warwick's Grammar and Finishing School, a couple of months before that, unaware she was the illegitimate daughter of a duke. Since then, the newlyweds had been busy overseeing renovations on the boarding school that catered to daughters of wealthy tradesmen, merchants, and a few barons. Classes had resumed in late September, and all the beds in the eight boarding houses had been claimed by new or returning students.

George saw to seating Elizabeth in the chair to his right, preferring to keep her at the same end of the long table as his carver was located. "I do not believe I have ever seen Teddy so happy," he remarked, deciding not to mention the time the bank clerk had won a hundred pounds in a game of whist.

Elizabeth beamed. "I am so glad to hear it."

"Or so frightened."

Elizabeth blinked. And blinked again. "Whatever do you mean?"

"Impending fatherhood has a tendency to do that to a man." He acknowledged the footman who poured the wine and regarded the soup course with appreciation.

A smile slowly spreading across her face, Elizabeth had

to wave a hand in front of her face as tears threatened. "Oh, George," she murmured. "This is such good news. Why, our babies will be born at almost the same time."

George allowed a shrug, not having thought of that particular detail. "You do realize this means he will have to hire a new headmistress?" he asked with an arched brow. He lifted his spoon to his lips and savored the lobster bisque before noting how Elizabeth gazed at her own bowl of soup. "Is something amiss?" he asked with a hint of alarm. "Shall I order you a different course?"

Elizabeth shook her head. "No. No, I'm fine." She looked up and gave him a brilliant smile. "This babe doesn't seem bothered by fish at all."

He finished another spoonful of soup before asking, "Then what about the soup has your attention so completely?"

Shaking her head, Elizabeth said, "Not the soup, but rather who could take Daisy Streater's place at Warwick's," she murmured.

His soup forgotten, George regarded his wife with interest. "Oh? Do tell," he encouraged.

Taking a breath and then holding it a moment, Elizabeth gave her head a quick shake. "Why, Mrs. Witherspoon, of course," she said with some excitement.

Not recognizing the name, George merely shrugged.

"She applied at the 'Finding Work for the Wounded'," she explained. "She was a field nurse, and although she was never wounded, she did run the Parker Hotel prior to her service on the Peninsula."

George returned his attention to his soup, not exactly impressed with the connection. "If she wasn't wounded, why did she seek assistance from your charity?"

Elizabeth allowed a shrug, absently dipping a spoon

into her bisque. "She is unmarried and doesn't wish to be a prostitute."

Thinking of at least a half-dozen other occupations that didn't require a woman to spread her legs—milliner, seamstress, teacher, nurse, maid, and housekeeper,—George was about to recite them when he noted the frown Elizabeth aimed in his direction. "Is she educated enough to be an accomptant?" he asked, remembering the boarding school required its headmistress to keep the books.

"She ran a hotel, George," Elizabeth countered. "And the only reason she cannot do it now is because the hotel was sold whilst she was playing nursemaid to soldiers, and the new owner is seeing to running the hotel himself."

George nodded his understanding. "Very well. Shall I suggest her to Teddy then?" he asked.

Taking a breath and then letting it out slowly, Elizabeth considered the query. "I will suggest her to Mrs. Streater," she said then.

George stopped his spoon in midair. "But what about Teddy?"

Furrowing a brow, Elizabeth gave her head a shake. "He doesn't run Warwick's, and I am quite sure he wants to keep it that way," she replied.

Allowing a grin, George finished his soup and nodded his agreement. "You have the right of it, my sweeting." He gave a sigh. "As usual."

If his wife could see to a new headmistress for Warwick's, the least he could do was see to a new husband for Charity Seward Wadsworth.

And he was fairly sure he knew exactly the man to fill the bill.

Chapter 8

A BALL SPENT WITH CHARITY

hree days later, Lord Attenborough's ball, Mayfair
"She's gorgeous, isn't she?" Marcus Batey, Viscount Lancaster, commented as his gaze took in the petite, blonde, blue-eyed Miss Analise Batey. Dressed in a bright white gown of fine lawn decorated with rows of white furbelows along the hemline and satin rosettes around the neckline, Analise was the epitome of the perfect English miss, fresh out of the school room and ready for her first Little Season.

Luke Merriweather, Viscount Wessex, furrowed his brows and followed his older friend's gaze until it settled onto a blonde of at least thirty. Her bright red satin ballgown, trimmed in black lace, was enhanced by a diamond cluster between her breasts. The gown fit to perfection and hinted at a pair of rather long legs. "Indeed," Luke agreed, despite the fact that she was entirely too old for his tastes —he was barely five-and-twenty.

Luke would have continued staring at the woman, if only because she was rather easy on the eyes, but her line of sight was about to intersect his, so he turned his attention back to the older viscount. "I didn't realize you were in the market for a mistress," he said, *sotto voce.*

Marcus blinked and turned his attention back to where the young viscount had been staring. Instead of the young lady in white—his daughter—Marcus realized Luke had been regarding the woman wearing a red satin ballgown.

A year out of widow's weeds and having raised both an heir and a spare for the late Earl of Wadsworth, the former Charity Seward was rarely seen at Society events. Many thought she still lived in one of the earldom's country estates, or had taken up residence in a dowager cottage next to the sea. "I wasn't referring to Lady Wadsworth," Marcus said in a scolding voice. Although, now that he gave *her* a second glance, he wondered how he could have missed her presence in the first place. He had been hoping to find her at tonight's entertainment. Lord Attenborough had assured him an invitation had been delivered to the widow.

A memory from a long time ago had his breath hitching and his body reacting in ways it hadn't done in many years. Just the thought of what he had at one time imagined doing with the woman, back when he was younger, had him allowing a sigh of frustration.

Responsibility and obligation had prevented him from approaching her during his university years. Then there was the unfortunate incident involving his former best friend. Edmund Fulton, then the future Earl of Wadsworth, decided he wanted Charity for himself and claimed he had ruined her. Explaining what he had done to the girl to her father ensured he would be granted her hand—and her dowry—in marriage, which precluded

Marcus from ever having a chance at courting the beautiful ingénue with the curly blonde hair.

His situation had changed, though.

And so had hers.

Charity Seward Wadsworth had buried her husband the same month his own wife had died in the childbed. His spare heir had survived the ordeal and was now ensconced in the nursery at Stanton House.

That is, if the tyke hadn't escaped from his nurse, as he had a tendency to do now that he was a toddler of two.

The boy had mastered door handles.

Marcus's arm no longer bore the black armband signifying he was in mourning. Now that his daughter was having her come-out—at this ball—Marcus was determined to socialize.

Luke frowned before his gaze finally settled on the young lady in white Marcus had mentioned first. "Rather young for you, isn't she?" he asked, his brows waggling. He knew the identity of the young lady, of course, but he enjoyed teasing the older viscount.

Marcus gave a snort. "I am not in the market for a mistress, and she—" he nodded in the direction of the young lady in white—"is my *daughter*," he countered before his expression changed, one that hinted of impending murder. "Have you had your sights on Analise?" he asked, his manner indignant, as if the very idea of Luke Merriweather paying his daughter any mind would result in pistols at dawn on a foggy Wimbledon Common—even if the young buck was the heir apparent to the Middleton earldom.

"I agree, she is gorgeous," Luke replied with a nod. "But even I know better than to believe you would ever allow the likes of me the privilege of courting her," he added in his own defense. "If you did, you would have introduced me to her."

Truth be told, he had been well aware of the young woman before he arrived at Lord Attenborough's mansion for that evening's ball. He had seen her on several occasions when he paid a call on Marcus at his house, although they had never been introduced. He had also seen her among her fellow students when she attended Warwick's Grammar and Finishing School, her happy expression and confident manner making her stand out from the young ladies who surrounded her. *Like bees to honey*, he thought.

Then he had paid witness to her dancing the very first cotillion earlier that evening. He had watched her dance the second set, a rousing Scottish reel, which had his usual dour expression lighting up in delight at her enthusiasm. As the crowd increased and it became harder to see all the dancers, Luke lost track of her until he had a brief flash of her performing the waltz. Poised and confident, she smiled as their eyes met.

And something twitched in his ribcage.

Now that he had a chance to really look at Analise Batey, Luke wished he hadn't been so quick with his comment to the older viscount. "You will have to allow *someone* to marry her, though," he argued, turning his attention back to Marcus. "Perhaps not this Season, of course, but next, just as Bostwick suggested that night we were at the club."

Marcus frowned, knowing the younger man had a point. "I could put her in a nunnery," he murmured.

"No, you cannot," Luke countered. "I have it on good authority she will be courted by no fewer than four of my peers with whom she has danced this evening," Luke claimed, his words a bit of a fib. He was quite sure she had danced all five sets. As for the identities of those who wished to court Miss Analise, he really had no idea. He just enjoyed watching the older viscount squirm.

"She danced?"

Luke blinked and wondered if he would lose his life if he mentioned Analise was quite stunning when dancing the first waltz of the ball. "Indeed. Whomever did you hire as her dance master? She's quite exquisite performing the waltz." He thought about closing his eyes, thinking the older viscount wouldn't punch him if he couldn't see the fist coming.

"She is?" Marcus countered.

Luke blinked again and stared at the older viscount. "She is," he affirmed, ready to take a step back should Marcus's arm come up with a closed fist at the end of it.

"But, I didn't hire a dance master for her," Marcus replied, his head shaking from side to side. "Which means... I suppose it was a good idea she attended Warwick's Grammar and Finishing School." After a second, he added, "I hired protection for her, of course. A rather burly sort who had experience in such matters."

One of Luke's eyebrows arched up in an approving manner. "Ah, well, since she went to school at Warwick's, then she had one of the Albright sisters—or both of them —as her dancing instructor," he said with a nod. He leaned in and added, "Ariley's daughters," in a hoarse whisper, one eyebrow arching up, as if he was imparting something secret.

Viscount Lancaster regarded his colleague for a long time while he considered this bit of information. "The Duke of Ariley allowed his daughters to teach at a... at a finishing school?" he asked in surprise.

Luke nodded. "Independent women, both of them.

But they're married now. Surely you heard Breckinridge took one of them as his wife."

Marcus furrowed a brow. "I heard he married an arithmetic teacher."

"He did. Diana Albright was her name. She's the younger daughter," Luke explained. "The new Lady Breckinridge was also the dance instructor at Warwick's. Probably your daughter's dance instructor until she married," he clarified. "Then, the older daughter, Lady Daisy, married Teddy Streater—the gentleman who joined us for drinks a few nights ago at White's—this past June. She's the headmistress of the school now, and while she did teach the dance class for a time, I happen to know someone else sees to that class now."

Marcus arched a brow. "Because you are pursuing the new dance instructor as a possible viscountess?" he guessed.

Luke's eyes widened. "Of course not! Mrs. Wheatley was my sister's governess," he replied, rather indignantly. "And she's old enough to be my mother."

Nodding his understanding, Marcus was rather glad Analise was done with finishing school. He had sent her to Warwick's after his wife, Joan, had died, thinking that to employ a governess to live in the home he had inherited—along with the viscountcy—might lead to scandal. Meanwhile, his oldest son, Andrew, was away at Cambridge for his college education, which meant Stanton House was occupied by just Analise, his two-year-old son, John, twelve servants, and him.

Although Marcus had missed his daughter during the weeks when she boarded at the school in Glasshouse Street, he had Analise's company on Sundays and holidays. By the time she had completed her schooling, he realized she had grown into an accomplished young woman, ready for the trials and tribulations of the *ton*.

Perhaps he really should see to a nunnery for her.

"You're staring at her again," Luke accused, glad the attention was off of him. He had been afraid his friend had paid witness to his appreciative perusal of Miss Analise.

Marcus blinked. "What?"

"Lady Wadsworth. You were staring at her. Aren't you a bit old for her?" he teased.

"Old?" Marcus repeated, his face displaying a hint of worry. Truth be told, he hadn't given a thought as to Charity Wadsworth's age, probably because he had secretly pined for her since his days at Cambridge. Then, as second sons were sometimes forced to do, he had married another—Joan Harrington—because he had been expected to do so from the time he was in leading strings.

His marriage and occasional time away from London hadn't lessened his fascination for Charity Seward, though. Instead, he imagined her just before he fell asleep from exhaustion. He woke up thinking of her, his initial thoughts in the morning comprised of how he might request an introduction. How he might come to know more about the mysterious woman who was rarely in London.

He winced at the reply she had sent him in response to his invitation to a ride in Hyde Park.

Although I am honored by your invitation, Lord Lancaster, I find I must decline as I have a previous obligation in the afternoons.

Obligation? What could be so obligating that she couldn't join him on an innocent ride in the park?

"She is why I decided not to move to my country estate," Marcus said with a sigh. Even if Charity wasn't in London, she couldn't be farther away than Suffolk. At least, that's where her late husband's earldom was based.

Luke eyed his friend with an expression of disbelief. "Are you speaking of Lady Wadsworth? Or your daughter?"

Marcus gave his head a shake. "My daughter, of course," he lied. He pretended to peruse the ballroom, just to discover if Charity was still holding court with two of the patronesses of Almack's.

She was not.

Marcus continued to scan the room, feeling a bit of panic when he couldn't find her either dancing or in conversation with anyone else. When he made the final turn, his attention still on the others in the room, he gave a start when he discovered Charity Seward Wadsworth regarding him with an elegantly arched eyebrow.

A beautiful, blonde eyebrow indicating either scorn or censure.

Certainly not approval.

"My lady," he said in alarm. His bow was immediate and deep. He reached for her hand, and she allowed him to brush his lips over her gloved knuckles before he straightened. "Lady Wadsworth. I haven't had the pleasure of an introduction," he managed to say, his eyes darting about them as if he was in search of someone to do the honors.

"You've been watching me," Charity accused. The words didn't hold any malice, nor did the hint of a question tinge them.

Marcus allowed a nod. "I admit, I have," he replied, deciding bravery was called for just then. He could have denied her claim, but she was finally speaking to him. He had her all to himself, if only for a moment or two. If she agreed to a dance, then he would have her for another half-hour. Perhaps after that, she would agree to a ride in the park.

From the way her expression faltered just then, Marcus realized she had been expecting a denial, or perhaps some excuse for why he was paying her so much attention. "I cannot help myself. I have found you to be one of the most beautiful women in all of London. Since the first time I paid witness to you when you were on a ride in Hyde Park. Back when I was... nineteen, I think it was?"

Charity blinked, her previously confident, almost haughty manner faltering. "Since I am poor at guessing men's ages, can you apprise me of how long ago that might have been?" she asked as she angled her head. She was about to add, "During the last century?" but thought better of it. The gentleman who stood before her, with his evening clothes fitting so perfectly and his dark hair precisely combed, with little in the way of sideburns, was certainly older than thirty. Maybe older than forty.

Hopefully not too much older than forty.

"One-and-twenty years, two months, and three days ago," Marcus replied, as if he didn't have to do the math but knew the numbers off the top of his head.

Charity blinked. She blinked again. Although arithmetic had never been her strong suit, she knew three things all at once: He was around forty years of age, he had seen her when she was sixteen, and it had been during the last century.

Not her best year, certainly. But not her worst. The

worst was the following year, when she learned she would be marrying Edmund Fulton, the future Earl of Wadsworth, because he had told her father that he had ruined her. They were to wed the following Season.

That is, if the older earl didn't keel over and die before their wedding day.

Unfortunately, he had waited until after eighteen years of marriage to manage that feat. Long enough for her to give birth to his heir and a spare. Although she loved them dearly—at least as much as a mother could love two spoiled rotten sons—she was glad the younger, Benjamin, was off to Eton for school and the older—Benedict, the current Earl of Wadsworth—had his own bachelor townhouse.

Although Benedict could have claimed his late father's mansion in Westminster, Benedict insisted Charity should continue to live there until such time as he took a wife. And since he wasn't planning to do so until he was at least thirty, she had at least a decade before she would have to either relocate to the dowager cottage in Suffolk or move to another Wadsworth property and suffer the title of Dowager Countess of Wadsworth.

"How is it I'm only learning of your... admiration now?" Charity asked, moving so she stood closer to him. The scent of his cologne—nothing special, but certainly not cloying or too floral—drifted past her nose.

"Circumstances beyond my control, of course," Marcus replied with a shrug. "University, marriage, Parliament, lack of invitations to the same social engagements." This last was truer than he should have admitted. Having only served in the House of Lords for the past two years, and since the death of his countess, his social calendar was more like that of a bachelor who toiled as a clerk in a warehouse day after day.

He had thought moving into the viscountcy's townhouse in Park Lane would help, but he went about life in London much like anyone else. "If you haven't promised the second waltz to anyone else, I would be honored to be your partner."

As if on cue, the orchestra played the opening strains of the supper dance, and Charity was forced to accept the man's offer. "I have not," she replied as she placed her hand on his proffered arm.

He led her onto the floor where other couples had already begun to prepare for the elegant dance. Once a few started to move and they had merged into the circle of dancers, Charity regarded him with an expression of doubt. "You do know I am a widow," she said.

Marcus nodded, leading her into a turn and then under his arm for the pirouette. "For two years and four days now," he replied. "Yes, I am aware." He wasn't about to apologize or give her his condolences. He knew perfectly well she had been in a loveless marriage. A marriage of convenience.

A marriage of inconvenience, if anyone asked him.

"You do know I am a widower," he half-asked, deciding he should mention it just in case she wasn't as aware of him as he was of her.

Charity was about to step out of his hold, say her apologies, and hurry off to the lady's retiring room, but there was something rather charming about a man who held her in such regard that he would know exactly how long she had been a widow.

And not a merry one.

"For two years..." Charity allowed the comment to

trail off, unable to remember the particulars since she hadn't been aware of Marcus Batey to the extent that he had apparently been aware of her.

And was his regard honorable? Or did he think she was available as a mistress? A merry widow?

Why was it aristocrats thought she would be an easy mark for illicit tumbles? That she would welcome their awkward advances, and act as if she should appreciate their lascivious attentions?

"I suppose you expect me to fall into bed with you later this evening," she accused, her body stiffening beneath his hold.

Marcus almost lost his place in the dance. He stutter stepped a bit to get them back in rhythm, apologizing under his breath before adding, "I would never expect such a wondrous event, my lady," he countered. "Even if I have prayed for it nearly every night for the past twenty years, two months, and three days."

That last part wasn't entirely true. There were nights his thoughts were on his wife, especially if she was sharing her bed with him. They had a pleasant marriage. Passionless, but pleasant. His wife had been a friend since childhood, after all.

Charity seemed to lose her place in the dance, but only for a moment.

When she didn't respond to his comment, the viscount sighed. "Oh, dear. Now I've gone and made you uncomfortable. I apologize. I—"

"Nonsense," Charity interrupted. "I find your manner rather refreshing," she said. "Mayhap you're a bit too enamored of me, though."

"Not possible," he countered as he managed to guide them past a couple who seemed to have lost a shoe or two during a pirouette. Her words about finding him refreshing had his heart soaring just then. "My devotion is unmatched. As is my determination to see you happy."

"Happy?" she repeated in disbelief. No one had ever said they wanted to see to her happiness. "What do you suppose would make me happy?"

Marcus angled his head just before he had her circling beneath his arm. When she was back in front of him, he asked, "What do you want more than anything else in the whole world?"

Charity blinked.

Apparently, no one had ever asked her *that* question before. She seemed to struggle to come up with an answer. "A... another child. A daughter," she whispered.

The Earl of Wadsworth had never gotten a girl on her. But then, he had at least one mistress he preferred and no desire to sire more children with her after the heir and spare had been born. Probably because he feared having to come up with a dowry for a daughter.

"Just one?" Marcus countered, his eyes darkening.

Charity swallowed. "I've thought these past two years that I might be too old to consider even one," she replied, her chin coming up a bit higher than the dance required.

"Nonsense," he replied, using her word. "Why, you only need look at the Countess of Torrington or Her Highness, the Queen of England, to know that isn't the case."

Charity regarded her dance partner for a moment before she was forced to break eye contact with him when she had to perform the pirouette beneath his arm again. When she returned to stand before him, she angled her head and said, "Well, now that we have the particulars sorted, I suppose you'll be proposing next." Although she wanted the words to come out sounding like a tease, they instead sounded sarcastic.

Marcus furrowed a brow. "I was thinking I should court you for a time before I propose," he replied. "Which is why I sent the invitation for a ride in the park." He gripped her waist and her hand a bit tighter when she seemed to stumble. "Oh, and now I've gone and made a cake of it. You wanted me to propose right now, didn't you?"

Charity couldn't help how her head swam just then. How dark flashes combined with bright sparks behind her eyes to have her blinking. Hunger had been gnawing in her belly since her arrival. The heat of the ballroom was suddenly so intense, she thought the room was afire. Dark gray surrounded her field of vision before she said, "I believe it's time I take my leave. I have somewhere I need to be in the morning," she murmured.

"Perhaps I could drive you there," Marcus offered. "Where do you need to be?"

Her eyes widened in an attempt to clear the gray at the edge of her vision. "30 Oxford Street." The address was out of her mouth before she could stop herself. She had recited the address at least fifty times in the last few days as she surreptitiously passed calling cards to unmarried seamstresses and servants, shopkeepers and costermongers. "Oh, I appreciate the offer, but my driver can take me," she replied. "Good night."

She stepped out of his hold, curtsied, and made her way in the direction of the entry of Lord Attenborough's mansion, all the while wondering what Lord Lancaster was thinking.

The man seemed lost in his thoughts.

Chapter 9

A CONVERSATION IN THE GARDENS

*N*ow, *Dear Readers, this is where we must remind you of our hero's tendency to employ his vivid imagination. Marcus Batey, Viscount Lancaster, cannot seem to help but daydream when circumstances allow it. Remember, we warned you.*

*A*few minutes later

Out in the gardens, the autumn air cool and barely lit with Japanese lanterns, Marcus carried the prone body of the Countess of Wadsworth to a bench and settled her onto it. Her head ended up in the small of his shoulder, which meant his nose ended up in the mass of curls that her lady's maid had pinned into place atop her head.

The scent of her engulfed Marcus, and he took a deep breath in an effort to capture as much of the floral and citrus scents as possible. At any moment, she would awaken and wonder how the hell she had ended up in the garden with an almost complete stranger.

He could tell her he had recognized the signs of an

impending fainting spell in the way her eyes were suddenly unfocused. He knew for certain when he was forced to hold up her body when her knees seemed about to buckle beneath her.

Expertly guiding Charity off the dance floor and to the back doors of the ballroom had been easy—her legs still seemed to work—but once they were just beyond them, she was in a dead faint. Hoping no one paid witness, he simply scooped her up in his arms—she was light as a feather—and hurried to the nearest bench.

He didn't have a vinaigrette, of course, and she didn't seem to have one in her hand, so Marcus merely waited until she finally stirred before he said, "That's never happened to me before."

Charity blinked awake and lifted her face to regard him in confusion. "And what might that be?" she murmured as she glanced around where they sat.

Marcus allowed a wan grin. "A woman fainting on me during a dance. You did it so beautifully. Like you were a ballerina performing as if you were a swan about to swoon..."

He knew his hold on her wouldn't last long. He knew she would come to her senses and probably berate him for taking liberties or some such. So he was ready when she suddenly straightened and regarded him with a look of alarm.

"Oh, no. What... what did I do?" Her eyebrows lifted and she once again glanced around where they sat. "What did you do?" Then her eyes rolled, and for a moment, Marcus thought she might faint again. "Did I say yes?"

Marcus blinked, rather wishing he had asked the obvious question—or any other, for that matter. "Uh, I hadn't yet given you the opportunity to respond one way or the other," he finally replied, deciding she must be referring to the marriage proposal he had mentioned earlier. "I would ask now, but it wouldn't be fair to you, seeing as how you're still recovering." He paused as he took a moment to gaze at her in the dim moonlight. "Tell me, though. It was the heat in the ballroom and not anything I said, I hope?" he half-asked. "I shouldn't think just speaking of marriage would send you into a swoon."

Charity allowed a sigh, and wonder of wonders, her head once again ended up in the small of his shoulder. "The heat, of course, but your..." She straightened, as if she just then realized where she was, and with whom she was sitting, and propriety was paramount. She stared at him a moment before her shoulders slumped.

"What is it?" he asked, his words quiet in the still night.

"I really should go back inside," she said, although she made no move to get up from the bench.

"Supper is being served. Would you join me?"

She seemed to consider his invitation for a moment before she finally gave her head a shake. "I should be getting home. I have to be at the office in the morning."

Marcus furrowed a brow. "Office?" he repeated. Then he remembered the address she had mentioned. *30 Oxford Street.*

Charity gave a shake of her head, as if she regretted her words. "I... I have a position. At a charity. 'Finding Wives for the Wounded'," she replied. "Tomorrow is one of the days I meet with potential clients."

The viscount seemed to consider her words for a time before he asked, "Isn't that Lady Bostwick's latest venture?"

Nodding, Charity said, "Indeed. I am the matchmaker."

Straightening on the bench, Marcus regarded her with an expression of surprise. "You're a matchmaker?"

Charity angled her head, about to defend her position, but the air seemed to leave her body for a moment before she said, "Please don't tell anyone."

"I... I won't," Marcus assured her. Truth be told, who would he tell? And who would believe him? No one would expect Charity, Countess of Wadsworth, to be employed in any sort of position. "May I ask how it is you became a matchmaker?"

About to get up from the bench, Charity regarded him for a moment before one shoulder lifted. "I paid a call on the office five days ago, intending to apply. Seems I didn't even have to interview with Lady Bostwick. I was hired on the spot."

"And how long have you been... matchmaking?"

"Just a few days," she replied. "But I've actually managed two matches so far. I have another pending, though. These things take time, you see, and they've only been accepting applications since Lady Bostwick started the charity at the beginning of summer."

Marcus nodded his understanding. "I didn't realize the wounded required help finding wives."

"Oh, but they do," Charity said earnestly, as she turned to face him. "These men have come back from the wars believing there isn't a woman who will find them worthy."

"Why ever not?"

She sighed. "Because they are missing limbs and think no one will have them. Or because they're embarrassed by their scars." She lowered her voice to a whisper and added, "Men can be so stupid."

Reeling, as if he'd been slapped in the face, Marcus

stared at her. He was about to chide her for the comment, but then his brows furrowed. "It's that obvious?" he asked, a hint of humor in his voice. "I thought we hid it rather well, but I suppose war brings out the worst in us. I've never been, nor was my late brother..." He paused as he fought the combination of sorrow and anger he felt every time he thought of Charles Batey.

"How did he die?" Charity asked, her voice still a whisper. "Forgive me, I was living in the country at the time and only heard of it from a neighbor."

"The ague, of all things," Marcus replied. "I would have thought him impervious to disease, given he was so unlikeable, but even he succumbed."

A battleground would have been a better setting for the sixth Viscount Lancaster to die. With his quick temper, determination, and reputation as a beast, Charles would have vanquished the enemy and shortened—or prevented—the final war against France. His poor widow, Elise, had been forced to put up with the philandering viscount who didn't even get a child on her. At least she was now happily married to Viscount Thorncastle. They were still on their wedding trip, one that had been extended several times since their departure from London. There were some in Parliament who claimed Godfrey Thorncastle would return to the capital with an heir and a spare, both conceived in Rome.

"I never expected to inherit the viscountcy," Marcus said then. "I always thought Charles would sire a son."

"He would have had to..." Charity paused, clamping her lips shut.

"What?"

Her eyes darted to one side. "Nothing. It's not important."

Marcus frowned. "Please, tell me what you were about to say."

Charity gave her head a shake. "You would have me speak poorly of the dead?"

His eyes darted to one side. "I already know my brother was not a good man. I know he was an unfaithful husband."

Charity hesitated a moment before she whispered, "I was about to say that he couldn't get a child on his wife because he was rarely in London. When he was, he was too drunk to bed her."

When she didn't continue, and he thought she knew more, Marcus said, "Go on."

Sighing, Charity gave her head a shake. "He was always at his hunting lodge. With his mistress. I know this because... because my husband was usually there with them and the other whores they employed to keep them entertained."

The vehement manner in which she imparted her words had Marcus jerking back on the bench. He had suspected his brother guilty of all manner of debaucheries, but he hadn't known of Lord Wadsworth's participation.

"Men are stupid," he said then, his brows furrowing. Although he felt sorry for the dowager countess, he also felt relief on her behalf. By surviving a rake like Wadsworth, she could finally live the life she desired.

Except she wanted another child. A daughter.

"Come have supper with me," he urged. "And then I'll see to getting you home safely." He had almost said, "See to getting a child on you," but caught himself at the last moment.

At her wide eyes and the hint of anger they contained, he added, "That is all I will do, I promise. At least, this evening." He paused a moment. "Unless you..." When her eyes once again flashed, he sighed. "It was worth a try," he said with a smirk.

The widowed countess finally allowed a nod and stood up with him. "I will go in with you for supper," she agreed. "But I shall be going home in my own coach. Alone."

Marcus lifted her gloved hand to his lips and kissed the back of it. "Then I shall follow in my own until I am assured you are safely in your house."

Charity sighed but didn't offer a rejoinder. She simply placed her hand on his arm, and Marcus led her back to ballroom.

Just in time to see Lord Haddon bent over his daughter, seemingly just about to kiss her.

Chapter 10

BACK IN THE BALLROOM

ow we return you, Gentle Reader, to the reality of the ballroom.

"Pardon me a moment," Marcus said to Charity as he pulled his arm from beneath hers and rushed over to where a young buck and Analise stood gazing at one another.

"Unhand my daughter this instant," he ordered, in a voice he struggled to keep as quiet as possible.

"Father!" Analise scolded, although her eyes widened when she realized how she and the marquess's son must have appeared to anyone paying them any mind. "Lord Haddon was just dancing with me," she added.

But Christopher Carlington, Earl of Haddon, stepped back and gave Marcus a deep bow. "Lord Lancaster. I assure you, I have done nothing but dance with your daughter. However, I was hoping to escort her to the supper. That is, if I have your permission, of course."

Marcus regarded the dark-haired, blue-eyed young buck who stood before him. He didn't immediately recognize the young man, but he thought he looked familiar. "And you are...?"

"Forgive me. Christopher Carlington. My father is Morganfield. I've just returned to London from Oxford, where I completed my studies in political affairs," the young man said as he gave a short bow.

Nodding his understanding, Marcus gave his daughter a quick glance before saying, "Lord Christopher." He paused, remembering the young man had an honorary title. "Lord Haddon, may I introduce you to my daughter, Miss Analise? And I am Lancaster."

Christopher afforded Analise a deep bow before saying, "It's very good to meet you, my lady."

Analise curtsied and said, "And you, my lord."

Marcus knew then that someone else had probably introduced them earlier in the evening. He gave a nod to the marquess's son and said, "You have my permission to escort her to supper."

*L*ord Haddon's eyes widened a fraction before they returned to normal. "Thank you, my lord," he managed, barely able to hide his astonishment. His gaze followed Marcus's retreat and attempt at a reunion with Lady Wadsworth—although the widow was no where to be found.

Having watched the viscount's waltz with the Countess of Wadsworth, Christopher now suppressed the urge to grin. He was reminded of how his father behaved in the company of his mother at a ball—as if he wanted nothing more than to get her alone in the library for a *tête-à-tête*.

The young earl turned his attention back to Analise.

"Now that I have his permission, I do hope you're not going to withdraw yours," he murmured.

Analise shook her head. "I'll do no such thing," she replied as she placed her hand on his proffered arm.

Not ever having seen her father in the company of another woman besides her mother, Analise couldn't help but wonder about Lady Wadsworth.

And her father.

How long had this been going on?

She had been tempted to ask just before her father disappeared into the crowd. Would her father give her an answer? Or would her query send him into another one of his daydreams?

She allowed Christopher to lead her into the supper room, deciding thoughts about her father could wait until later that night.

Chapter 11

CONTEMPLATING A VISCOUNT

A few minutes later

Charity, Countess of Wadsworth, had been lost in thought the entire trip back to the mansion she called home whilst she was in London. Before the Little Season started, she had thought she might return to Suffolk if life in London proved too difficult. A series of unusual circumstances had changed her mind, though. Circumstances that included the discovery of limited funds on which she was supposed to subsist for the rest of her life.

Her oldest son, Benedict, had done what he could to shore up the Wadsworth accounts, including firing the earldom's man of business and seeing to it rents were collected. With no property available to sell, he warned her that her allowance might not be as much as it had been when her husband was alive. *I'll do what I can to make Wadsworth solvent again, but it will take time*, he warned.

She had been left with little in the way of an inheritance from Wadsworth—the cur had gambled away all of the unentailed properties associated with the earldom—so the need to line up a position that would afford her an income made itself apparent. Since she had no desire to become someone's mistress, the position had to make it appear as if she wasn't working, exactly, but merely donating her time toward some worthy cause.

The matchmaking position was perfect. Viscountess Bostwick had assured her no one would learn she was being paid for her services. The bit of blunt a soldier paid towards the search for his wife probably wouldn't cover her salary, but Charity knew Lady Bostwick's main charity, 'Finding Work for the Wounded,' was well funded. Those who had been placed in positions eventually paid back the amounts the charity incurred on their behalf—costs for a suit or appropriate work clothing as well as the bribe sometimes necessary to place them in a position. Those funds simply went back into the charity so it could continue its work for other soldiers unable to find employment in the capital.

As for Viscount Lancaster, she didn't know what to think. There was a time earlier that evening, when she was enduring a lecture on the proper behavior for a widow by one of the patronesses of Almack's, that she had thought to simply leave the ball.

And then, because she was angry and hurt by the countess's insinuations, Charity was ready to do the same to the man she had caught staring at her.

His words of adoration had caught her completely off guard. Left her nearly speechless. Why, if it hadn't been for the attentions of the new Viscount Lancaster, Charity might have left the ball, returned to Wadsworth Hall, and had her lady's maid pack up her traveling trunk so they could return to Suffolk on the morrow—matchmaker position or not.

Lancaster's words about her—about how he had pined for her long ago—had been said with such earnest. Such devotion. She almost said she would be happy to join him in his bed, but then thought better of it.

She knew nothing—or rather, very little—about the viscount who so expertly led her through a waltz. When the dance was near its end, she almost hoped he would ask her to join him for the supper. Instead, he had nearly asked for her hand in marriage! With the rising temperature in the ballroom, was it any wonder she had nearly fainted?

She had no idea how she was supposed to respond to Marcus Batey's query, so she was relieved when his attention was diverted to the young heir to the Morganfield marquessate. Apparently Christopher Carlington, newly armed with a degree from Cambridge, had taken too much interest in Lancaster's daughter.

On the one hand, Charity had to admire the viscount for his protective stance when it came to Miss Analise. She would expect nothing less from a father. But on the other... being left at the edge of the dance floor after the waltz, with barely an apology from him, had her feeling abandoned.

And yet, what should she have expected? The dance was done. She had curtsied to his bow.

The coach jerked to a halt in front of the mansion, pulling Charity from her reverie. Allowing a quiet sigh, she stepped down with the help of a groom and made her way inside.

As for returning to Suffolk, she decided against it. She had a position now. One that paid enough to see to her expenses—for now.

Chapter 12

AN APPLICANT IN NEED
OF MORE

The following day
Roger Weatherby regarded his master with a critical eye—or rather the clothes in which he had just dressed him. "When you are next at your tailor's, may I suggest you acquire a waistcoat in a dark green?" he said. "This bright blue is just a bit too much for the Nankeen breeches."

Luke Merriweather glanced in the cheval mirror and immediately understood his valet's comment. The man had an eye for color and was quick in his choices of appropriate clothing. "Indeed. I shall make a trip to St. James Street to see to it after we're done in Parliament today," he replied. He glanced around his bedchamber, deciding there wasn't anything else he could do to prepare for that day's agenda. "Pray tell, what are your plans?"

The valet allowed a shrug as he made his way to the dressing room with a pile of topcoats, his limp causing him to list dangerously to one side. Luke feared the man might topple over, but Weatherby made it to the dressing room and disappeared for a moment.

Luke's attention went to the man's cane, a simple wooden stick with a rounded ball top. He made a mental note to shop for something more decorative for the valet he had employed since his move to London. He often wondered who he might have ended up dressing him had he not agreed to hire the veteran of the Peninsular Wars.

Lady Bostwick had recommended the young man when Luke had approached the viscountess, thinking her charity might have someone he could employ as opposed to relying on an agency to send him someone.

In the two years Weatherby had been in service at Luke's small townhouse in South Audley Street, the valet had proved knowledgable and eager to please. He had even taken over the duties of butler given the townhouse didn't come with one, overseeing the one footman and small kitchen staff.

He also seemed terribly lonely.

Reminded of Lady Bostwick's charity to help find work for wounded soldiers, Luke then wondered if perhaps the valet could benefit from her newest charity.

The viscount didn't employ many servants. The housekeeper was older and married to a butler from a nearby residence, and the only footman and the only housemaid were married to one other. The scullery maid was apparently carrying on with a groom from the mews behind the townhouse, and the cook had informed him on more than one occasion that she had no use for a husband.

The cook was also old enough to be Roger's mother.

Or my mother, he amended as he gave it some more thought.

When Roger reappeared from the dressing room, Luke broached the subject. "Have you been courting anyone?"

Roger straightened as best he could and regarded his master with a look of shock. "I have not," he replied.

"Do you... wish to?" Luke pressed. "I ask only because you seem of an age to take a wife."

The valet angled his head and said, "Begging your pardon, my lord, but if I am of an age to take a wife, then so are you."

Luke chuckled as he bobbed his head in agreement. "I am guilty as charged. However, I do have a young lady in mind. I think I may have to see to courting her very soon."

"Oh?" Roger responded, fussing with the knot in Luke's cravat.

"Last night's ball reminded me of duty and such," Luke murmured. Indeed, the sight of Lady Analise had stirred something in him that was most unexpected.

Desire.

Which had him wondering just why. Most young ladies her age were annoying in their behavioral when among the young bucks, their titters and constant blushing making them seem far too young to be considered seriously as marriage prospects.

Analise behaved far differently from the others who had made their come-out during the Little Season. She exuded a kind of confidence that suggested she was older than her seventeen years. An ease with conversation, even when addressed by those older than her. And she displayed poise regardless of who she with.

Luke nearly winced when he remembered how pleasant she managed to be when Lord Albert approached her for a dance. The pimply-faced prick of an earl's son always behaved as if he were another Prinny.

Perhaps it was because her mother had died and her

father had felt compelled to send her to a boarding school. Perhaps it was because her father had only recently inherited his viscountcy, and Analise hadn't yet spent enough time around other daughters of the *ton* to have adopted their annoying behavioral traits.

He thought of the eight years that separated them and winced.

"Is something amiss?" Roger asked. He stepped back to regard the mail coach knot he had managed to create in the viscount's cravat.

"Eight years is a long time, is it not?" Luke asked.

Roger furrowed a brow. "That depends, I suppose. To what are you referring?"

Luke considered waving off the query, but finally said, "The difference in age between me and the young lady I am considering."

Roger's eyes darted to one side before he finally sighed. "Then she must have had her come-out recently," he remarked. "Since I cannot see you considering a silly chit or a bluestocking, then she must be a diamond of the first water."

Luke blinked, deciding to put voice to an argument as it applied to the comment about a bluestocking. "Sommers did rather well by marrying Lady Evangeline," he argued. "Says they never lack for topics of conversation."

"He's a baron, my lord," Roger reminded him.

Angling his head left and then right, Luke finally allowed a slight shrug, deciding his valet did have a point about a silly chit. "She's not a silly chit, but she's not the daughter of a duke, either."

"But she is an aristocrat's daughter?" Roger half-asked.

"She is," Luke affirmed. "A viscount's daughter, in fact."

"Very good, my lord," Roger replied. "She will no doubt already be prepared for life as a viscountess."

"True," Luke agreed, not having thought about it from that perspective. The prospect of courting Analise Batey wasn't so daunting now. He just had to gain Lancaster's approval.

Well, he could work on that once he determined if Miss Analise was even interested in being courted.

Frowning, he wondered how to encourage his valet to begin the search for a wife. "Is there a reason *you* haven't courted anyone since your return from the wars?"

Roger's eyes darted about until they came to rest on his cane. "Can't be thinking a proper young lady would want to walk in public with the likes of me, given my limp and all," he replied with a shrug.

Furrowing his brows, Luke realized he had the perfect response. "Lady Bostwick's new charity can find you the perfect mate," he countered. "The viscountess has hired another matchmaker that I here is all the crack."

Roger stilled his features, hoping his face wasn't displaying the tell-tale color of embarrassment. "Well, perhaps I'll pay a call on my day off," Roger replied, although there wasn't any conviction behind the words.

He wasn't about to admit he had already paid a call on the new matchmaker who had begun work there a few days ago. Even though she didn't have a young woman in mind for him at the time of his appointment, Mrs. Seward had mentioned she would be paying calls on young misses in the hopes of finding matches for her many applicants. Apparently, the charity had been without a matchmaker for over a week, and the new one was left with a backlog of single men in search of wives.

"Go today," Luke encouraged him. "And should she

find you a wife, you can move into the larger quarters at the end of the servants' floor."

Roger's eyes widened. He hadn't even considered accommodations. "I appreciate the offer, my lord," he replied.

"Look, if I end up married in the next few months, I'd rather not be the only newlywed man in the house, if you catch my meaning," Luke said in a quiet voice.

Allowing a nod, Roger replied, "I'll pay a call on the matchmaker. But, my lord, I won't be allowing my hopes to get too high."

Luke straightened. "Understood." He sighed. "Well, I guess I'm off to Parliament now."

The valet frowned. "No breakfast, sir?"

The viscount allowed a grin. "After breakfast," he agreed, deciding he could mentally compose a note to Miss Analise asking if she might be available for a ride in the park. And then, after Parliament, he would see to taking pen to paper and writing it down.

"Very good, sir. But I should warn you, the cook is out of honey. She hopes to locate some when she goes to market later today."

Disappointed, Luke allowed a shrug. "I'll live," he replied, his mind still on the note he needed to compose. As for the delivery of the note, well, he might have someone else see to that.

He didn't want his servants spreading the news that he was in the market for a wife.

Chapter 13

IN PURSUIT OF A WIFE

ater that morning

"So, when is the wedding?" Luke Merriweather asked, just as he and Marcus were about to enter the House of Lords.

"Whose wedding?" the older viscount countered, pausing a moment to adjust his robes.

"Yours, of course. You spent enough time waltzing with Lady Wadsworth to court her, propose, and set a date," the younger viscount teased.

Luke was never pleased with dance sets lasting a half-hour or more. If he ended up with a partner who was a dullard or who couldn't tell her left foot from her right, then he was stuck for the duration of the dance with no way out—short of breaking a heel or spraining an ankle.

Now, had he been in the company of Miss Analise, he might not mind the long dance sets. The young woman was a breath of fresh air when it came to those who had made their come-outs so far this Little Season. Her happy countenance and unblemished complexion had him thinking of her as a daisy with perfect white petals splayed out from a bright yellow middle. That would make him a bee, of course, and he could think of nothing more satisfying than being the one to pollinate her. They would make the most delicious honey together.

Luke rolled his eyes at the analogy. What the hell had gotten into him? Perhaps he really did miss having honey in his tea this morning.

"Your impertinence has been noted, Merriweather," the older viscount replied in response to his teasing about Lady Wadsworth. Marcus's brows furrowed. "Why are you here? Your father didn't die last night, did he?"

Luke Merriweather rolled his eyes. "I accepted a writ of acceleration, which I am beginning to regret. Apparently there are too many ancient lords presiding these days. I decided I would prefer knowing what I would be getting myself into when I finally have to inherit the earldom. Besides, I have difficulty sleeping past nine o'clock in the morning."

Marcus's annoyance was evident in how he screwed up his face. "Prefer a number of naps during the day, instead?" he teased. "Because that's what's in store for you here," he warned.

"This isn't my first session," Luke argued. "And, unlike you, I am rather fascinated by what happens in there," he added as he he aimed his chin toward the door to the Chamber of Lords.

"I almost wish you were courting my daughter."

Luke's eyebrows lifted in shock. *Now from where had that comment come?* "Almost because...?" he prompted, wondering how he might make it so.

"Because I've heard quite enough about Lord Haddon on this day," Marcus replied, his response making him sound cranky.

"Ah, yes, I noticed Christopher was back from Oxford. Quite popular with the young ladies, too," he murmured. He wasn't exactly jealous of the young man, but he had been annoyed to watch as he escorted Miss Analise into the supper.

Marcus went on as if he didn't hear the younger viscount's remark. "In fact, I am sorry I gave Morganfield's whelp permission to escort my daughter to the supper last night. She could speak of no one else and nothing else in the coach on the way home last night." He inhaled and let out the breath before adding, "To think—he'll be a marquess when Morganfield has a coronary and finally dies from too much—"

"Shhh," Luke interrupted, knowing exactly what Marcus was about to say. *Sexual intercourse.* The marquess and his wife were hopelessly in love with one another and took every opportunity to prove it. "Someone will hear you ranting and think you're jealous."

Dipping his head, Marcus apologized. "Still, I wasn't expecting my daughter to be so enamored of him."

Not having considered Analise Batey a potential wife —nor any other daughter of the *ton*, for that matter, until the night before—Luke was struck by the pang of jealousy that had him frowning just then. *Faith!* He hadn't even danced with the young lady. He had certainly kept an eye on her all evening, but how could he not? She was strikingly lovely. Confident, and possessed of a demeanor that suggested she would be easy to please and eager to please.

He had a passing wonder if that eagerness to please would ever extend to the marriage bed.

Managing to mask the odd sound he emitted just then by clearing his throat, Luke regarded Marcus in a new light.

That of the father of the young woman for whom he was smitten. "I rather doubt he's going to be in search of a wife anytime soon," Luke murmured, referring to Lord Haddon. "He just finished his studies. He'll want to spend a few years sowing his oats—"

"Not in my daughter, he won't," Marcus stated, his face reddening in anger.

Luke recoiled at the vehemence of the older viscount's response. "I'm quite sure he'll employ a mistress or two," he said. Although he'd had a mistress for a couple of years, Luke had grown bored with the woman who constantly complained of not having enough of anything, whether it be jewelry or gowns or pin money. When their second contract ended, he made no attempt to renew it, and neither did she.

At the thought that Lord Haddon would employ a mistress instead of courting young ladies like Miss Analise, Luke found he hoped that would indeed be the case. Given his thoughts of courting Miss Analise earlier that morning—and encouraging his valet along those same lines—the thought of marriage no longer had him cringing.

In fact, the thought of courting Analise Batey wasn't such a far-fetched idea.

The thought of marrying her wasn't the least bit daunting, either.

Indeed, the idea of taking Analise Batey as his wife was suddenly an idea well worth his consideration.

Honey, indeed.

Would it be an idea Lord Lancaster could abide, though?

"Might I put forth a suggestion?" Luke asked then, wincing when one of the words came out sounding a bit strangled. When a footman opened the doors, the two made their way into the chambers. "Perhaps I could invite Miss Analise for a ride in the park?" Luke suggested. "Or otherwise ensure she's engaged so that she won't be available to spend time in Lord Haddon's company."

His eyes rounding at hearing the offer, Marcus stepped up and stood in front of his seat. "You would do that?" he asked in a whisper. "That's rather sporting of you."

Luke gave a one-shouldered shrug. "It's the least I can do to keep Miss Analise safe from the earl."

Marcus gave the younger viscount an approving glance. "Then please do."

Rather satisfied with how he had manipulated the situation, Luke gave a nod and moved to take his own seat. If the session proved boring, he only need think of Analise to pass the time.

Rather pleased at how Lord Wessex had stepped up and offered his services, Marcus considered the ramifications. For if Analise was in another's conveyance, she couldn't be in Lord Haddon's phaeton. And if she was in Luke's phaeton—or whatever he was driving these days—Marcus could have Lady Wadsworth all to himself in his curricle.

That is, if he could ever get her to agree on a ride in the park.

Chapter 14

A VISIT TO A CHARITY TO
SEE CHARITY

*L*ater *that day*

Top hat in hand, Marcus entered the offices of 'Lady E's Finding Work for the Wounded' and 'Finding Wives for the Wounded.' His gaze went first to a tall gentleman who was getting up from behind a corner desk. Then it went to a shorter gentleman seated at another desk next to where a poorly dressed older man was perched on a wooden chair.

The reason for his visit was seated behind a desk in the opposite corner, her attention on a sheaf of paper.

"May I help you?" Nicholas Barnaby asked as he hurried up to the viscount. He knew from the visitor's clothes that he wasn't there about finding a position, but sometimes those with positions to fill stopped by the office to enquire about available laborers.

Marcus nodded toward where Charity sat. "I was hoping I might have a word with Lady Wadsworth," he murmured.

Nicholas furrowed a brow, his suspicion evident. "There's no Lady Wadsworth here," he countered.

Marcus blinked as his gaze went back to where Charity sat. "Sorry. I meant to say Miss Seward."

"Do you have an appointment, sir?"

The viscount dipped his head. "I do not. Perhaps I could speak with her about setting one up," he suggested.

Allowing a sigh, Nicholas angled his head in Charity's direction. "Don't be keeping her long, sir. She's a busy lady these days."

Marcus shook his head. "I shall be quick," he promised before he headed back to the corner.

When Charity looked up from her paper, surprise showing in her eyes, he said, "My lady, I wish to apologize for having abandoned you last night. I feel awful about it—"

"Abandoned me?" she repeated. "Why, I've no idea what you're talking about."

Marcus furrowed a brow. "After our time in the garden, when I discovered Lord Christopher—Lord Haddon, rather—with my daughter," he said as he gave a slight bow. He reached for her hand, intending to brush a kiss over the back of it.

After a moment, she allowed him the courtesy, but pulled her hand away when she thought he might be lingering over it too long. Then she inhaled very slowly and gave a quick glance in the direction of Mr. Barnaby. "I'm quite sure I don't know what you mean," she said in hushed tones. "Perhaps you have me confused with someone else?" She was about to accuse him of having been too drunk to remember, but she didn't recall him smelling of alcohol, nor did he seem addled in any way during their waltz.

Marcus blinked. "Do you... do you not remember our time in the gardens?"

It was Charity's turn to blink. "My lord, I am quite certain we did not spend any time in the gardens." In fact, she hadn't been with anyone in any gardens since Lady Morganfield's garden party back in 1810.

She had intended to avoid dancing the night before, preferring instead to hide in the lady's retiring room while gentlemen were searching for their next dance partner, but she hadn't made it that far when he had asked her to dance.

"What about the waltz? The supper dance?" Marcus whispered, his eyes darting to where Mr. Barnaby stood with his beefy arms crossed over his rather impressive chest. "You fainted, and I escorted you to the gardens..." He stopped when she continued to display a blank expression. "Oh, dear," he murmured.

"I'm almost afraid to ask," Charity said with a sigh.

The viscount allowed a grunt of frustration. "None of it happened, did it?"

Charity leaned over the desk, her fingers interlinked as she rested her elbows on the edge of the desk. "You were there," she said quietly. "And I was there. I admit that we did dance a waltz, but after it ended, I took my leave of the ball. And not by way of the gardens."

Marcus nearly rolled his eyes in relief. At least he hadn't imagined seeing her at the ball. He hadn't imagined dancing with her.

But apparently he had imagined everything else.

It had all seemed so real!

"Did you... did you approach me to... to chide me for having stared at you?" he stammered, in an attempt to learn exactly where reality ended and his vivid imagination had taken over. He couldn't have imagined her scolding him, could he? She seemed so incensed. So real as she confronted him. "I deserved the scold, of course, because I *was* staring at you."

"I didn't *scold* you," Charity countered in her own defense. With another glance in the direction of Mr. Barnaby, she waved Marcus to the chair that was placed at the end of her desk. "Sit down, please, Lord Lancaster. Perhaps I may be able help you remember exactly what happened last night."

Marcus was about to refuse her offer, but then realized he had been given an opportunity to spend time in her company in a manner he had never been able to before.

He took the proffered chair and gave her a nod. "I am relieved we danced the waltz, but then I was sure you were about to faint, so I hurried you out of the ballroom and into the gardens..." He stopped when he paid witness to her elevated eyebrows and look of disbelief.

"Oh, do go on," she encouraged him. "I'm rather curious as to what I might have allowed you to do in the gardens when I was no doubt already in my town coach and on my way home."

Marcus's eyes widened in alarm. "But, you didn't... that is to say, I didn't attempt anything untoward, I assure you," he replied. "You had your head in the crook of my arm, but then, if you hadn't, you might have fallen to the ground."

For some reason Charity couldn't explain just then, the idea of resting her head in the small of Lord Lancaster's rather impressive shoulder seemed rather appealing. "For how long?" she asked with a furrowed eyebrow.

"Oh, no more than..." He sighed as his broad shoulders slumped. "Well, until you woke up, but even then, you continued to use it to rest your head until we decided we really had to make our way back to the ballroom," he explained. "For propriety's sake, of course."

Daring a glance at the small of his shoulder—both of them—Charity decided either would have worked well for a place to rest her head while she recovered from a faint. But she wasn't about to admit it. "What did we talk about?"

Marcus was about to mention marriage, but thought better of it. "I said that no one had ever fainted on me before, and you seemed quite concerned and asked how you might have looked. I told you it was as if you were a ballerina playing a swan about to swoon—"

"A ballerina?" she repeated in disbelief. Well, at least she hadn't looked like a sack of potatoes in satin.

"Oh, it was an elegant swoon," he assured her. "It didn't happen instantly, of course, because I was able to walk you out the French doors of the ballroom. That's when you completely fainted, so I scooped you into my arms—you're light as a feather, so it was no trouble at all —and I carried you to a stone bench and set you down."

Charity was about to chide the viscount for his overactive imagination, but she found his tale of the imagined event rather entertaining. "And that's when my head ended up in the small of your shoulder," she murmured with a sigh.

He straightened and regarded her with a baleful look. "You think me a fool," he said sadly.

"Unlike your daughter, I am not fresh out of the school room, Lord Lancaster," Charity interrupted, setting aside a sheet of paper on which a number of details were written about one of her clients. "I arrived home safe and sound, and you'll be relieved to know, *alone*." This last was said with a roll of her eyes, as if she might be teasing him.

"Still, I am sorry. *I* should have escorted you home."

Despite her initial annoyance with the viscount, Charity couldn't help her reaction to hearing this tidbit. "I admit I am flattered," she allowed. "But I am left wondering if perhaps we shouldn't find you a new wife," she added as she angled her head. "You, my lord, strike me as a man who is in need of a wife."

Marcus blinked. He did miss having a woman in his life. His daughter was a joy to have in his home now that she was done with finishing school, but life had been rather lonely this past year. "Although I really liked Joan— Lady Joan... Joan Harrington—we were never really a love match," he said in a whisper. "I had known her since we were children. Sort of like marrying a sister, I suppose," he murmured.

A shiver raced through Charity. She knew exactly what he meant by those words. Her marriage had been much the same until her husband had lost interest. "So, you would like to find a love match," she said as she pulled a sheet of blank parchment from the opposite side of her desk. She dipped her quill into an ink pot and regarded him for a moment.

The viscount angled his head to one side. "Still, I... I wish to make it up to you. Would you be amenable to a ride in the park during the fashionable hour? Later today, perhaps?"

Charity couldn't help the frisson that shot through her body just then. She had managed to live for two years without the company of a man—not that she had much of her husband's when he was alive—and just a few moments in the company of the one who sat next to her desk had her body responding even if her mind didn't want to have anything to do with him.

"I believe my maid will be washing my hair about that time," she replied with a smirk. But when she paid witness to his obvious disappointment, a pang of guilt had her adding, "But I probably could tomorrow. Once I'm finished here at the office."

She was shocked by how his entire countenance changed with those simple words. A brilliant smile appeared, youthening his features and once again setting off the most unusual sensations deep in her body. That's when she noticed his eyes. They were golden brown, almost the color of chocolate and just as warm. When her eyes took in his hair—she had noticed the style the night before—she realized it was the same color. She supposed under sunlight the golden shades became more evident.

Marcus gave a vigorous nod. "May I meet you here then? I can bring my phaeton or a... or a curricle, if you prefer. Then I can see to returning you back here... or to your home, whichever is more convenient, when we're finished." He thought about adding other possibilities— like a quick trip to Gretna Green, or at least as quick as a trip to Scotland could be—but he didn't want her changing her mind about their ride in Hyde Park.

Charity couldn't help the grin that softened her own expression. "You may come at four o'clock, but no sooner."

"I'll come for you at one minute after the hour," he countered, giving her a wink when he noted her look of chagrin. Then he reached over, lifted a bare hand, and brushed his lips over the back of it. "Oh, and if you have a soldier looking for a wife, my butler has informed me that one of my housemaids could really use a husband."

Her interest piqued—she hadn't yet had many female

applicants appear at the office—Charity arched an eyebrow. "Oh? Has *she* said so?"

Marcus screwed up his face a bit before saying, "Not exactly. But apparently she has... she has pleasantly exhausted all the footmen, if you catch my meaning. I figure it's best she be married in the event she ends up with child." This last was said in a whisper, at the same time his face took on a decidedly reddish cast.

Charity resisted the urge to blink several times when she not only caught his meaning but knew exactly which one of her clients might suit the randy maid. "It's possible I may have someone perfect for that situation," she murmured.

"My housekeeper would be ever so grateful."

"Oh, I... I thought you said she was a housemaid."

"Oh, it is a housemaid who is in need of a husband," Marcus assured her. "Mary Baker is her name. Mrs. Barstow, the housekeeper, is the one who wants her to *be* married," he explained, hoping his reddening face wasn't too apparent.

"I thought you said it was your butler who informed you," Charity said, her dark brows furrowing with her confusion.

Marcus angled his head first one way and then the other. "He informed me because she informed him. Now, had I a wife, I'm quite certain Mrs. Barstow would have gone to her as opposed to the butler, and then I would know nothing of any of it, but... there you have it."

Charity nodded her understanding, amused that his face still displayed his blush. "Would I be allowed to pay a call on Miss Baker at your home? In order to interview her? I shouldn't think it would take more than a half-hour out of her day."

Nodding, Marcus said he would see to letting the housekeeper know when he returned to Stanton House.

"I'll see what I can do," Charity promised. "And in the meantime, I expect I'll see you again tomorrow at one minute past four o'clock."

Dipping his head, Marcus allowed a wan grin. "I look forward to it." With that, he got up from the chair, gave a bow, and took his leave of Charity and of the charity's office.

Charity stared after the viscount, now wishing she hadn't agreed to a ride in the park. She certainly didn't want to encourage Lord Lancaster. But there was something about the viscount that had her intrigued.

Entertained, even.

Chapter 15

AN INVITATION TO RIDE
PROVES DIFFICULT TO WRITE

M *eanwhile, in South Audley Street*

Luke Merriweather regarded the blank parchment before him, his quill threatening to ruin it by dropping a dot of ink before he had a chance to consider his first words.

Again.

He had formed the message for the note in his head at least a dozen times during the morning's session of Parliament. He had refined the words over the early afternoon when he drove his phaeton back to his townhouse. And now that he was ready to write them, he found the words wouldn't come.

He wanted to begin with "My dearest Analise," but knew that was a bit presumptuous. They hadn't really been formally introduced. They hadn't been introduced at all, truth be told. A situation Luke now decided was entirely Viscount Lancaster's fault—the man had had every opportunity to do the honors on any one of the many occasions he had paid a call at Stanton House to join Marcus.

To be fair, Analise wasn't always there. But Marcus

could have introduced them the night before, at the ball. Given his attentions were directed at Lady Wadsworth, Marcus Batey had somehow kept his daughter from Luke.

Or rather, all her partners in the dances had.

The younger viscount remembered the older viscount's rebuke when he had made a comment about the gorgeous young lady the night before. Although it was evident Lancaster didn't want his daughter being courted by just anyone—or anyone at all—he seemed determined that Luke not consider her. Once Lord Haddon made an appearance, though, Lancaster's manner had changed entirely.

Now he seemed to welcome Luke's suggestion that he court Analise. And Luke wasn't about to squander the opportunity.

Dear Miss Analise,

Although we were both in attendance at Lord Attenborough's ball last night, I realized too late that your father failed to introduce us...

Luke rolled his eyes. Although the blame did fall at Lord Lancaster's feet, he shouldn't exactly say it. He crossed out the "failed to introduce us" and wrote "*overlooked the opportunity to introduce us.*"

There. That was better.

I would like the opportunity to spend time in your company and wondered if you might join me for a ride in the park tomorrow afternoon? I, of course, have your father's permission to drive you. I will come for you at four o'clock in the hopes you can join me.

Yours in service,

Luke Merriweather

Luke reread the note several times, deciding it would do. As for how he could see to its delivery to Stanton House, he thought of his footman and quickly dismissed the idea. He didn't want the older man knowing he was writing to a young lady—the servant would tell his wife, and by tomorrow at this time, every servant in every household in South Audley Street would know he was courting. They would probably all line up outside their houses and watch as he made his way in his old, black phaeton, waving and wishing him luck.

And they would all know the identity of his intended.

No. The footman would not be delivering this missive.

A thought of sending his valet had him cringing. It would be cruel to expect the old fogey to make the walk to Park Lane given his limp.

In the end, Luke called for Weatherby and asked for his horse, making it sound as if he intended to ride in the park during the fashionable hour. By the time he made it to Stanton House, it was just past four o'clock.

He lifted the brass knocker with the intention of giving it a couple of *whacks* when Harrison, Lancaster's butler, answered before he could knock at all. "Good afternoon, sir," Harrison said.

"Lord Merriweather for Lancaster. Is he in?" He passed the note to the servant along with his calling card. "And this is for his daughter."

Harrison regarded the viscount and then the note. "Neither are in at the moment, my lord." He glanced out and noted the man's horse next to the pavement. "They just left for the park."

A bit of panic set in when Luke thought of Lord

Haddon taking Analise in his sporty phaeton—or whatever the honorary earl was driving these days. He had thought from Lancaster's earlier words that Christopher Carlington would not be allowed such an honor.

"Pray tell, do you know who Miss Analise is with?"

The butler's eyebrows lifted into a bushy caterpillar across his forehead. "The Simpsons, I believe," he answered, although he did so reluctantly.

Luke let out a sigh of relief. Although he didn't know any 'Simpsons', they weren't Lord Haddon.

"If you hurry, you can probably catch them before they go through the gates, my lord," Harrison suggested.

At first offended by the idea of chasing down the Simpsons, Luke thought to scold the butler. But his idea had merit. If he arrived at the gates at the same time as their carriage, he could ride alongside. Engage the young lady in conversation. Keep her safe from Lord Haddon should the earl decide to do the same thing.

"Capital idea," he replied. Luke mounted his horse and was off at a gallop even before Harrison had closed the door.

Chapter 16

A DAUGHTER KNOWS BEST

A few minutes earlier, at four o'clock in the afternoon
When Marcus returned to his townhouse in Park Lane, he watched his daughter descend the stairs wearing a green carriage gown. She carried a folded parasol in one hand. "And just where might you be going, young lady?" he asked as he met her at the base of the stairs.

Analise reached up and bussed him on the cheek. "I've been invited for a ride in Hyde Park," she said with a huge smile.

Marcus swallowed. *And so it begins*, he thought in despair. "With Morganfield's son?" he guessed, an expression of pain crossing his face.

Angling her head to one side, Analise sighed. She had only danced with Christopher Carlington the one time, but she supposed since he was the only young buck her father had noticed in her company the night before, probably because the earl escorted her to supper, his comment was to be expected.

She had sung the young man's praises the entire ride home from the ball. Although she had no intention of encouraging the son of a marquess, Analise thought to tease her father just a bit. Prior to last night's ball, he hadn't seemed the least bit interested in her marriage prospects. But then, after the waltz, he suddenly did take an interest.

What was it about Lord Haddon that had him so riled?

"Of course not," she replied.

Analise wouldn't mind riding with the heir to the Morganfield marquessate. But given Lord Haddon's age—he was just out of university—she doubted he had marriage in mind. Probably wouldn't until he was closer to thirty. "I'm going with the Simpsons. Hannah's father is driving us."

Marcus's attempt to remember who the Simpsons might be was met with a quelling glance. "Remind me again—"

"The Simpsons in Kingly Street. They are proprietors of the terraces on both sides of the street."

Marcus blinked and gave his head a shake, clearly not making any connections in his head.

"Hannah's mother was a Burroughs and is the Duke of Ariley's aunt. Hannah has a twin brother who is *gorgeous*, but how can he not be when her parents are so beautiful?" Analise asked rhetorically. "Her older brother is Gregory Grandby—"

"Ah, you're practically going with royalty then," Marcus replied with a smirk. "Do have a good time." He decided it was better he not ask if the gorgeous twin brother would be joining them on the ride.

Analise was about to argue the Simpsons weren't royalty, but her father had been acting rather odd lately. When she gave it more thought, she wondered if it had anything to do with his having inherited the Lancaster viscountcy from her late uncle the year before. Losing his wife two years before that certainly didn't help the situation.

For the first year after her mother's death, her father had been in mourning, his countenance rather sad even on the days she joined him whilst she attended Warwick's.

Although she, too, missed her mother, her enrollment in Warwick's meant she lived with other girls her own age. Ate dinner with them every night. Attended classes and plays together. Learned to dance, and paint, and draw. Practiced comportment, although it wasn't her favorite pastime—walking about with a large book on one's head seemed ever so ridiculous—and played the *piano-forté*. Arithmetic wasn't so bad once she had memorized her tables. And she had even learned to sew, a skill her mother had never taught her because she couldn't do it well and said a maid would see to clothing repairs. Analise hadn't any idea how beautiful stitcheries could be when done with silk thread on the proper fabric.

After her first year at the school, her mother had become a pleasant memory. When Analise wanted to be with family, her father would escort her when she paid calls on one of her many aunts. There were four of them just on the Harrington side alone.

Her father wasn't nearly as sociable, though. She wondered if he was even a member of a men's club. Then she remembered she hadn't lived with him for most of the past two years. Perhaps he did go to a club every night. Perhaps he had taken a mistress. Perhaps he had already begun courting a potential wife.

Analise rather doubted the last, if only because he

hadn't left the house at night but once since her return from Warwick's.

As for what her father and mother had been like together, Analise had never believed her parents were *in love* with one another. They always behaved as if they were merely friends. Good friends, of course. They never fought. They never argued about anything. But their friendship was without the passion she decided her father required now.

One thing she knew for certain—her father needed a new wife. And not one who was merely a friend. He needed someone for whom he could be truly, deeply, passionately in love with.

Someone as unlike her mother as possible.

A knock at the front door interrupted her reverie. "Would you like to meet Mr. Simpson?" she asked, just as the butler saw to opening the door. "I'm sure he would appreciate meeting you."

Her father inhaled, about to decline the opportunity, but then thought better of it. "Yes. Yes, I would." He offered his arm. "I'll escort you to their carriage."

Grinning, Analise placed her arm on his. The two took the few steps to the pavement, where a rather distinguished gentleman held the reins of two matched greys. Next to him sat the young man Marcus decided must be the 'gorgeous twin'. And in the plush seat behind them sat two of the loveliest ladies he had seen in a very long time.

Well, since last night's ball.

"Lady Simpson, may I introduce you to my father, Marcus Batey, Viscount Lancaster?"

Sarah Burroughs Grandby Simpson smiled and extended a gloved hand. "So good to finally meet you, Lord Lancaster."

Marcus bowed over her hand and kissed the knuckles. "The pleasure is all mine." He turned his attention to the young lady seated next to Sarah. "And you must be Miss Hannah."

Hannah dipped her head. "Thank you for allowing Miss Analise to join us," she said. "May I introduce my father, James Simpson, and my brother, Henry?"

Marcus shook hands with the two. He couldn't help but notice the age difference between Henry and his father. Although especially handsome, James looked as if was old enough to be the twins' grandfather. As for Sarah, it was impossible to tell her age, but then the Burroughs women were all like that.

"Good to meet you, Lancaster. Would you care to join us? I believe we can make room," James offered.

Marcus helped his daughter into the curricle so the two younger ladies were situated on either side of Lady Simpson. "I thank you for the offer, but I believe I shall ride today. My horse could use the exercise."

Surprised by his comment, Analise gave him a brilliant smile. "Then I shall look forward to seeing you in the park," she said.

Marcus gave a wave as the equipage pulled away.

Truth be told, he had only given a thought to riding in Hyde Park during the fashionable hour if he could do so with Lady Wadsworth, so he wasn't sure from where his comment had come. When he returned to the house, he mentioned it to Harrison, who assured him his horse would be ready shortly.

"I suppose this means I should change into riding clothes," Marcus said with a sigh. "Do I even own riding clothes?"

Harrison seemed to think on the question a moment

before saying, "I'll send your valet to your apartment immediately."

On his way up to his bedchamber—it was still uncomfortable to think of this townhouse as his—Marcus decided he had an ulterior motive for riding this afternoon.

He hoped to see Lady Wadsworth. Her comment about her maid washing her hair was no doubt made in jest.

As to what he might say to her that he hadn't already said, he wasn't sure.

He knew *what* he wanted to say to her. What he wanted to be doing with her. The trouble was, the saying would get him into trouble from which he might never recover. She might slap him so hard, he would be seeing stars for days.

As for the doing...

He sighed and rolled his eyes.

The doing might leave her speechless. Breathless. Boneless. Open to whatever he wanted to spend a night doing with her.

It might leave him in the same condition.

He could only hope.

"Would you like the navy blue coat? Or the hunter green?" his valet asked.

Marcus stared at Frears for a full five seconds before he comprehended the man's words. "Which will make me appear irresistible?" he asked as lightly as he could manage. He didn't want his servant thinking he was serious with the query, even if he was.

Frears regarded him and then the two garments for a moment before discarding the hunter green coat onto the bed. "The blue brings out your eye color, my lord," he commented. "Which means the buff breeches will be best."

Deciding he was in good hands, Marcus shed his top coach and breeches with the help of Frears and went about redressing. At the sight of the Hessians his valet brought forth from the dressing room, Marcus feared he might look like an officer in one of the armies of the new United States. But once he gazed at his reflection in the cheval mirror, he decided the buff breeches were dark enough to prevent the association from being made.

"Your horse has been brought round front, my lord," the butler said from the other side of his bedchamber door.

"Your gloves and crop, my lord," Frears said as he pressed the accessories into his master's hand. He disappeared into the dressing room for a moment and emerged with a short top hat. He placed it on Marcus's head and regarded the viscount with a critical eye. "If she does not accept an offer of a ride in the park on the morrow, then she is not worth pursuing," he said with a nod.

Marcus blinked and stared at the valet. "She who?"

Frears furrowed a brow. "The woman who is to be your next wife?" he guessed.

Angling his head to one side, Marcus grinned. "Your optimism is refreshing, Frears." With that, he took his leave of Stanton House, mounted his horse, and headed in the direction of Hyde Park at a full gallop.

Chapter 17

A RIDE IN THE PARK

An hour later in Hyde Park

On a pleasant day in Rotten Row, the fashionable hour featured all manner of equipage driven by aristocrats dressed to impress and in which their passengers rode with the intention of being seen. Those on horseback had the advantage, for they could wind their way through the heavy traffic and converse with those in carriages at their leisure.

Marcus had never ridden a horse in Rotten Row during the fashionable hour. His late wife preferred riding in the comfort of their curricle, and since he enjoyed driving, Marcus never gave their trips to the park a second thought.

Once he passed several carriages, he understood why his peers did such a thing. Why it was the young bucks chose horses over phaetons. Why even some young ladies opted for riding habits and jaunty hats and their favorite steed over the comfort of a carriage.

The experience was rather enjoyable.

To see as well as to be seen was a daily ritual for those

who participated. If Marcus wanted to see someone again, he could simply turn his horse around and trot to the back of the line and move forward all over again.

When he was on his second return to the front gates, he spotted Lady Wadsworth in the back of a barouche driven by a man wearing livery. Although a parasol occasionally hid her from prying eyes, he recognized the Wadsworth livery before he determined she was riding in the barouche.

"Good afternoon, my lady," he said when he had his horse trotting alongside the Wadsworth equipage. "You look even more beautiful than you did when last I saw you." He had to inhale a bit at his words. He had never in his life made such a bold statement to a lady before. She would probably think him a rake!

Charity regarded him with suspicion. "Why, Lord Lancaster, what a surprise."

"Indeed," he replied. "But a pleasant one, I hope?" At her lack of immediate response, Marcus's confidence waned. Why did he have to sound so bold? He was never bold. Never so forward with his remarks about a member of the female sex. "I apologize. I did not intend for my words—"

"It is a pleasant surprise," Charity interrupted him, folding her parasol and resting it on her lap. "I have now been in your company three times in less than a day. Why, I am left wondering if you are following me," she said with an arched brow.

Marcus was forced to halt his horse when the barouche stopped to allow another carriage to move in front of it. "I admit to hoping I might see you again on this fine day," he said sheepishly. "Why, I would be happy to see you every day for the rest of my life."

"Oh?" Her expression displayed a hint of alarm.

"After our discussion this afternoon at your office, I thought to discover if I might employ you."

Charity's eyes widened in alarm. After what they had discussed this afternoon, he thought to offer her *carte blanche?* "How dare you!"

Marcus blinked, just then realizing what she thought he meant. His eyes rounded to match hers. "Oh, no, no, my lady. Not like that!" he countered, just as the barouche lurched forward. He managed to get his horse in motion until he was once again abreast of the barouche. "For your skills."

Now, Dear Reader, Marcus Lancaster really should have been more careful in his choice of words. He really should have considered how she would interpret his meaning. But, alas, he did not and only realized too late how his words sounded to a widow, the understanding even more complete when her parasol suddenly whipped out and walloped his Hessian hard enough to send his horse into a gallop and nearly into the back of Lord Devonville's yellow phaeton.

"If I ever see you again—for the rest of my life— it will be too soon," Charity said from clenched teeth, managing to keep her expression pleasant despite her words.

For the first time that afternoon, Marcus regretted having ridden his horse. Regretted having made the trip to Hyde Park. "You have my humblest apologies, Lady Wadsworth," he said in his most pleading voice. "I am not a rake. I am not a brigand nor a scoundrel. I merely..." He had to cease his comment when the Wadsworth barouche took an opportunity to turn off of Rotten Row and make its way out of the park.

Before Marcus could redirect his mount to follow, another carriage had filled the void, a carriage he recognized as the one belonging to Mr. Simpson. His daughter's attention was on a rider on the other side—a man he recognized from the night before. Christopher Carlington, Earl of Haddon, was regarding Analise as if she were the only occupant in the Simpson equipage.

"Why, Lord Lancaster. I wondered if we might see you again," Mrs. Simpson said from where she sat between the young ladies. "Have you made the rounds already?"

Marcus tipped his top hat. "Indeed. I believe I'm on my third go-round," he replied. He tried hard to keep his expression friendly, but the sting of Lady Wadsworth's dismissal—and his daughter's intense attention on Morganfield's son—made it difficult.

How had he bungled it so?

"Lady Wadsworth has had a trying day," Sarah Simpson said as she leaned in his direction.

Trying day? He wondered if his visit to the 'Finding Wives for the Wounded' had been the cause. "I do hope I didn't add to her distress," he commented.

Sarah dared a quick glance in his daughter's direction, apparently to ensure her attention was still on Christopher Carlington. When Sarah turned back to him, she said, "One of her clients suffered a set-back, and I fear she is taking it far too seriously."

Marcus nodded his understanding. "I do hope she understands how important her work is."

Sarah arched an eyebrow. "Perhaps too well. Tell an

old, nosy woman if you will, how long have you and Charity been spending time in one another's company?"

His horse nearly halted on its own in response to hearing her query. Marcus pulled up on the reins if only because the question was so unexpected. Unfortunately, his daughter overheard the query, for she turned and gawked.

"Father!" she said in surprise, either because she had just then noticed his presence or because she had overheard Mrs. Simpson's query.

Probably because she had overheard Mrs. Simpson's words.

"We have not been," he countered, loud enough for both ladies to hear. "I only danced with her last night at the ball. And then I saw her this afternoon when I paid a call at her office."

Analise, apparently forgetting the Earl of Haddon was only a few feet from where she sat, furrowed a brow as she regarded him. "Are you courting her?" she asked, her voice suggesting more curiosity than alarm.

Marcus's eyebrows lifted nearly to his hairline. "No!" When it became apparent none of the ladies in the carriage believed him—even Hannah and Henry cast him looks of disbelief—he added, "Not... not yet, at least."

A small smile appeared on Mrs. Simpson's lips. "She'll require a bit of time is all," she said, just before turning her attention to the earl. "As will Miss Analise."

Christopher gave a reluctant nod. "I understand, my lady." With that, he tipped his hat and then he spurred his horse so it moved up to flank the Devonville phaeton.

The disappointment on Analise's face could not be ignored, which had Marcus feeling even more alarm than he had experienced the night before.

Was the Earl of Haddon more interested in Analise than he had let on at Lord Attenborough's ball?

And worse, was Analise interested in him?

few minutes later
Breathless and his heart beating far too fast, Luke directed his horse beneath the gates of Hyde Park. He had passed a parade of all manner of equipage on the way, surreptitiously surveying the occupants of each—especially the curricles and barouches—in an effort to find the one that carried Miss Analise.

He wasn't paying any attention to those on horseback, so Luke was shocked when he heard "Merriweather?" called out by someone to his right. Glancing in that direction, he found Marcus Batey regarding him with a look of surprise.

"Lancaster? I didn't know you were going to ride today," Luke said as he pulled up alongside the older viscount's bay.

"I didn't know you knew how to ride," Marcus countered, his manner suggesting impatience, just before his gaze went to a carriage that had left the rest of those parading along Rotten Row.

Frowning, Luke followed Marcus's line of sight. From this distance, he didn't recognize the older equipage, nor the horses that pulled it, but a thought as to who might be in it had him glancing back at Marcus with an arched brow. "Lady Wadsworth, perhaps?"

Marcus allowed a sigh of frustration. "Indeed. She... she is a bit miffed with me. A misunderstanding, is all." He glanced to his left and found his daughter scowling at him. "On two accounts, I believe."

Luke slowed his mount and directed his attention to the Simpson carriage, heartened to see Miss Analise sitting next to Lady Simpson. Her expression was anything but pleasant, however, a combination of disappointment and anger making her eyes flash in a most arresting manner.

Although he didn't wish for her to ever look at him in that way, he fought the wave of desire that gripped him just then.

"Lady Simpson! Miss Hannah! So good to see you on this fine day," he called out, well aware when Analise's attention turned from her father to him. Her expression changed to one of curiosity.

"Why, Merriweather," Lady Simpson replied, her blue eyes bright with recognition. "I haven't seen you in an age. Or Laura. How is your mother?"

Luke allowed a shrug. "Still in Epping, I fear. She refuses to come to London for the Little Season but says she will join Father for the Season come spring." He turned his attention on Hannah. "Are you still attending Warwick's, Miss Hannah?"

The young lady nodded her head. "I'm in my last year, Lord Merriweather. I hear congratulations are in order." She turned her gaze onto Analise. "Lord Merriweather accepted a writ of acceleration and is already serving in Parliament," she explained.

Analise redirected her attention to the young viscount. "I've not had the pleasure of an introduction."

Lady Simpson beamed in delight. "Then allow me," she said, giving Marcus a quick glance. "Miss Analise Batey, may I introduce you to Luke Merriweather, Viscount Merriweather? You might be acquainted with his sister, Eleanor, the Countess of Wakefield."

Luke watched as Analise's eyes widened a fraction, and

his heart skipped a beat as what appeared to be a genuine smile lit her face. "It's a pleasure to finally meet you, Lord Merriweather," she said.

Luke lifted his top hat and gave a nod. "Merriweather, please. And the pleasure is all mine. I had hoped your father might introduce us at Attenborough's ball, but you must have danced every set last night."

Her eyes rounding at his comment—she was obviously unaware anyone but her father had been keeping track of her the night before—Analise gave a slight shake of her head. "Not every dance," she said, a becoming blush pinking her face.

"Then the blame lies solely on your father, for he neglected to introduce us," he replied in a light-hearted jab at Marcus.

Analise's eyes flashed in the direction of her father. "He has been keeping much from me, it seems," she said. "May I expect to dance with you at the next ball?"

Luke allowed a slow smile. "Indeed. The waltz. Both of them, if there are two."

"Now, you needn't be greedy, Merriweather," Lady Simpson chided, although she was smiling as she said the words.

"I should say not," Marcus put in, as if he was just then joining their conversation. His attention had been on something up ahead, as if he were lost in thought. He lowered his voice. "Greedy about what?" he asked in a hoarse whisper.

Blinking at the query, Luke decided he could fib with his answer. "Two waltzes with Miss Hannah." The older viscount didn't need to learn the truth just then. Luke had only earned his permission to call on Miss Analise earlier that day.

Marcus nodded his understanding and then turned his attention to those in the carriage. "I am going to ride up ahead and pay my respects to Devonville. Good day." He tipped his hat.

A chorus of 'good-byes' followed him and Luke as they spurred their horses forward.

"Whatever did you say to earn such a withering stare?" Luke asked after he had rejoined Marcus. They were nearly abreast of the Devonville phaeton.

Marcus allowed a shrug before he indicated a horse and rider up ahead. "My daughter thinks I've been courting Lady Wadsworth—which I am not," he replied. Yet," he added, deciding he wasn't about to give up on the countess. "And I believe she has deduced I disapprove of Haddon." He lowered his voice. "I may have said something to discourage his attentions."

The younger viscount allowed a grin. "Thank you for that. I stopped at Stanton House to deliver an invitation for her to ride with me on the morrow. Perhaps I can keep her mind off the earl."

Marcus gave him a withering stare. "I cannot believe you are doing this on my behalf," he said. "Surely you have someone in mind to make your viscountess. This is no doubt taking you away from her."

Luke allowed a shrug. "Not at all. I have yet to set my cap on anyone," he replied lightly. "Now, whatever happened with Lady Wadsworth?" he asked in an attempt to take the older viscount's attention away from his daughter.

Giving his head a shake, Marcus said, "She thinks I was trying to offer *carte blanche*—which I was not—and my attempt to clarify why I wished to speak with her further only made matters worse."

Hearing the disappointment in Lancaster's response had Luke realizing there was more to his interest in Charity Wadsworth than what the man had intimated the night before. "Do you wish to make her your viscountess?" he asked. "Or your mistress?"

Marcus nearly halted his horse at hearing the bold query. "Viscountess, of course. And yes, as a matter of fact, I do. Not that it's any of your business."

"Perhaps if you mention your intention first, then she will not assume you are after a mistress," Luke replied, his tone helpful rather than spiteful.

"I thought I made it very clear..." Marcus stopped when he remembered that not everything he had said to Charity had been said with her actually *present*. Some of it had been said to the Charity with whom he had spent that half-hour in the gardens the night before.

The Charity in his imagination.

"But apparently not," he continued in a whisper. Then he remembered Lady Simpson's comment about Charity.

Lady Wadsworth has had a trying day.

He glanced over at his colleague with new-found appreciation. "You are right, of course. I shall try that approach next."

Feigning shock at hearing he was right about anything, Luke allowed a grin. "Do be sure to let me know how it goes." Even as he said the words, though, he knew Lancaster was lost in thought, for the older viscount was staring off where Lady Wadsworth's coach had long since disappeared. Deciding his presence wouldn't be missed, he spurred his horse to quicken it's trot and left Lancaster to ruminate by himself.

Marcus was well aware that Luke had pulled up ahead, but in his current state, he wasn't feeling particularly sociable. In fact, he was imagining any number of scenarios he might try on the delectable Lady Wadsworth.

Perhaps he would don a mask and enter her bedchamber in the middle of the night. He wouldn't be intent on stealing her jewels, though, opting instead to ravish her before he took his leave at dawn. He would worship her body with his lips and tongue, his black leather-gloved fingers smoothing over her heated skin and inciting a million darts of pleasure beneath the surface. Perhaps he would secure an invitation to visit her again. And again.

He groaned in frustration, turned his mount in the direction of the gate, and rode home.

Chapter 18

A CHARITY DOUBTING HER CHARITY

eanwhile...
Her anger at Lord Lancaster slowly abating—how could the viscount be so bold as to offer *carte blanche* and do so with so many aristocrats nearby?—Charity dared a glance back at Rotten Row and gave a *huff.*

At least she had managed to speak with a few ladies regarding their unmarried servants, asking if they might know of anyone in need of a spouse. She, of course, had to quickly explain that she was seeing to Lady E's 'Finding Wives for the Wounded' as its new matchmaker, lest anyone think she was after something else.

Or someone else.

Thinking Lady Pettigrew would be the perfect person to spread the word about the need for unmarried servants to contact her, Charity was just about to have her driver converge on Lady Pettigrew's coach when Lord Lancaster appeared. He looked ever so regal in his riding clothes, his breeches snug around his thighs, his boots polished to a shine.

And then he had started to speak. And say things she couldn't believe she was hearing!

Perhaps she had overestimated the viscount. Earlier that day, she had come to appreciate his attentions, strange as they were. That he would have imagined her in the gardens with him—apparently he had conjured a rather cozy image of the two of them on a stone bench—Charity found she was curious as to just how cozy he had imagined their time together.

Had they kissed? Murmured sweet nothings? Told each other their deepest, darkest secrets? Made a date for a secret assignation? If so, she wondered where that might be. She couldn't imagine the viscount would arrange anything at his townhouse given his daughter lived with him. Which meant he was probably thinking of paying a call on her at her house!

The cur.

How dare he?

About to curse out loud, Charity had to remind herself she really didn't know what the viscount intended. She was only there in his imagination.

Which meant he probably imagined a perfect version of her. Unblemished and slightly blushed, with her curly, dark blonde hair splayed out as if it was caught in a gentle breeze. Her naked body a model of female perfection atop a velvet counterpane. Her lips murmuring words of encouragement and invitation. One crooked finger beckoning him to join her. The floral and spicy scent surrounding her slowly surrounding him, capturing him and pulling him in.

And him quite willing to be caught in her net.

Charity allowed a mischievous grin. Oh, the naughty things she could do with a willing man such as him!

As to her deepest, darkest secret, she furrowed a brow when she realized she really didn't harbor a secret that could be considered deep or dark. Everyone knew she didn't feel affection for her late husband. But who knew she always wished a masked man might enter her bedchamber in the middle of the night, intent on stealing her jewels and instead ravishing her before he took his leave without going near her jewel box? How he would worship her body with his lips and tongue, his black leather-gloved fingers smoothing over her heated skin and inciting a million darts of pleasure beneath the surface.

"Milady?"

Charity was about to allow a moan of sensual satisfaction, about to beg for more, when she realized the voice didn't belong to her masked man. In fact, the voice belonged to one of the grooms from the stable behind her house. "Yes?" she replied, trying hard not to sound too annoyed.

The groom held out a hand. "I'll see to the horses," he said.

Charity blinked, a sense of melancholy settling over her when she realized where she was. And it wasn't on a velvet counterpane in her bedchamber with a masked man hovering over her.

"Very well," she said as she took his proffered hand and stepped down from the carriage.

She was already in her house when she realized she had been guilty of possessing the very same sort of imagination Lord Lancaster claimed to suffer with.

Oh, no, she thought in a fit of despair.

After another moment, she allowed a long sigh and decided she might have to give Lord Lancaster another chance. At least until she knew exactly what he had imagined.

Chapter 19

A VISCOUNT IMAGINES MUCH

*L*ater that night
A note of apology, Marcus thought as a footman brought in the first course of dinner. *I'll write it as soon as dinner is done and then have a footman deliver it.*

"What plans are you making for this evening?"

The query had Marcus blinking. "Plans?" he repeated, wondering how his daughter would guess that's exactly what he was doing. Making plans.

Analise was seated to his right, looking luminescent after her ride in the park. Her yellow corded silk dinner gown, adorned with dainty embroidered flowers and gros grain ribbons fashioned into flowers along the neckline, fit her to perfection. She looked so much like her late mother, Marcus did a double-take.

"You've been daydreaming again," Analise accused with a grin, lifting a soup spoon from her place setting. She knew if she hadn't said something, her father would be lost in thought and probably miss the opportunity to eat his soup.

"I apologize, he murmured as he blinked at the sight of the bowl of soup before him. He was about to ask how long it had been sitting there when he noticed tendrils of steam rising from the surface. Not long then. "Which is the very subject of what I was daydreaming about," he admitted.

Analise paused in lifting her spoon to her lips and regarded him with a raised brow. "Apologies?"

He nodded. "I owe one to someone who I have apparently vexed. I wish to clear up the matter before she's had a chance to think about it too much and form a poor opinion of me," he explained. He took to eating his soup and then paused when he noted Analise still watched him. "What is it?"

"Lady Wadsworth?" Analise guessed, returning her attention to her soup. She quirked a lip when she caught her father's look of shock from the corner of her eye. "Really, Father. I saw how you looked at her last night," she murmured. "While you were dancing with her. So I suppose I shouldn't have been so shocked to learn you were courting her."

Marcus was about to put voice to a protest, but he instead allowed a sigh. "I'm not courting her," he replied. "But would it bother you if I might wish to court her? I had the distinct impression you were... displeased with me this afternoon in the park."

Her eyes widening with her surprise—on two counts —Analise started to respond and then stopped. She hadn't thought her father was of a mind to court the widow. She hadn't considered her father would ever remarry. He seemed content as a widower. She thought she would have him all to herself, at least until she married and moved into her husband's household. "Bother me?" she finally repeated. "Of course not. It's just a bit... unexpected is all."

"Unexpected?" he repeated.

Analise gripped her spoon tighter. "I didn't realize you were considering remarriage. But I think you should."

Marcus gave a start. "You do? I wasn't. That is, I wasn't considering it until just recently."

Until just last night, he nearly added, but thought better of it.

"What happened to change your mind?" Analise asked.

"Nothing."

At her arched eyebrow and look of disbelief, Marcus finally relented. "I watched the Morganfields dance last night," he said, remembering how David and Adelaide Carlington held one another during the waltz. Far too close, their eyes never leaving one another. He was sure their wordless stare was a prelude to an assignation. Probably in the Attenborough's library. Or perhaps in the gardens.

Before that moment, he had only been concerned about how Analise fared with her dance card. About how the Morganfield's son, Lord Haddon, gazed at her. About how he was thinking of her as an innocent lamb about to be devoured by a wolf. About how he might have to send her to a convent. About how he might have to move to the country and take her with him.

And then he had spotted Lady Wadsworth and all thoughts of Analise and the Carlingtons flew from his head.

What had she been doing that had him so intrigued?

When Analise continued to stare at him, Marcus gave a quick shake of his head and added, "And I saw that Lady Wadsworth was without a dance partner, so I..."

When he didn't finished the sentence, Analise's eyes rounded again. "You didn't," she said in a hoarse whisper.

Marcus blinked. "Didn't what?"

"Imagine her as your wife. Round with your third heir and fawning over you as you went about your daily life. On your arm as you walked about town shopping. Kissing you good morning every day in the breakfast parlor like Mother used to do—"

"I did no such thing," he argued, rather shocked she could come up with such an intriguing scenario. And one that wasn't too far off the mark. He slumped in his carver. "At least, I didn't get quite as far with the..." He waved his hand in a rolling motion. "... the shopping and the kisses before breakfast," he said quietly. "The domestic considerations."

It was Analise's turn to blink. Twice. "You feel affection for her," she murmured as her normally ramrod straight back fell against her chair back.

About to put voice to a protest, Marcus found he couldn't. Analise had guessed his situation correctly. As for the 'round with heir', he would be satisfied with another daughter, if only to see the look on Charity's face when she held their babe.

"And it wasn't another heir I imagined, but rather a girl. Lady Wadsworth would like a daughter, you see," he whispered.

Analise straightened at the same moment the footman entered to remove their soup bowls. "She cannot have me," she said, just before she realized how spoiled she sounded.

"She doesn't want..." Marcus stopped and stared at his

daughter, horrified by what he had almost said. "She's always wanted a daughter. Wadsworth only ever got two sons on her."

Relieved she wasn't about to gain a doting mother in the next few minutes, Analise allowed a sigh. "I met the new Earl of Wadsworth earlier this year," she said then, her brows furrowed. At her father's expression of curiosity, she added, "It was just after he had been officially declared the new Earl of Wadsworth. He was at Warwick's to pay a call on someone there, and all the girls nearly fainted, they were so excited by his presence."

Marcus frowned. "Did you faint?" he asked.

Analise resisted the urge to leave the table. "I was not the least bit affected by Lord Wadsworth, I assure you," she said with annoyance. "Nor was the young lady on whom he paid a call. At least, not like that."

"His betrothed?" Marcus guessed.

Shaking her head, Analise said, "Cousin, or so he called her, although he did so in a most demeaning tone of voice. Told her she could no longer attend Warwick's. Said he wasn't going to pay her tuition now that he was the earl. That she was to go home to her..." Here, she stopped, realizing she couldn't repeat what the cur had said within her hearing.

The only reason she had heard Benedict Wadsworth's words was because she was in the same classroom as Marguerite Fulton. Most of the others had already taken their leave. She and Hannah Simpson had been left to pay witness to the earl's treatment of Marguerite, his words making it clear he thought her a bastard.

His father's bastard.

Marcus was sure she was about to say, "Mother," when

he noted Analise's expression. "Home to her...?" he prompted.

"She is really his *sister*," Analise said softly, ignoring his query. "We weren't supposed to know, but everyone at school knew she was Lord Wadsworth's daughter."

Arching an eyebrow, Marcus gave a shake of his head. While they had been dancing, the countess had made it quite clear that she had never had a girl. That she wished for one. "But Charity doesn't have a daughter. Why, she told me..." He halted his remark when several footmen delivered the next course and poured wine, the same moment he understood the implication of his own daughter's words.

Marguerite Fulton wasn't Charity's daughter. Which meant she was a by-blow. An illegitimate daughter.

Did Charity know about Marguerite? He felt a twinge of regret on the countess's behalf, for if she did, she must have felt doubly deprived that one of Wadsworth's mistresses would be allowed to bear him a daughter when she was not.

"Wadsworth refuses to acknowledge her?" he asked when the last footman had disappeared behind the door to the butler's pantry. Then he gave a *huff*. This sort of discussion with his daughter was entirely inappropriate.

"He refuses to continue the arrangement his father made on the girl's behalf," Analise whispered. "Marguerite was heart-broken. Her mother cannot afford the tuition. She was supported by the late earl, too, and Wadsworth has seen to cutting her off."

His eyes darting to one side, Marcus had a mind to ask Analise just how much she knew of such arrangements. She shouldn't know anything, but he supposed there were other illegitimate daughters who attended Warwick's

Grammar and Finishing School at the expense of their fathers.

Marcus felt relief at never having sired a bastard. Although he would have gladly recognized the child as his own, he knew their life would never be as good as a legitimate child's life. And he knew he hadn't fathered a bastard because he had never employed a mistress. Before he inherited, he couldn't afford the lease on a townhouse and the accoutrements a mistress would demand in addition to pin money.

He wasn't sure he could afford one even now.

"I'm sure Miss Fulton's mother will find a new... arrangement," Marcus murmured, thinking there was usually another man who wanted what someone else had. "Although if she meant anything to Wadsworth, he surely would have made provisions for her in his will."

Analise stared at her dinner plate. "Her living until she married, and then a dowry, which the new Lord Wadsworth claimed he would not pay."

Furrowing a brow, Marcus regarded his daughter for a moment before he realized just how annoyed he was with Benedict Fulton, Earl of Wadsworth. Why, if he was still a practicing solicitor, he might seek justice on behalf of Marguerite just because he could.

In fact, the more he thought about it, the more he was tempted to confront the young earl and make his position clear. If Edmund Fulton had made provisions in his will on behalf of his illegitimate daughter, then it was Benedict's duty to see to it those provisions were carried out.

And if he refused?

Marcus imagined how he might bring up the topic with the young earl. Introduce himself, since he had never been formally introduced to the cur. Make a bit of small talk, mention the weather and remark on the fact that the earl's sister and his daughter were classmates at Warwick's.

If the earl feigned no knowledge of a sister, then Marcus would be sure to apprise him not only of the girl's existence, but also of the late earl's arrangements on her behalf. "You do realize you must honor those obligations?" he would ask. Or tell, rather. In a firm voice that gave no choice in the matter. "Or be prepared to find yourself forced to pay more should your malfeasance be discovered."

Oh, he liked championing a cause such as this. Why, he might have to come out of retirement for this very case!

"You're doing it again," Analise said as she placed her fork on her plate. She had finished nearly all her fish and most of the potatoes.

"Doing what?" Marcus asked as he shook himself from his reverie. He glanced down at his plate, realizing the fish course had been served and was now probably cold.

"Daydreaming," she accused. "I do hope it was something having to do with Mother."

Marcus felt a twinge of regret. "Actually, I was thinking of what I might do for Marguerite Fulton," he replied. "From a legal perspective."

Analise's face brightened as she allowed a smile. "You would do that? For me?" she replied as she sat up straighter and nearly bounced in her chair.

"I would do it for *her*," Marcus responded in a quiet voice. He frowned suddenly. "Except I would need to be sure of the provisions of the late Wadsworth's will." His furrowed brows nearly joined one another into a single line. "I don't suppose you have a copy in your possession?" he teased.

Her food forgotten, Analise looked as if she was trying

to decide whether to humor her father or leave the table. "I do not, but Miss Fulton has a copy. Or rather, her mother does. She found it in an escritoire, all rolled up and marked with a seal and several signatures."

Without seeing the document in question, Marcus couldn't know if it was an official copy of the late earl's will. "I must make an appointment to meet with Miss Fulton's mother, but I cannot be seen calling on her at her house, of course. Nor can she come here," he added when it appeared as if Analise was about to suggest it.

"Can you meet with Marguerite? I can invite her for tea and ask that she bring the document," Analise suggested.

"Without her mother's knowledge?" he asked, wondering if the mistress might already be pursuing assistance from a solicitor. Perhaps his help wasn't required.

"Her mother..." Analise paused, slumping once again in her chair. "She cannot read, at least, not well, so Miss Fulton said she has just believed what she's been told."

Marcus frowned. "And what might that be?"

Analise sighed. "That the late Lord Wadsworth made provisions for her and for Marguerite. A living for them both, at least until Marguerite married, and then a dowry of not less than five-thousand pounds."

Marcus allowed a shrug. "Seems fair," he hedged. "So... was the Earl of Wadsworth the bearer of this news, or did he send someone else with the information?" he asked, not expecting Analise to know. He was already rather surprised at just how much she did know.

"A solicitor paid a call on Miss Fulton's mother two days after the earl's death. He gave her a box, mostly of small gifts she had bestowed on the earl, and some jewelry as well as a necklace for Marguerite. He explained every-thing, and Marguerite said they have lived comfortably for nearly two years. And then, after Lord Wadsworth paid a call on her at the school, the monthly payments stopped."

His eyes darting to one side, Marcus felt a hint of anger. Wadsworth had no right to circumvent the terms of his father's will. "It's all rather odd he waited nearly two years before he ceased the funds," he murmured. He had a thought that perhaps the Wadsworth earldom couldn't afford the monthly payments, but he hadn't heard the new earl was in financial straits. Most lords had recovered from the debacle brought on by the Year of No Summer, their tenants unable to farm or pay the rents on their lands due to the inclement weather of 1816.

What if the Wadsworth earldom had not?

Marcus shook his head. Wadsworth had coal mines. Forests. At least a sawmill or two.

So maybe Wadsworth had suffered losses at the gaming tables. Spread vowels all over London and no longer had the funds to cover them. Or perhaps his man of business had been helping himself to more than he was entitled.

Surely I would have heard something, Marcus thought.

Then he realized he had no idea if the earldom had suffered because Benedict Wadsworth was an inveterate gambler or not. He hadn't been at his men's club more than a few nights since his wife's death, and Parliament had only reconvened last week.

Analise leaned over the table and lowered her voice. "You're doing it again," she accused.

Marcus angled towards her and whispered. "I am trying to reason why it is Wadsworth would suddenly take an interest in a rather small monthly cost to his earldom," he replied.

"You're excused then," Analise said, her lips quirking a moment before she once again sobered. "Her mother is beside herself with worry. She claims she is too old to attract a suitor—"

"Invite Miss Fulton for tea. Be sure she brings the will, and we shall see what we can do," he said before he settled back into his carver, just as the footmen appeared with the next dinner course.

"I shall do so. Right before I take a ride in the park," she said as she tucked into her food. "With whomever asks me to accompany them."

But she knew her father wasn't listening. He once again appeared lost in thought.

What she didn't know is that he was musing as to how it was she knew things she shouldn't at her age.

Chapter 20

A NOTE OF APOLOGY

*T*he following morning Marcus reread his note of apology to Charity for the sixth time, frowning when he realized how messy it looked. With so many words crossed out and blotches of ink obliterating his best words, he knew he had to start over.

At least he had some time before he needed to leave for Westminster. He wanted desperately to finish and have the note delivered to the countess's office before noon. It wouldn't do to have Charity think the worst of him for any longer.

He drew another sheet of stationery before him and copied from his original letter.

Dearest Lady Wadsworth,

Will you please accept my humblest apologies for the poor choice of words I used in your company yesterday? Although their meaning was clear in my mind, they were obviously misconstrued in yours, and you had every right to feel offense.

First, let me be perfectly clear. I wish to employ you. Not as a mistress, but in your capacity as a matchmaker.

You see, I have reason to believe Lord Haddon has set his cap on my daughter, Analise. I wish said cap to be set on someone else. Anyone else but my daughter.

Second, my first reason for asking you to go riding with me in the park was so that we might spend time in one another's company. Perhaps you would come to realize I am not a rake and that my intentions and my affections are sincere.

Third, there is a matter of some concern and delicacy which involves your oldest son. I hesitate to bring it up with you for I know it may cause undue pain, but in the interest of justice for the injured parties, I feel it is my duty to pursue their cause.

May I still call upon you at one minute past four o'clock today at your office as we discussed yesterday? Or somewhere else? I will have instructed the footman to await your reply.

Your humblest servant,
Marcus, Viscount Lancaster

Marcus stared at the finished letter, wondering if the second half made it sound too ominous. Perhaps Charity Wadsworth knew nothing of her son's machinations. Perhaps the two were estranged. Benedict, Earl of Wadsworth, didn't even live at Wadsworth Hall. But Marcus thought she needed to know what the earl had done. Far better Charity learn of the issue before the gossip rags started printing word of what he had learned.

The last thing he wanted to do was embarrass the widowed countess.

Chapter 21

MATCHMAKING AS A MEANS
OF MAINTAINING

*M*eanwhile

Determined to forget Lord Lancaster and his *faux pax* in the park the day before, Charity arrived at 30 Oxford Street just as Mr. Barnaby was unlocking the door.

"Mornin', milady. You're rather early," he commented as he opened the door for her. The two had arrived at the office at the same time, Mr. Barnaby from having escorted his new wife to Warwick's Grammar and Finishing School, where she was a teacher.

"There's much to do," Charity replied. In her hands, she clutched a number of missives that had been delivered to her home last evening. Before it had been brought to an abrupt halt by Lord Lancaster's comments, her time in the park had given her the opportunity to ask other riders if they might have servants in need of spouses, especially housekeepers, maids, and kitchen staff.

Having read the responses, Charity knew she was onto something. Apparently, Lancaster's randy maid wasn't a unique situation. Lady Attenborough mentioned she had two young housemaids who were pining for husbands. Lady Carlington's lady's maid wanted a spouse (but not one that was so old, he required nursing, for she didn't want to lose the lady's maid's services). And Lady Devonville's youngest kitchen maid required a husband because the fast girl had exhausted all the footmen so they were "useless in all their duties but one". Charity briefly wondered what that one duty might be, but decided perhaps she didn't wish to know.

Then there was a note from Lord Torrington, who claimed his butler needed a wife but didn't know it yet.

Charity wasn't about to guess what that might be all about. She had met Bernard in his capacity as butler of Worthington House but didn't get the impression he was necessarily in *need* of a wife.

If she couldn't arrange for the servants to pay her a call at the office, Charity would simply pay a call on them at their place of work—should permission be granted by their employers. In any case, notes needed to be written to all involved so that she might begin matchmaking.

Having completed several of her letters and about to start another, she was interrupted by a rather tall, ginger-haired footman who appeared on the other side of her desk just before eleven o'clock. "Yes?" she asked as she looked up. And up, until she was staring into extremely blue eyes.

"My lady," the footman said as he gave a bow. He held out a sealed missive. "I am from Stanton House with a note for your ladyship. His lordship asked that I wait for a reply."

Charity took the note from him and immediately recognized the seal. She gave a sigh before she broke the wax and then frowned when she saw that it wasn't a simple question. She expected an invitation to ride in the park, not a letter hinting at something awful.

"Where are you to deliver my reply?" she asked. She wondered if this might be one of the footmen with whom Lancaster's housemaid had been intimate. He didn't appear pleasantly exhausted.

"Parliament, my lady. That is, if I can get there 'afore three o'clock."

Charity glanced at the mantle clock over the room's only fireplace, deciding she could keep her responses short. "Tell his lordship that he can collect me at four o'clock," she said. "But I must have you deliver a missive on my behalf to Lord Wadsworth. He should be at Parliament as well. Can you do that?"

"I... I think so," the footman replied with a nod.

Pulling a sheet of paper from her small allotment, Charity wrote:

Dear Benedict,
  What have you done?
  Your loving mother

She folded the sheet into quarters but didn't bother sealing it, and then wrote *Benedict, Earl of Wadsworth* on the outside. She doubted the footman could read, but he might be forced to show it to others in order to locate her son amongst the other lords. "Give this to Lord Wadsworth."

"Yes, milady," Rodney replied. He gave a deep bow and was about to take his leave when Charity held up a staying hand.

"Are you familiar with a maid in your household named Mary Baker?" she asked.

Rodney blinked before his eyes darted to one side. "I am, in every way. If you catch my meaning, my lady," he replied, one of this eyebrows waggling. Then he suddenly sobered. "That is to say—"

"How would you describe her?" Charity interrupted, ignoring the implication of his claim—and the eyebrow.

Inhaling and then blowing air out of his mouth, the footman seemed to consider the question for too long before saying, "Verra pretty. Long dark hair. Short." He held his hand out at chest height to indicate the maid's height. "Happy. Well, that is to say, she was happy until the housekeeper told her she had to carry her own coal buckets. I was glad to do it for her—"

"Yes, well, thank you for your insight. You may go now," Charity said, hoping her face wasn't displaying the blush she felt coming on just then. She watched the footman take his leave and wondered if her messages would be delivered.

With that thought came the reminder that she had her own letters that needed delivering.

Mr. Overby, who was perusing the latest *Morning Chronicle* in search of job postings, was eager to make the deliveries on her behalf. "A walk will be good for me," he claimed as he collected the missives from her.

Remembering how he displayed a noticeable limp when she had seen him walk, Charity gave him a quelling glance. "Take a hackney, at least to the end of South Audley, and you can walk from there," she suggested.

Watching Mr. Overby take his leave, his limp more of a gait that had him bobbing up and down with each step, Charity thought of Mary Baker and her coal buckets.

And the rather odd look the footman had aimed in her direction when she asked about the maid.

Concern? Alarm? Or was that jealousy she saw?

Well, no matter. She had a job to do, and she was determined to do it.

Chapter 22

AN INVITATION TO RIDE IN
THE PARK PROVES
DIVERTING

*L*ater that day

Analise regarded the just-delivered note Harrison had brought to her bedchamber, a combination of excitement and foreboding causing her to hesitate to open it.

"Apologies, my lady, but this was delivered yesterday afternoon. I left it in your father's study and just discovered it was still where I left it," Harrison explained, one of his bushy gray eyebrows arching up in concern.

"My father was distracted last night," she said as she studied the missive. "No harm done, I'm quite sure."

The butler bowed and closed the door, leaving Analise feeling a combination of excitement and dread.

She really needed to learn the crests of the various aristocratic families, for she didn't recognize the one that was embossed in the dark red wax on the back of the missive. The handwriting was masculine, though, which had her guessing it was from Lord Haddon.

Breaking the wax, she carefully unfolded the note and began to read.

Dear Miss Analise,

Although we were both in attendance at Lord Attenborough's ball, I realized too late that your father ~~failed to introduce us~~ *overlooked the opportunity to introduce us. Again. Although I have called your father a friend this past year—we are both new to our roles as viscounts—it seems there has never been a time where you were in residence at the same time as was I.*

Analise looked up from the letter and stared at her reflection in the dressing table mirror. The missive had obviously been written and delivered the day before—well before the ride in the park. Lady Simpson had done the honors and formally introduced her to Lord Wessex.

As for his comment about her not being in residence when he was there, that wasn't exactly correct. She had been to Stanton House on many occasions when her father and the newly-minted viscount were in the study. The two spent hours discussing matters of a political nature and arguing about which party they wished to align themselves with once the next session of Parliament convened. She never wondered why father hadn't called her from her bedchamber or from the library to meet his guest. Perhaps he simply thought she would be bored by the younger viscount.

Or perhaps he feared what might happen if he did introduce them.

Analise returned her attention to the letter.

He has assured me that he will do the honors upon our next meeting. I am hoping that meeting can take place on the morrow.

In addition, I would like the opportunity to spend

*time in your company and wondered if you might join me
for a ride in the park tomorrow afternoon? I, of course,
have your father's permission to drive you. I will come for
you at four o'clock in the hopes you can join me.*

Yours in service,

Luke Merriweather

Postscriptum: Your maid will join us, of course.

Analise let out a squeal of delight.

Her new lady's maid let out a cry of fright. "Whatever
is it?" Parker asked in alarm as she emerged from the
dressing room with several dinner gowns draped over her
arms. Parker, a former housemaid at Stanton House, had
secured the position when Analise finished her studies at
Warwick's Grammar and Finishing School.

Forcing a more passive expression on her face, Analise
said, "I've been invited for a ride in the park." *On the
morrow*, she reread. Given the missive was delivered yesterday, that meant the ride was *today*. "As have you. Please
say you can," she begged the lady's maid.

The curly-haired Parker allowed a grin. "I can," she
replied, wondering what the young mistress of the house
thought she might be doing otherwise. "And who will be
your escort? The heir to the Morganfield marquessate,
perhaps?"

Analise furrowed her brows, wondering how it was
Parker would guess Lord Haddon. And then she remembered how she had behaved that night when she had
returned from her come-out ball. "No. The heir to the
Middleton earldom," she said, once again having to
restrain herself from squealing.

Placing the gowns on the end of the bed, Parker

displayed an expression of disappointment. "That will be the viscount's doing, I imagine."

Her eyes rounding at this comment, Analise asked, "What are you saying?"

Her lady's maid shrugged. "I accidentally overheard the Lords Lancaster and Wessex talking about the Morganfield boy. Your father's none to happy about you spending time in his company, prob'ly because he fears the young buck will ruin you," she explained. "So when Lord Wessex offered to drive you so you wouldn't be available for Lord Haddon's invitation, your father was quick to agree."

Analise blinked, at first rather hurt her father would do such a thing.

Then she grinned in delight.

"Oh, this is rich," she murmured.

Parker regarded her a moment, wondering why the young lady wasn't more disappointed. Why she didn't seem disappointed at all. She was sure Analise *liked* the honorary earl who had just returned to London after years away at university. She had talked of nothing else the night of the ball. "How so?" she asked, her voice kept low, despite the butler having closed the door.

"I like Lord Haddon, I *do*," Analise admitted. "But not... not like *that*. He's devilishly clever and ever so friendly, very handsome, but... he's young. He is *young*."

"He's older than you," Parker countered, giving her head a shake. The halo of blonde curls that surrounded her face bobbed about as she did so.

"By only a few years," Analise argued. "Now that he's in London, he will want to spend his evenings at clubs and carouse and gamble, and do the naughty things young bucks do before they're of a mind to marry."

Parker's eyes widened. "What do you know of naughty things?" she asked in alarm.

Analise felt a blush coming on and hurried to sit at her dressing table, hoping the lady's maid couldn't see her cheeks aflame. "I may have heard some tales whilst at school," she admitted, just as Parker moved to take down her hair and redress it for the ride in the park.

"Why, I haven't seen you blush like this. Ever," Parker remarked. She may have just become Analise's lady's maid last June, but she was a housemaid for several years before that. "Are you quite sure you don't feel affection for Lord Haddon?"

Analise regarded her lady's maid's reflection in the dressing table mirror. "Quite sure."

Parker rolled Analise's hair into a bun atop her head, making sure to leave the hair at her temples loose so that she might curl them into spirals with an iron. She inserted several pins into the bun to hold it secure. "So you must feel affection for Lord Wessex then," she guessed, once she was sure her creation wasn't about to tumble down from the young woman's head.

Rolling her eyes as her face once again took on a pinkish cast, Analise said, "I was only just introduced to him yesterday. Lady Simpson saw to it when he rode up on horseback," she replied.

Which was the truth.

They hadn't been formally introduced before that. As to why her father had never introduced them, she couldn't say. But given how long he and her father had been friends outside of Parliament—at least a year now—she decided it was well past time she spent time in the man's company.

And apparently Lord Wessex was of the same mind.

Chapter 23

A VISCOUNT MAKES
HIS MOVE

An hour later

Harrison was expecting someone to call that afternoon. The missive he had delivered to Miss Analise was no doubt from a young gentleman wishing to escort her for a ride.

Just because it came by the way of Lord Wessex wasn't necessarily an indicator of the author of said letter. He was sure the viscount was merely the messenger, agreeing to deliver the missive only because he was already on his way to pay a call on Lord Lancaster.

The butler wasn't sure just which young gentleman, though. There were several eligible young bucks this Little Season. Young men who had completed their terms at university, like Lord Haddon. Or some who hadn't even begun their schooling at Oxford or Cambridge, like Henry Simpson. So he was entirely unprepared when he opened the door to discover Luke Merriweather, Viscount Wessex, standing on the stoop.

"Lord Wessex for Lady Analise," Luke said as he held out his calling card.

"My lord," Harrison said as he gave a slight bow and stepped aside. "I'll see if Miss Analise is in," he added as he left the viscount in the vestibule.

If she's in?

Luke wondered at the words. He hadn't received a reply and had simply assumed the young lady would be joining him. What if she had made other plans, though? What if she never got the missive? He imagined it still on the salver on Lancaster's desk and was about to allow a groan of disappointment when his gaze went to the top of the stairs.

Lady Analise was making her way down, her bright coral carriage gown a perfect complement to her blushed cheeks and lips.

"Lord Wessex. I hope I haven't kept you waiting long," she said when she moved to join him at the threshold of the vestibule.

Luke blinked. "I've only just arrived," he said, giving her a deep bow. "And call me Wessex if you would."

Analise curtsied and offered her hand, which Luke was quick to take. He kissed the back of it and then tucked it in the crook of his arm.

"I was expecting my father to be home by now."

"He's otherwise engaged, my lady," Luke replied, not exactly sure Marcus was in the company of Lady Wadsworth. If he wasn't, then the older viscount was probably at the club licking his wounds.

"Is he with Lady Wadsworth then?" At Luke's look of surprise, she added, "He told me he would like to court her."

Luke allowed a nod. "You're not disappointed?" He hadn't been sure of her reaction when she learned of it during yesterday's ride in the park.

"Not disappointed as much as I was surprised, I suppose. He hadn't said a word about wanting to remarry," she explained.

He led her out of the house and to his phaeton before glancing behind them. "Where is your—? Ah, here she is."

Analise paused next to the step of the phaeton and turned around to find Parker hurrying to join her.

"My apologies," Parker said as she regarded the equipage. Her eyes widened. "Am I to sit way up there?"

"Next to me," Analise replied as she allowed Luke to assist her onto the bench. He smelled of Bay Rum and wool and citrus, and she had to suppress the urge to lean closer so that she might inhale the scents once more.

She watched as he assisted the petite maid up and onto the bench, his manner never once suggesting he was bothered by the maid joining them on the ride.

Luke bounded up to the bench from the other side of the phaeton and took up the reins. Given the phaeton was meant to seat only two comfortably, there was no room to spare on the bench. He didn't mind, but he wasn't sure about his passengers. "I apologize for the lack of room," he murmured, when he noticed how the maid had interlinked her arm with Analise as well as clutched the pole next to the bench. Perhaps she thought she would be bounced off during the ride.

"It's merely cozy," Analise replied. "And high. I don't believe my father's phaeton is nearly this tall."

Luke thrilled at hearing the excitement in her voice. Her smile was infectious. "Once we're in the park, you can take the reins, if you'd like," he offered, urging the matched pair forward before merging them into traffic. They headed toward the gate that led to Rotten Row.

Her smile broadening, Analise gave a shake of her

head. "You are kind to offer, but I shall leave the ribbons in your capable hands."

"Your father has never allowed you to drive?" he asked in surprise. The young woman seemed far older than he knew her to be, perhaps because her mother had died and she had been forced to grow up a bit faster than others her age.

"He wouldn't dream of it," Analise replied. She furrowed a brow. "And if he did, he would probably imagine the worst."

Luke knew exactly what she meant. "Let me guess. You're proceeding along quite brilliantly—"

"And then something spooks the horses," she said, using the dramatic voice she had learned in theatre class.

"A runaway team, threatening everyone and everything in its path," Luke said, imitating her dramatic delivery.

"Rearing up and neighing," she said, as one gloved hand pantomimed a rearing horse. "The reins escaping my hold and dragging on the street below."

"Your father jumping onto a horse to take control—"

"Settling both horses until they come to a halt right in front of our destination," she finished with a musical laugh.

She turned to find the viscount gazing at her. A frisson shot through her body and she sighed, knowing full well her bonnet did nothing to hide her blush.

"And where might that destination be?" Luke asked, his voice barely audible above the sounds of the horses' hooves.

The delightful grin reappeared. "Gunther's Tea Shop," she replied with a giggle. "Where he'll order a bergamot pear ice."

Luke angled his head. "What will you order?"

"Lemon. Or strawberry," she murmured, her manner sobering.

"Why not both?" he countered, wondering if he could get away with taking her there for an ice that very moment.

She gave a sound of disbelief and then shrugged. "I've never thought to ask."

As they took the sharp turn to go through the gate, Parker let out a squeak, her precarious position on the bench made more so. She tightened her hold on Analise's arm, which had Analise jerked sideways—away from Luke. Reacting without thinking, Luke wrapped an arm around her waist and pulled her back against him. "I've got you!" he assured her, just as their thighs collided.

When his hand remained gripping the side of her waist, Analise turned to stare up at him. Parker, still overcome with fright, didn't even notice how the viscount held onto her mistress. "Thank you, my lord," Analise whispered, tempted to lean a bit more in his direction so she could end up pressed against his entire side, her head tucked into the small of his shoulder.

"Wessex," he whispered. "Or Luke, when we're alone."

Analise stared at him a moment, wondering when that might be. She blinked when she heard shouts of greeting from another carriage that had come up alongside them.

Aware of how cozy they must appear, Analise wrapped a gloved hand across her waist to cover the evidence of his black kid-gloved hand that rested there. "Hello," she called out as she leaned forward to see beyond Parker. All four of the Simpsons exchanged greetings with them.

Analise resisted the urge to mewl when the arm behind her waist pulled away, but she did nothing to reposition herself on the bench.

"You're looking lovely as ever," Luke said, his attention on Lady Simpson as he tipped his hat using the previously pre-occupied hand. "If my mother ever again deigned to live in the capital, she would be green with envy."

Sarah Simpson dimpled. "You're a bounder, Wessex," she said, leaning over her daughter, Hannah, to make the good-natured accusation. "Please let her know I insist she pay a call if she ever does come to London. It's been an *age* since I've seen Laura."

Luke nodded. "I will, my lady," he replied, at the same moment he noticed Miss Hannah and Analise exchanging meaningful glances. He was sure Hannah had pursed her lips to imitate a kiss, but he had no idea how Analise had responded. The edge of her bonnet hid her face from his view.

Hannah's brother, Henry, who had also been watching the two young women, merely rolled his eyes before catching Luke's gaze. He lifted his head in acknowledgement, although Luke had the distinct impression he was not happy to see Analise in his company. "Pull on ahead, Mr. Simpson, and we'll follow you," Luke said when the older gentleman gave a wave.

"Much obliged," James Simpson said just before he urged his matched pair to quicken their pace.

Once they were in line with the other carriages making up the parade on Rotten Row, Luke angled his head in Analise's direction. "Has Miss Hannah's brother always held a candle for you?" he asked in a hoarse whisper.

Analise turned to regard him, her shock apparent. "*Henry?*" the word said in obvious disbelief. "He's but a friend. I have known him since... since we were in leading strings, I suppose," she explained.

Luke allowed a grin. "Hmm."

Analise's eyes widened. "What do you know?"

The viscount continued to grin as he regarded her, his gaze darting to the horses to ensure they stayed in line behind the Simpsons' equipage. "I had the distinct impression that if his eyes had been capable of shooting daggers at me, I would now be full of them."

Although her first thought was to deny there was—or ever would be—any attraction between her and Henry Simpson, Analise instead said, "He'll be an excellent catch for any young lady, once he's a bit older and has finished his education."

The Green Monster made a quick visit to Luke just then, and he struggled to keep a pleasant expression on his face. "Does that include you?"

Analise inhaled sharply and regarded the viscount for perhaps a moment too long. *How dense could a man be?* Didn't Wessex know that if she had wanted to spend time in Henry's company, she would be riding in their carriage instead of with him on his phaeton? Then she let out the breath she'd been holding and gave her head a shake. "It does not include me," she admitted.

"And Lord Haddon? Will you be riding with him on the morrow?"

Blinking in alarm—Analise was sure she heard jealousy tinge his query—she was about to allow her indignation to show. She thought better of it, though, deciding she didn't want to torture the man if he really did have feelings for her. If he wasn't just taking her for this ride to appease her father, as Parker had suggested earlier that afternoon.

Angling her head in an effort to see more of the viscount's face, Analise said, "Not that it's any of your concern, but Lord Haddon hasn't invited me to ride with him."

Luke frowned. "He hasn't?"

Analise shook her head. "Not yet," she said, deciding she could tease him just a bit. She slumped then. "I apologize if you're only doing this because my father put you up to it—"

"He did no such thing." When Luke saw her look of disbelief, he added, "*I* was the one who suggested it."

Unable to stop her mouth from dropping open, Analise stared at him for a moment before she schooled her features into a pleasant expression. "But, why?"

It was Luke's turn to slump a bit, a muscle in his jaw twitching. He directed the horses to pull over to the side of the road before bringing them to a halt. "I don't want Christopher Carlington anywhere near you." *Henry Simpson, either,* he thought to add, but didn't put voice to it.

Surprise had Analise's eyes widening, their cornflower blue irises nearly the color of the afternoon sky. "Oh?" she managed to say, at the same moment he looked in her direction.

With her head turned as it was, her bonnet no longer hid her face from him. He was momentarily mesmerized when their eyes met. "Not that I think he will try anything —he would be a fool to do so—but..." He sighed and was about to lean closer when he was aware of how Parker was staring at him. "Perhaps we could go for a walk?" he suggested.

"I'd like that," Analise murmured. Sitting so close as they were, she was well aware of the heat of his body, of his thighs still pressed against hers. And poor Parker was probably hanging onto the bench for dear life.

Luke paused a moment before he stepped down and tied the reins to the post. Then he came around and helped Parker down, noting how she seemed relieved to have solid ground beneath her feet.

When Analise moved to step down, he simply lifted her beneath the arms and lowered her until her slippered feet touched the lawn below. "Thank you," she murmured. She placed her hand atop his proffered arm and allowed him to lead her along a crushed granite path. Parker followed a few steps behind.

"I have reason to believe your father doesn't want you to wed," Luke began in preamble.

"He's just teasing me," Analise countered.

Luke didn't look convinced and said, "But I think he would be amenable to your betrothal should he find a new wife."

Analise narrowed her eyes. "Are you referring to Lady Wadsworth?" she asked.

He nodded. "I have known your father for some time, and I have never known him to pay any mind to a woman since your mother died," he commented. "But since the Attenborough ball..."

"He's in love with her," Analise finished for him.

Allowing a wan grin, Luke said, "So you're aware?" he half-asked.

"We talked of it during dinner."

They walked in silence for a time, passing by trees and hedgerows until they were no longer visible from Rotten Row. "Does it... does it bother you that he wishes to take another wife?" Luke asked.

Analise shook her head. "When I first learned of it, I suppose. But only because he said Lady Wadsworth wanted a daughter."

"And you don't wish to be hers?"

Angling her head to one side, Analise considered the

query for a time. "I suppose I should feel differently, but I had a mother I loved very much, so I admit my reaction was not very nice." She paused. "In fact, I was a bit cruel to him."

Luke gave her a quelling glance. "I don't believe that."

Ignoring his comment, Analise continued. "But then he said the countess wants a daughter of her own, and that he'd like to be the one to give her what she wants."

Luke had to suppress the urge to grin. Poor Lancaster! The man was truly in love.

"Would you accept a child of theirs as your sibling?" he asked then, rather surprised by how personal his questions were and how willing she seemed to be answering them.

Analise made a sound in the back of her throat. "Of course I would," she said finally. "By the time that happens, I might be married. I might have a child of my own."

Had he heard such words just a few weeks ago, Luke would have been relieved at knowing he wasn't the one who had fathered said child. But just then, he had an overwhelming desire to *be* that father.

What the hell?

Before he even knew what he was doing, Luke paused and turned to regard Analise. She stared up at him, a look of surprise once again widening her eyes. "I would like to kiss you," he said in a voice he didn't recognize as his own. Apparently he had forgotten the lady's maid was with them.

Analise blinked. She glanced over at Parker and was stunned when the maid dipped a curtsy and simply turned around to face the other direction.

When she turned back to face Luke, his head lowered

until his forehead rested against the top of her bonnet. A moment later, and his lips brushed over hers.

Feather light and barely there, the touch of their lips ended far too quickly. So when her hand reached up to grip his lapel for support, she raised herself on tiptoes and did the same to him, this time gratified when his lips captured hers more completely.

Lost in the moment and in the scent of honeysuckle that seemed to surround them, Luke wrapped an arm around the back of her waist and held her up, returning her kiss for several seconds before finally pulling away. "I wish I could do that every day."

Analise swallowed, her gaze going between his heavy-lidded eyes and his lips. She was aware of his arousal, aware of how his cologne had changed to include a hint of musk. And aware that his expression had turned to one of lust. "Why do you make it sound as if you cannot?" she asked in a whisper.

Luke blinked. *Why indeed?* "Your father will have my head—"

"My father needn't know."

Analise could barely believe what she had just said. Luke must already think her fast. She had allowed him to kiss her in broad daylight.

And she had kissed him back!

A quick glance in Parker's direction showed the lady's maid had wandered off the path to a flower garden, her attention on the mums that were still in bloom.

Luke raised his face to the sky and took a deep breath. He chuckled and allowed a sound of disbelief. And then he lowered his head back down to hers and kissed her again, this time placing a hand along her jaw, then sliding it down her neck.

When he finally pulled away, he regarded Analise with an expression of wonder. "I do hope your lady's maid can be trusted to keep quiet," he murmured. "Or I really shall be a dead man."

Analise allowed a wan grin. "I'll speak with her, of course," she replied, before her expression changed. "Do you think me... fast?"

Luke frowned and shook his head. "Of course not." He knew she hadn't been kissed before. Knew she hadn't kissed another man before, at least on the lips. Her manner had been too tentative, too careful. There had been a sense of wonder surrounding their kisses. A sense of innocence he found refreshing. "Was mine your first kiss?"

A blush colored her face and she dipped her head. "Was it that obvious?"

Luke's smile brightened his face as he once again kissed her, this time a stolen kiss she barely had time to return. "It was perfect."

She looked at him in disbelief. "That bad, huh?"

He laughed then and pulled her into a hug. "You're going to steal my heart, aren't you?"

Sobering, Analise dipped her head. "I cannot steal it if it's freely offered."

Damn, but he couldn't believe what was happening. They were speaking of hearts, which meant they felt affection for one another. "And what about yours?"

"A bit afraid of being broken," she replied.

"As is mine."

"Do you feel affection for another?"

"I do not," he replied with a shake of his head. "And you?" After all their talk of Lord Haddon and Henry Simpson, he would feel like an utter fool if she mentioned someone else.

"Of course not. I've only just had my come-out," she replied with a grin.

Luke inhaled and said, "Then let us spend some time in courting and discover what we must of each other."

Analise nodded and gave him a brilliant smile. "Agreed."

"And hope your father doesn't kill me."

Her gaze once again going to where Parker stood next to the garden of mums, she said in her dramatic voice, "Fear not, for I will defend you, my love."

Unable to help himself, Luke laughed.

At least he would die a happy man.

Chapter 24

TEA FOR THREE AND A WILL

The following afternoon Marcus returned from Parliament to find his daughter waiting for him in the parlor. Another young lady was with her, a shy girl who appeared almost frightened by his appearance on the threshold.

"Miss Fulton, may I introduce you to my father, Lord Lancaster?" Analise said after she had bussed Marcus on the cheek.

Although she seemed glad to see him, Marcus was startled by his daughter's lack of a smile. Her usual happy countenance wasn't in evidence.

He bowed and reached for Marguerite's hand, brushing his lips over the back of it. When she dipped a curtsy, he noted how her gown was cut from fabric of quality, and the shoes that peeked out from beneath her hem were covered in satin.

"It's very good to meet you, my lord," Marguerite said with a nod. After a moment, she offered him the document she had been holding in her other hand.

Gripping in her other hand.

From the bruises in the parchment, he could tell she had been holding onto it as if her life depended on it.

Perhaps it did.

Marcus took the document and then a seat directly across from Marguerite. He was heartened when his daughter poured him a cup of tea. The two young ladies had already finished at least a cup of the aromatic brew, and the crumbs on their plates suggested they had finished a biscuit or two as well.

"Thank you, my dear," he murmured as he unfolded the multi-page document. He made an appreciative sound and then, his attention on the will, said, "According to my daughter, your father made arrangements for you and your mother that your brother has since rescinded. Is that what this is about?"

Marguerite's eyes widened, and she nodded. "It is, my lord. I've read the will, and I believe the terms are spelled out quite clearly."

Having scanned the first few paragraphs of the document, Marcus lifted his gaze to hers. "This was written not long before his death," he murmured, having noted the date.

"Mother said he knew he was not long for this earth when he met with his solicitor. His physician..." She stopped, swallowing hard at the memory of learning her father was expected to die before she reached her majority. "He told him to see to his affairs."

Marcus suppressed the urge to wince at the word *affairs*. Edmund Fulton, Earl of Wadsworth, had apparently engaged in many of them over the years, although, towards the end, he had settled with just the one mistress, presumedly Marguerite's mother. "Fortuitous he did so," Marcus murmured, his gaze once again going to the will.

Although he secretly hated Edmund Fulton for having ruined and then married Charity all those years ago, he had to respect the man for having seen to those who relied on him for their livings. "Tell me, do you and your mother have... accommodations?" he asked.

She nodded. "He let a townhouse on our behalf. Saw to a two-year lease even. But the rent is only paid through the end of the month. After that..." She blinked back tears. "My mother thinks she is too old to secure another man's protection," she whispered, her eyes darting sideways when she realized she shouldn't speak of such things with Analise present.

"And funds? Do you have any?" Marcus asked, keeping his voice as businesslike as possible. He didn't want to be frightening the girl anymore than she already seemed, but he didn't want to offer sympathy, either. At least, not until he knew the full story.

He cringed when he thought of Charity. Perhaps he was the wrong man to take on this case. By doing so, he was sure he would lose any chance of making a life with the widow. This young lady was evidence of her late husband's infidelity, not to mention a version of the daughter Charity might have given birth to if her husband hadn't taken a mistress or two. He couldn't blame her if she'd hate him.

The oddest pain in his chest had him suppressing a grunt just then.

"He gave me some money the week before he died," Marguerite said. "A hundred pounds. Said I should use it for a modiste. To have clothes made for my come-out, and for the subscription to the Wednesday night balls at Almack's."

"And did you?"

She shook her head. "I won't be of an age to make my come-out until this next Season," she explained. "When Benedict—that is to say, Lord Wadsworth—paid a call on me at Warwick's this past spring, I knew my mother and I would require those funds for food."

Marcus regarded her with a wan grin. "Wise girl," he murmured. "I understand Lord Wadsworth told you of his plans to cut you off whilst you were in school. Tell me. Had you met your brother before that day at Warwick's?"

Marguerite nodded. "Many times, when we were children."

This bit of news surprised Marcus, and he straightened in his chair. "Indeed?"

She nodded. "We... used to play together, although he's a few years older than me, his brother, Benjamin, and I got along quite well."

"Did you... did you *know* they were your half-brothers?" Marcus asked, rather surprised the children had been allowed to know one other.

"Oh, of course. Father always referred to them as such when he spoke to me," she replied. "Is that... is that not usual?"

Marcus blinked, not sure how to respond. He didn't have any by-blows of his own, but he knew others who did. "It depends," he hedged. *On if the wives would put up with the knowing or not*, he didn't add. He held up the will. "Might I keep this? Just for this evening? So that I might take notes before I inform Lord Wadsworth I'll be suing him on your behalf?"

Marguerite's eyes rounded. "Suing him?" she repeated in alarm. She turned to Analise and then back to Marcus. "I don't wish to make trouble for him," she said in a hoarse whisper.

Frowning, Marcus regarded the young woman a moment before he said, "Well, only if it's necessary. It may not be. Wadsworth might be compelled to do the right thing without this having to proceed in the legal sense."

Tears once again threatened, and Analise allowed an audible sigh. "You must allow my father to do what he can for you," she murmured to her friend. "We can't have you and your mother cast out of your home."

The word 'home' had Marcus deep in thought. He knew Wadsworth Hall was an entailed property of the earldom. Benedict lived in a townhouse. But did Wadsworth have other houses in London? Entailed properties he would have been unable to lose whilst gambling? If he proposed one of those to Benedict, perhaps the young man would allow the women to move into it. The cost wouldn't be so great to the earldom, then, if rent monies were an issue.

And if not, he thought of the house Charity occupied. If she married him, she would move into Stanton House. Benedict could occupy Wadsworth Hall, and that would free up his townhouse so Marguerite and her mother could move into it.

Or there was the house in Suffolk. The one Charity had lived in by herself all those years her husband was in London with his mistresses. If it was an entailed property, then perhaps they could move there.

Could all this happen in just a few weeks, though?

He blinked when Analise's hand passed in front of his face.

"You're doing it again, Father," she said in a whisper.

Marcus blinked. "Indeed, but for good reason." He turned his attention back to Marguerite. "If a suitable arrangement cannot be made before the end of the month, you and your mother shall move into this house," he stated. "At least until a townhouse can be arranged."

"Father!" Analise said in awe, a smile lighting her face for the first time that afternoon.

"However, I do believe I can encourage Wadsworth to do the right thing."

Marguerite nodded. "Then you may keep the will," she said quietly. "But I would like it back."

"And you will have it," Marcus replied. He moved to stand up. "I'll leave you two to discuss the matter of suitors," he teased, and then he suddenly sobered. "Well, not seriously, I hope," he added as he gave a bow and took his leave of the parlor.

Analise blushed a bright pink before Marguerite smiled for the first time that afternoon.

Chapter 25

A VISCOUNT AND COUNTESS DISCUSS AN EARL'S MOTIVES

Four o'clock in the afternoon, 30 Oxford Street

Having driven his curricle to 'Finding Wives for the Wounded,' Marcus glanced about in search of a street urchin to see to his horse. He didn't expect to be in the charity's office long, but he didn't dare leave the equipage unattended.

"I can see to your horse," a liveried groom said as he stepped forward.

Marcus turned to find one of the Wadsworth Hall grooms holding out his hand. Behind him was a town coach, apparently the one belonging to Charity. "Much obliged," he said, fishing a coin from his waistcoat pocket. "Has she been here all day?" he asked.

The groom shook his head. "She had me take her to a few shops in Bond Street in the middle of the day, so she could pass out cards." He lowered his voice. "She's been after eligible ladies," he added, a self-conscious grin displaying a broken tooth. "An hour later, and three of 'em were waiting for her here at the office."

Marcus nodded his understanding. Apparently the

countess had found a way to encourage young, unmarried women to seek her out so she had possible matches for all the men who had already applied for wives. He briefly thought of his randy maid and wondered if there would be a match in her future.

He rather doubted there would be one in his. Not after what he was about to tell Charity.

He made his way into the office and held his hat in both hands as he watched Charity finish a conversation with a petite brunette. Although the young woman was plain of face, she was dressed rather fine, and her posture appeared perfect as she made her way past him to the door. He hurried to open it for her and then turned his attention back to where Charity was sitting.

Except she wasn't.

She was pulling on her pelisse even as she made her way in his direction.

He gave a bow. "Good afternoon, my lady," he said before taking her hand in his.

"Yes, it most certainly is," she replied, her manner suggesting she might actually be pleased to see him.

"I was hoping for a moment of your time," he hedged, realizing she was in a hurry to get out.

"You have it. In fact, you can have an hour if you'd like."

Marcus blinked, his eyes following her retreat from the office before his legs had a chance to catch up. "Does that mean you will join me for that ride in the park?" he asked.

She seemed to give the query a moment of thought before she said, "How about a walk in Berkeley Square? I really need some air."

His eyes widened with mischief. "And an ice at

Gunther's Tea Shop?" he countered, as he helped her into his curricle.

Her eyes widened, as if she hadn't remembered the confectionary.

"Follow us to Berkeley Square," she said to the groom who held the reins. "You can take me home from there."

Once they were both settled, Marcus had the curricle merging into the late afternoon traffic in Oxford Street. "May I ask what made this day especially good for you?" he asked.

Charity grinned, but kept her attention on the equipage in front of them. "I made some matches today," she said proudly. "Three of them. Two I am quite sure will work."

"And the third?"

"Possible, but doubtful. It would work if he weren't so tall and she wasn't so short, I think. They seemed to really like one another, though, so I suppose it could work."

Marcus was about to imagine what sexual congress might be like for such a couple, but had to keep his mind on the here and now. He didn't want to be lost in his thoughts whilst in the company of Charity. Not when he finally had her in his curricle.

"Congratulations are in order then," he said. "And your favorite flavor of ice."

Charity sighed. "Would you believe me if I said I had never been to Gunther's?" she asked.

He was about to say 'no' when he realized she was telling the truth. "May I ask why not?"

Sighing, Charity regarded him for a moment before she finally allowed a shrug. "I've been in Suffolk so long, and I can't say as I've been of a mind for such an outing since my return to the capital." She didn't add that she didn't think she could afford the extravagance.

Money had been far too tight these past few months, and she hoped Benedict had been successful in staunching the losses the earldom seemed to have suffered under his father. The Year of No Summer couldn't have been responsible for all of them. "How are things in Parliament?"

He allowed a shrug. "Boring, sometimes. Interesting at other times," he replied, deciding he had the perfect opportunity to broach the topic of Wadsworth's will. "I've actually had to return to my former profession to take on an interesting case, one I hope doesn't result in any legal action on my part."

Charity frowned, noting the seriousness in his voice. "Someone hired you to be their solicitor?" she guessed.

Taking a deep breath, Marcus decided this was the moment he'd been dreading. "Something like that. Tell me, were you ever shown a copy of Wadsworth's will?" he asked.

Her head swiveled in his direction so fast, her hat was nearly pulled from its pins. "His will?" she repeated. "Of course not. What's this about?"

Marcus cleared his throat. "I read it yesterday," he said. "Twice."

Charity gave her head a shake. "But, why?"

"I've taken a client. One who is mentioned in the will. She... and her mother... were promised a certain sum. It's spelled out quite clearly in the will, but it seems the current Earl of Wadsworth has seen to cutting them off."

Her eyes wide, Charity stared at Marcus for a moment before she faced straight ahead. "He must have had a good reason," she suggested, thinking she should be angry with the viscount for having brought up the matter with her.

"Possibly," Marcus agreed. When she turned to regard him again, he added, "There are rumors that the Wadsworth earldom... suffered some losses—"

"They are not rumors," Charity interrupted. "Benedict has discovered a number of... *inconsistencies* in the accounts. It seems my late husband's man of business was benefitting from the earldom far more than he was entitled. Thought he could hide what he was taking by simply writing it off... as if it were a gambling loss," she explained. "Losses, I should say."

Alarmed, Marcus was about to steer the curricle to the curb so he could better concentrate on the conversation. He saw the square up ahead, though, and waited until they were under the shade of a plane tree across from Gunther's before turning to regard her. "Has he done anything to recover the stolen funds?" he asked. "Sued the man? Or had him arrested for embezzlement?"

Charity shook her head. "I... I don't know. He's managed to learn the books. Knows the businesses—has a head for it, even—but I don't know that he has the contacts or the means to do anything about the man who stole the money. He's only eighteen years of age."

"So, he hasn't reported it?"

She gave a shake of her head. "I'm sure I would have heard something," she murmured. There was a reason she had a subscription to *The Times* and *The Tattler*. She took a deep breath and let it out just as a waiter ran up to take their order.

"I meant for us to go inside," Marcus said to the waiter.

"Let's not," Charity said, motioning for the waiter to stay. She didn't want to become the next *on-dit* in Mayfair parlors, although being seen in the curricle with Lord

Lancaster might have tongues wagging as much as sitting together in Gunther's.

"You're not too cold?"

"I'm fine. Truly," she replied, noting his look of concern. "But I've no idea what to order."

Marcus regarded her with a wry grin. "What's your favorite flavor of all the fruits you have tried?"

Charity dipped her head. "Strawberry, I suppose," she hedged.

"One strawberry ice and one bergamot pear ice," Marcus stated. The waiter nodded and hurried off into the tea shop.

They sat in silence for a time before they both started to speak at the same time. "You go first," Marcus said, knowing his words would ruin an otherwise perfect outing.

"I was going to ask you about the will. About the woman you said my son has cut off."

"Women, actually," Marcus clarified, wincing as he said the words. He allowed a long sigh.

"Is Marguerite one of them?"

Marcus's eyes rounded before he turned to regard the widowed countess. "You know about Marguerite?" He stared at her a moment and then gave his head a shake. "Of course you would. Your boys would have mentioned her, since they played together as children," he murmured. "I'm so sorry about this—"

"You needn't be," she interrupted. "But I don't understand what it is Benedict did."

Marcus furrowed a brow. "According to Miss Fulton, he went to Warwick's last June and informed her he was cutting her off. That she wasn't due anything from the earldom." He paused a moment. "My daughter paid witness to it because she is a friend of Marguerite's and was there in the classroom when Benedict made his appearance."

Charity seemed to have trouble breathing for a moment. "Did he do it in front of a whole class?"

Shaking his head, Marcus said, "No. The others had all left. The issue is, she and her mother are in a townhouse that Wadsworth let on their behalf. Before he died. The lease is up at the end of the month. They have little in the way of funds."

"What will they do?"

Marcus held his breath a moment, rather surprised that Charity didn't demand he let her out of the curricle. Her own coach was parked directly behind them. She could take her leave of him and be off in just moments. "Well, if Wadsworth cannot see to renewing the lease and giving them the living that was promised in the will—five-hundred pounds per annum—then I will be forced to sue your son on their behalf."

Charity squeezed her eyes shut in an effort to control the myriad of emotions his words incited just then. She was about to lash out in anger, but the waiter had returned with their order, and she found she simply didn't have the energy. The sight of the ices had her mouth watering and her stomach reminding her she hadn't eaten anything since early that morning, and then only toast and tea.

Marcus gave her a dish of pink ice and a spoon while he saw to paying the waiter. When the man stepped away, he noted how tears had begun streaming down Charity's temples.

One-handed—he had to hold onto his own ice— Marcus pulled out a handkerchief and dabbed at her cheeks. "Oh, Charity," he breathed. "I am so very sorry."

She sniffled and lifted her chin. "I don't know why I'm crying," she whispered. "It's not as if I am at fault." She turned her attention on the ice and lifted a spoonful of the pink confection to her lips. She tasted it and let out a sigh of pleasure. "Oh, this is good. This is very good," she said.

"Just don't eat it too fast, or your head will hurt," Marcus warned, noting how she had already brought another spoonful to her lips. "You don't have to give me an answer, because it's really none of my business, but has your son been able to... to see to *your* allowance?"

Charity nodded. "He has. He increased it quite substantially..." She was about to say "last summer" when it dawned on her just why that could be. "Oh," she breathed. She turned her attention on the viscount. "Oh, dear," she said in a whisper.

Marcus thought she was about to faint and set his ice on the seat next to him so that he could take hers from her trembling fingers. "What is it, Charity?" he asked. He snaked an arm behind her back and pulled her closer, alarmed by how light she felt. How terribly thin she was. "When was the last time you had a decent meal?"

But Charity didn't hear his query. She was thinking about how it was all making so much sense now! How it was that Benedict had been able to pay the servants. Arrange for some much needed repairs of Wadsworth Hall. But this past month had been much like it was when she first moved to London, which meant the pantry wasn't as full and the servants were forced to eat more lobster.

Marcus furrowed a brow as he watched her get lost in her thoughts. He supposed she looked much like he did when he allowed his imagination to get the best of him. The moment allowed him to gaze at her without fear of repercussion.

She was thinner then he remembered. Her collar bones had been evident the night of the ball, the design of her gown doing nothing to hide them. He was sure she had been light-headed after their waltz, probably because she was starving.

When her head fell onto his shoulder, Marcus remembered her ice and fed a spoonful to her. "Eat, my sweet," he encouraged. She did as she was told, making humming sounds in the back of her throat. "I'm going to take you to my house for dinner this evening," he said, just before he turned around to look for the groom.

When the servant noticed, he hurried up alongside the curricle, frowning when he saw how Charity was slumped against the viscount. "My lord?"

"She needs something to eat," he announced.

"Very good, my lord."

Marcus furrowed a brow, wondering if all the servants in Wadsworth Hall knew their mistress was wasting away. "I'm taking her to Stanton House for dinner. I'll see to getting her back to Wadsworth Hall later tonight," Marcus explained. "No need for you to have to wait for her. Go on back to Wadsworth Hall."

The groom hesitated but finally gave a nod. "Very good, my lord." He returned to the Wadsworth town coach. After another minute, the coach pulled away and headed south.

"Can you eat any more?" Marcus asked, returning his attention to Charity. He wished she wasn't wearing a hat. He wanted desperately to rest his cheek on her head.

She stirred and took the spoon from him, finishing off the rest of what was in her dish. Marcus set it aside and then offered her what was left of his. "Eat this one, too," he ordered.

Charity did as she was told, and after a few minutes, she straightened in the squabs. "I apologize. I don't know what came over me," she whispered. The waiter had returned to take the dishes, giving a bow before he returned to the shop.

"Hunger, my sweet," Marcus said as he got the horses into motion. After a moment, he asked, "How many houses does the Wadsworth earldom own here in London?"

Charity regarded him with a furrowed brow. "Three, I think. We used to live in a small one over in Bruton Street before Wadsworth—before Edmund—inherited. That's when we moved to Wadsworth Hall," she explained. "And the dowager countess moved to Suffolk."

"And the one your son lives in now?"

She gave a shrug. "A small terrace close to Parliament. Wadsworth used to stay there on occasion. I think one of his mistresses might have lived there back in the day," she added in disgust.

"Marguerite and her mother need a place to live," he stated.

She allowed a sigh, understanding now why he had brought up the topic of houses. Her brain was fuzzy, as if she had drunk too much champagne, and despite being warned not to eat the ice too quickly, she had done so. Now a sudden headache had her grimacing. "I'll speak with Benedict," Charity said. "Find out if the house in Bruton Street is available or if he can simply renew the lease on the house they are in." She glanced back and then looked around in alarm. "Where's my coach?"

Marcus gave a start, sure she had been conscious enough to know he had sent it to her home. "On the way back to Wadsworth Hall."

"What? Why? Where are you taking me?"

"To Stanton House," he replied. "So you can have a decent meal."

"You're kidnapping me?" she half-accused.

For some reason, Marcus was tempted to reply in the affirmative, just because the idea was so ludicrous. But he shook his head. "As much as I want to, I am not," he said.

"I'm not dressed appropriately for a dinner," she argued.

Suppressing the urge to chuckle, Marcus regarded her for as long a he could before he had to return his attention to the road ahead. "My sweet, it wouldn't matter what you wore to dinner. You always look resplendent."

Charity was about to argue, but decided she didn't have the energy. She did want the last word, however. "Bounder," she replied.

Marcus allowed a grin and hurried the horses into a faster pace.

Charity slumped into the squabs and decided to simply enjoy the ride.

Chapter 26

A COUNTESS PAYS A CALL ON HER SON

he following day

Benedict, Earl of Wadsworth, girded his loins when he spotted the Wadsworth town coach pulling up in front of his bachelor's quarters. His mother's cryptic note had piqued his curiosity, although not enough to have him too concerned.

He hadn't done anything of note, other than seeing to the business of the earldom—when he wasn't suffering from extreme boredom in Parliament. If one could die of boredom, he was quite sure his younger brother would have inherited the earldom by now.

He rather wished the two of them could exchange places, if for no other reason than he could go back to university and continue his studies. If it weren't for the business side of the earldom, which he found interesting, he might put a gun to his head.

Watching Charity make her way to the front door of his townhouse, Benedict frowned. She appeared far too thin. Frail, almost. But she had a look of determination about her that had him a bit cowed.

He thought he might have a moment or two to compose a proper welcome, but Charity didn't allow his butler to take her pelisse. She simply breezed in and stood regarding him.

"Mother," he said with a bow. He captured her hand in his and was about to kiss the back of it when she pulled it away and simply wrapped an arm around his middle and hugged him.

"Oh, Benedict, what have you done?" she whispered.

Startled by her hold on him, Benedict did the only thing he knew to do. He returned the hug, alarmed by the evidence of the bones of her shoulders and ribs beneath his arms. He lessened his hold lest he crush her before he finally pulled away.

"When was the last time you ate a decent meal, Mother?" he asked in a whisper.

Charity furrowed a brow, remembering the words from the afternoon before. Spoken by the man with whom she had dined. The meal at Stanton House reminded her of what life in London had been like back when Benedict was younger. Before he had left for Eton. Before his younger brother, Benjamin, had started school. At least seven courses every night. More food than she could possibly eat.

There had been good company at Stanton House, given Lancaster's daughter was in attendance, as was his friend and fellow viscount, Lord Wessex.

She could have sworn there was something going on between the daughter and Wessex—the air seemed to crackle with their attraction to one another—but nothing had been said about a possible match.

Perhaps her presence precluded an announcement or a

query by Wessex. If so, Lancaster seemed completely unaware anything was afoot.

"I had dinner last night, at Stanton House," she replied, lifting her chin.

Benedict frowned. "Lancaster's townhouse?" he guessed as he turned and led her up the flight of stairs to the first floor parlor.

"Indeed," she replied, and then realized she could mention a good excuse for being there. "One of his maids is in need of a husband, and I have a number of men who are looking for wives," she explained, just before she settled onto the settee. Although the parlor was small, it was warm and cozy.

Benedict's butler carried in a tea tray, setting it before her and giving a bow before he hurried out.

"Will you do the honors, Mother?" Benedict asked, just before he leaned over to snag a Dutch biscuit. "And tell me what I've done to vex you? Your note was rather cryptic."

Charity allowed a sigh and prepared two cups of tea. "It's about Marguerite. And her mother," she replied, handing over a cup and saucer to him.

Benedict stiffened. "I did what I had to. I cannot afford—"

"You will honor the terms of your father's will," she stated.

Giving a start, as if she had slapped him across the face, Benedict frowned. "I... I cannot—"

"You must, or you will be sued," she countered.

His frown deepening, Benedict regarded her in alarm. "What do you know?"

Charity sighed before she took a sip of tea. Why was it tea always seemed to make things seem better? Even if they weren't? "I know that Marguerite and her mother are owed their livings at the sum of five-hundred pounds per year. I know you approached Marguerite whilst she was at school and told her she was no longer your sister and that you weren't going to honor the terms of the will," she went on.

"She told you about that?" he asked, his anger becoming apparent.

Her eyes narrowing, Charity shook her head. "*She* did not. I learned of it from a solicitor acting on her behalf," she replied, hoping her look of annoyance would force him to rein in his anger.

The words did the trick.

"I didn't know what to do," he said with a shake of his head.

"Whatever do you mean?"

A grimace crossed his face. "I saw you. Saw how you were starving, and how Wadsworth Hall was leaking like a sieve, and I couldn't abide it—"

"Did you hear one word of complaint from me?" Charity asked in a hoarse whisper.

Benedict looked as if he'd been slapped. "Never, in fact. But I wasn't about to allow you to live as father would have you living."

"And yet you would have your sister living like that?" she countered, her voice rising in defiance. "She and her mother have no place to go, Benedict. No money. No means of making any money." Before he would have a chance to mention the former mistress's profession, she added, "She's too old to attract another protector. And now that you've seen to it Marguerite can no longer attend school, it's doubtful she can attract a suitable match in the marriage mart."

Benedict slumped in his chair. "You would have me

use funds that should go to you, go to her instead?" he questioned.

Charity inhaled and then sighed. "Yes, of course. I have a position now. I earn enough pin money at 'Finding Wives for the Wounded' to cover some of the expenses. You only need cover the servants' wages and the repairs of Wadsworth Hall when necessary," she explained.

"Mother," he said on a sigh.

"She's your sister," Charity implored.

Benedict furrowed a brow. "I thought you would hate her," he whispered. "I thought you would want me to give her the cut direct. To absolve our family of any connection to her and her mother."

"You cannot absolve the family of what your father did," she argued. "Especially when he saw to making provisions for them," she added. "In writing."

"I thought you would hate her," he whispered again.

Charity dipped her head. "It's true I hated the *idea* of her," she admitted. "But only because I wished she had been *my* daughter."

Her son's eyes rounded at her words. "I wasn't aware you wanted a daughter," he murmured. He finally allowed a nod. "Because you insist, I will see to it the lease is renewed on their townhouse," he said then.

"Or you can have them move into one of the earldom's townhouses," she suggested. "Isn't there another here in capital?"

He shook his head. "I've let it to a baron for the year. I needed the rent monies."

Charity sighed. Well, at least he was making something from the entailed property. "Then see to it the lease is renewed on their home."

"Yes, Mother."

"Can you also see to giving them fifty pounds as soon as possible?"

He nodded, his reluctance apparent. "I can. I will do so on the morrow."

"You will do so *today*," Charity ordered. "And it would be good of you to offer an apology. If not to her mother, at least to Marguerite."

Taken aback by his mother's tone of voice, he relented and said, "Very well." His conflicted thoughts had his face displaying a variety of emotions before he finally admitted, "She is my sister."

"The only one you'll ever have," Charity said in a quiet voice. She took a sip of tea and finally allowed a watery smile. "Now. Tell me how things are with you," she said. "Is there a countess in your future?"

Benedict rolled his eyes. "If there is, she is far in the future, or I've not met her yet," he replied. "Besides, until I can ensure the earldom is once again flush with funds, I can't exactly afford a wife."

Finishing her tea, Charity leaned forward and said in a quiet voice. "Well, when you're ready, I might know of a matchmaker who can assist in introducing you to a—"

"Mother," he warned, just before he allowed a chuckle. "Perhaps *you* should be using those skills to find another husband? So that you don't starve to death."

Charity stared at the bottom of her teacup, as if she thought there might be answers in the few leaves that rested there. "Point taken," she whispered.

Chapter 27

AN EARL'S LETTER TO HIS SISTER

*L*ater that day

Marguerite opened the missive even before the door closed on the footman who had delivered it. She didn't recognize the handwriting, but she certainly recognized the seal embossed in the dark red wax on the back.

"Who is it from?" her mother asked. The older woman joined her in the small vestibule, her hands clutching her skirts as if she thought someone might attempt to take them from her.

"Benedict," Marguerite murmured, once she had the parchment completely unfolded. A small paper fluttered on its way to the floor and nearly made it there before she managed to snag it between a thumb and forefinger.

"What is it?"

Marguerite stared at the bank draft. "Fifty pounds," she murmured. Her gaze darted over to the letter, and she scanned the script. She realized almost immediately she would have to read it in its entirety—she couldn't determine the message from the few words she could make out. "Come. Let's sit down for this," she encouraged, making her way into the ground floor parlor that faced Curzon Street.

Once the two were settled, she angled the paper so the light from the front window made it easier to see.

Dear Miss Fulton,

After careful consideration regarding my call on you last spring at Warwick's, I have come to understand my actions were rash. They were made in haste and were a result of my disbelief of the facts—that I do indeed have a sister, and that you are she.

Can you ever forgive me?

I have read—in its entirety—a copy of my father's will. In deference to his wishes, I am compelled to abide by the conditions he has set forth for your welfare. That is to say, a living for your mother, Miss Fulton, and a living for you in the amount of five-hundred pounds per year, as well as a dowry in the amount of five-thousand pounds for you, payable to your betrothed at the time of your marriage.

You need not vacate your home. The lease on the townhouse has been renewed for another year.

Although not all of the funds are available at this time (I will not share with you the frustration I have experienced in trying to sort my our late father's accounts), I have been successful in seeing to some of this year's living. The funds have been set aside in an account at Barings Bank, accessible by an agent representing either you or your mother.

In the meantime, there is a bank draft included here so that you may gain immediate funds. It is my sincere hope

*that the monies for the dowry will be available in that
same account sometime next year.*

*I do expect to have some say in who you marry, if for
no other reason than you are my sister, and I do not wish
you to end up wed to a scoundrel or a fortune hunter.*

Marguerite lifted her head and turned to stare at her
mother. "I can barely believe it," she whispered.

Maria dipped her head. "It seems Wadsworth did raise
a fine boy," she murmured.

Her daughter shook her head. "I rather doubt my
father had as much to do with it as her ladyship," she
replied, remembering Lord Lancaster's comment about
Lady Wadsworth. Apparently the woman had been
appalled when she learned what Benedict had done, even
though it meant acknowledging the existence of her late
husband's by-blow. "And I do hope Benedict is able to
afford his mother's living."

Her brows furrowing at hearing this comment, Maria
asked, "What are you saying?"

Marguerite realized she had said too much. "It seems
Benedict paid a call on his mother when she moved to
Westminster a few months ago—a welcome call, if you
will—and discovered she was starving. Or, at least, that is
what he thought. Wadsworth Hall was in poor condition.
The roof was leaking. There were very few servants because
she could not afford them—"

"Because she lived beyond her means in Suffolk?"
Maria challenged.

"Oh, no, Mother. Because father did not see to
treating her as well as he treated us," she replied, a bit too
forcibly. "While he gifted you jewels, he gave her paste."

She remembered how shocked she had felt at meeting the woman. Charity Wadsworth seemed far too thin—frail, almost—and despite the fichu she wore, her collar bones were in evidence. "She has even taken a position as a matchmaker to earn a living."

Suitably chastised, Maria dipped her head. "I did not know. Your father spoke only of his sons," she said on a sigh.

"He did not speak poorly of her," Marguerite reminded her mother.

"He did not speak of her at all," Maria corrected her. She regarded her daughter for a moment before her attention went back to the letter she held. "What else did he write?"

Marguerite gave a start, her gaze going back to the long parchment. When she found where she had left off, she continued reciting Benedict's words.

> *"Should you wonder what has occurred to change my mind on the matter, you have my mother to thank. She reminded me that family must come first in all considerations, and you, Marguerite, and my brother, and my mother, are my family.*
>
> *Yours in service,*
> *Benedict, Earl of Wadsworth*

Marguerite lifted her head and gave a watery grin as her eyes blurred with tears. "Oh, dear. I do believe I must forgive him," she whispered.

Her mother nodded in agreement. "Perhaps you will write a letter then? To let him know?"

Fishing a hanky from a pocket, she dabbed at the

corners of her eyes. "I will," Marguerite agreed. "But first I wish to pay a call on Miss Analise. To let her know, and to thank her father for what he had done on our behalf."

"And Lady Wadsworth, too?" Maria reminded her.

Marguerite nodded. "And her, too."

Chapter 28

OF PURSES AND PROPRIETY

The following afternoon
With the unusually fine weather in the late afternoons came the larger contingent of aristocrats parading down Rotten Row. The better weather—and the brief visit that morning by Marguerite Fulton—also had Charity pining for a chance to be out in it.

The news that Benedict had done what she insisted wasn't so much a surprise as Marguerite's other words.

Although I love my mother, if I had to choose another, it would be you.

Who would have ever thought a husband's illegitimate daughter could leave her happier than she had felt since returning to London? Charity was considering this and more when a footman appeared at her desk and confirmed her identify. He gave a deep bow and handed her a note.

"Who is this from?" she asked before the servant could step away from her desk. Even as she asked the question, she knew the answer.

She recognized the handwriting.

"Lord Lancaster, my lady."

"You're not going to wait for a reply?"

The footman's eyes darted to one side. "No, my lady. I was just instructed to make the delivery." With that, he bowed again and took his leave of the charity's office.

As she had no clients waiting in line at that moment, Charity popped the wax seal and unfolded the long note.

Dear Lady Wadsworth,

Having arranged for the afternoon to be sunny, may I request the honor of your presence in my curricle so that we might take a ride in the park?

Charity straightened as she allowed a sound of disbelief. Apparently Lord Lancaster thought he had some sort of arrangement with the weather gods!

There is no need for you to send a reply as I shall collect you from your office at four o'clock this afternoon. I have already received permission from your employer to do so with the understanding you are to be returned to said office sometime tomorrow.

Her mouth dropped open at this particular bit of news, and Charity gave a huff. *How dare he?* Why he implied she would be spending the rest of the afternoon— indeed the entire *night*—in his company!

I, of course, can provide transportation for your return to the office directly after our ride in the park (if that is your preference) as I do not believe Lord Bostwick conveyed Lady Bostwick's words quite right. (You must think me the very worst libertine if you read the viscount's words the way I heard them, which is how I wrote them.)(Which I now realize was the most very wrong thing to do—can you forgive me?)

Lifting her head and glancing about the office, as if she thought she was being watched by everyone else there, Charity allowed a sigh of relief at finding Mr. Barnaby and Mr. Overby engrossed in the papers on their desks. She was sure her face was bright red, for she had thought exactly as Lancaster claimed in the missive.

And just what did Viscount Bostwick have to do with this? Lancaster's words made it sound as if the younger viscount was merely the messenger.

Although I would like nothing more than to spend an entire afternoon and night and morning in your company, I rather doubt I shall have that opportunity.

Well. He had that right!

At least, not yet.

Charity rolled her eyes. She crumpled the note in one hand without reading the rest, well aware someone else had moved to stand next to her desk.

"Would it really be so awful to take a ride with him? Lady Bostwick fears you may be spending too much time in your new avocation."

Inhaling sharply, Charity looked up to find George Bennett-Jones regarding her with an expression of sadness.

"Lord Bostwick," she said as she moved to stand up. He held out a hand though, indicating she should remain seated. He settled into the chair next to her desk as she regarded him with a look of confusion. "I... no, it would not be awful to take a ride with him, I suppose," she agreed. "The weather is fine, and it's really rather kind of him to offer. Again."

George was about to allow an expression of relief, until he heard this last bit. "Again?" he repeated. A brow furrowed. "How many times has he asked?"

Charity lifted a shoulder. "This is the third invitation since Lord Attenborough's ball," she replied as she held up the crumpled paper. "We danced the one time, but I cannot sort just why he wishes to spend more time in my company. He even paid a call here at the office the afternoon following the ball."

She decided not to mention the ride to Berkeley Square or the dinner at Stanton House, or the ride back to her house once dinner was finished, all because of what her son had done.

Her eyelids heavy from having eaten a larger than usual dinner, Marcus had seen to returning Charity to Wadsworth Hall the night before last. Making his apologies to Lord Wessex, he asked that the younger viscount join Analise in the parlor until such time as he returned and they could imbibe in a glass of port.

His request was gladly received by Wessex, but then, why would it not? The younger viscount seemed happy to spend time in Analise's company. And she in his.

Charity had to allow a grin at remembering just how the atmosphere in the dining room fairly sizzled with their mutual attraction. One that seemed to go completely unnoticed by Marcus.

"Ah," George responded to her accounting of Lord Lancaster's attempts to spend time in her company, his head nodding. "In the hope persistence would pay off, no doubt. Well, is there anything I might do to help?"

About to give her head a shake, Charity suddenly straightened. "Perhaps," she hedged. "It seems Lord Lancaster knows much about me while I have absolutely no knowledge of his interests—"

"Archaeology," the viscount interrupted. At her look of astonishment, he added, "If he hadn't inherited the viscountcy, he would probably be off collecting artifacts in the Kingdom of the Two Sicilies, or in Greece, or..." He allowed a shrug. "Egypt or Timbuktu, for that matter."

Charity considered this bit of news. She never would have guessed the man with whom she had spent an evening in the Attenborough's garden—in his imagination —would be caught digging in the dirt. "I see," she replied in a quiet voice, remembering there were a few ancient artifacts on display in the Stanton House parlor.

She thought of the number of times she had visited the British Museum, her preference to spend time among the ancient statuary and pottery. She wondered briefly if the viscount might have contributed any relics to the collections on display. "Any other interests? Closer to home, perhaps?"

Emboldened by the query, George leaned toward her and lowered his voice. "His children, of course, but I have the distinct impression he would like more of them." He said this last as a brow arched, as if he were confiding a secret. "Now that his oldest boy is off at school and his daughter might marry in the next year, he'll only have his young son at Stanton House," he explained. "I think he was hoping for a larger family."

Dipping her head slightly, Charity considered how unusual such a sentiment seemed for a gentleman of the *ton*. Most were satisfied with an heir and a spare—daughters be damned—for any additional children were simply a drain on the coffers. "I met your children last week," she murmured. "Your daughter is... is an angel."

George heard the longing in her voice, but couldn't help saying what first came to mind. "I am so relieved she gives that impression to callers, for her mother is of the opinion she will be a hoyden." He was about to say 'hellion,' but thought better of it. It wouldn't be proper to say such a thing to the widowed countess. "You're welcome to visit the nursery whenever you wish," he offered.

Charity allowed an impish grin. "Be careful, Lord Bostwick, or you may find I have taken up permanent residence in your nursery." She inhaled and then sighed, her gaze going to the crumpled note she still held in her hand. "I shall go on this ride with Lancaster this afternoon."

Allowing a grin to lighten his face, George gave a nod. "I am very glad to hear it," he replied. "If you'd like, I can escort you to his curricle."

Blinking, Charity turned her attention to the front of the office, but she couldn't see the street beyond the front door. "Is he... is he already here?"

George nodded. "He is." He glanced at his chronometer. "A bit early," he commented, not about to tell her it was only half-past three. "But better early than late."

Charity glanced at the papers on her desk and allowed a shrug. "I suppose I can leave early today," she said, rather glad no one had come in seeking her services this afternoon.

George helped her into her pelisse, and she wrapped the cord of her reticule around a wrist.

"Tell me, Lord Bostwick, was it really Lady Bostwick's opinion that I should take a ride in the park with Lord Lancaster?"

Offering an arm, George nodded. "Of course," he replied as he settled his beaver on his head and led her out of the office. The Lancaster curricle was parked at the curb.

Marcus Batey sat holding the reins of a matched pair of blacks, but he stood up at her appearance and offered a bow. "So good of you to join me, my lady," he said with a nervous smile.

Charity dipped a curtsy and accepted George's offer of a hand as she climbed into the conveyance. Her reticule ended up on the seat between her and Marcus, its contents providing a suitable barrier betwixt their bodies. Turning to the other viscount, she gave George a nod. "Good day to you, Bostwick. And please give my regards to Lady Bostwick, won't you?"

George tipped his hat. "I shall," he called out as Marcus put the horses in motion.

"How are you on this fine day?" Marcus asked, once he had the equipage merged into the traffic in Oxford Street.

Charity regarded him a moment. "You are persistent," she accused.

His pleasant expression faltering, Marcus dared a glance in her direction. "Had I learned you needed only one more invitation, and I had stopped at two, I never would have forgiven myself," he replied.

Considering his words a moment, Charity finally settled into the squabs. "I am doing rather well on this fine day," she said then, deciding she should at least try to get along with the viscount. "And you?"

"Capital," he said with a grin. "Mostly because of what I suspect you did."

"Oh?"

"Miss Fulton paid a call at Stanton House this morning. Wadsworth has seen to honoring the terms of his father's will, so she and her mother are no longer in danger of being thrown out on the street."

Charity dipped her head. "I rather doubt it would have come to that."

"Was there an entailed property they could have moved into instead?" he asked.

Shaking her head, Charity said, "My son has already let it to a baron for the year. If he hadn't agreed, or if he didn't have the funds necessary to extend the lease on their townhouse, I might have had them move into Wadsworth Hall." She took a deep breath. "I expect you've already guessed this isn't all my late husband's fault," she said.

"Mismanagement on the part of his man of business, perhaps?" Marcus asked.

"More like embezzlement." Before this week, she hadn't even known the meaning of the word.

"Then Wadsworth needs to sue the man responsible. Recover what he can of whatever's been stolen." If he was still a full-time solicitor, he would have gladly taken the case.

Knowing her son would need to decide for himself what action to take, she said, "Marguerite paid a call on me, as well."

When she didn't say more, Marcus dared a glance in her direction. "Did you... receive her?"

"I did. She's a fine young woman. She'll make a great match some day."

"Perhaps with your help?" he half-asked.

"She'll probably end up married to a rich merchant or a banker," Charity replied with a grin. "Maybe even a baron."

Marcus inhaled and said, "On the subject of young women, I find I am in a bit of a quandary with respect to reticules."

Charity dared a glance at her own misshapen reticule, wincing at the thought of how much she had stuffed into it over the course of the past week. The seams very nearly strained at their task of keeping everything inside. "Does my reticule bother you?"

Marcus blinked, his gaze going to the velvet purse decorated with beads and embroidery. "Oh, not at all," he replied. "I have been told a reticule would make a good gift for my daughter. She will be eighteen years of age on the morrow, and I was considering where I might shop for one."

"Ah," Charity responded with a nod. "And you've no idea where to start such a search."

"I thought of New Bond Street."

Giving him a look of approval, Charity allowed an impish grin. "And yet, if you remain on this very street, you will come upon a small shop full of fripperies. Just on that corner up there," she remarked, indicating a stuccoed building with mullioned windows. Behind the windows was a riot of color, although from this distance, the items contributing to the colorful interior couldn't be discerned.

"Forsham's Fripperies," he murmured. "Would you mind very much if we stop? Perhaps you can... assist me in the search? I fear there will be much to dig through to find the perfect purse."

Charity regarded him a moment. "Of course, but you

needn't make it sound like an archaeological expedition," she teased.

Marcus jerked his head in her direction, wondering if she knew of his interest in ancient artifacts. "I suppose not."

"Unless it makes it easier to abide," she countered. "The searching, I mean."

He sighed as he parked the blacks at the curb. A young boy ran up, and he tossed him a coin to hold the reins while they shopped. "It puts it in a context I am better prepared to face," he agreed, just before he stepped down from the equipage. He hurried around the back of curricle and then helped her down from the other side.

"Archaeology, you mean?" she replied, placing her arm on the one he offered. "I understand it's your avocation."

Marcus nodded, realizing Viscount Bostwick must have said something. "It was, before my brother died and I inherited the viscountcy," he replied. "I am a solicitor, but I used to take the family to the Greek islands in the winter, so I might dig up bits of antiquities," he explained, his expression wistful. He sobered and then sighed. "Can't do that anymore, what with Parliament and all."

When he opened the door to the shop, Charity stepped in and waited until he rejoined her. "Greek islands," she murmured. "It sounds so exotic." She had never been outside of England. The wars with France had prevented travel to the Continent for half her adult life, and during he early years of her marriage, her husband had preferred to stay in Suffolk when he wasn't expected in the capital.

Marcus watched as Charity's expression changed with her words. He loved seeing her eyes light up, the color come into her cheeks. He was about to imagine what it might be like to take her to the park, to park the curricle and find a secluded spot in which they might kiss one another.

He was precluded from doing so when Charity pointed to a display of reticules. "Now, does Miss Analise need something for the day, or something more formal for the evening?" she asked as she reached for a tasteful fabric bag with a simple drawstring closure.

Perusing the various styles, Marcus gave a shake of his head. "Day, I should think." He frowned as he studied a beaded reticule. "Unless, she would consider this special?" he asked as he pulled it from the shelf. The entire bag seemed to be made up of colored beads intricately woven into a floral design. As a result, it was heavier than expected, and he nearly dropped it.

Charity regarded the one he held and gave a shake of her head. "She might use it once or twice. For the theatre or a *soirée*," she commented.

"She could use it as a weapon," he remarked, hefting it in his hands as if to determine what kind of damage it might do if thrown at a man's face.

"It would have a more profound effect if she swung it by the handle," Charity remarked. "Then she would still have possession of it after it did its damage." She dimpled when she noted his look of surprise at hearing this. Perhaps he was considering her own stuffed reticule and what she might do to him with it should he annoy her overmuch.

"I take your warning and thank you for it." He reached up and fingered several bags that were displayed in a long line. "This one looks as if it's made of shells," he murmured, holding another small bag so he could examine it more closely. "I wonder from what beach these shells might have come?" He redirected his gaze onto Charity. "There are some excellent examples of ancient shells down by Lyme Regis."

Charity recognized the name of the town in which Mary Anning lived. The young woman was famous for her discovery of fossils, including that of a dinosaur. Selling shells and fossils was how Miss Anning made her meager living. Some of her finds were even featured in the British Museum. "If you don't mind me asking, how did you come to be interested in archaeology?"

Marcus regarded her with appreciation. No one had ever asked him such a question before. "Oh, I don't mind at all. It was my mother, if you can believe it." He gave a short guffaw. "And her reticule, of all things."

Pausing in her attempt to pull a reticule from a higher shelf, Charity regarded the viscount in surprise. "Her reticule?" she repeated. But from Marcus's slack jaw and the fact that his gaze wasn't focused on anything in particular, she realized he was lost in thought.

"*W*hat do you think you're doing, young man?"

Marcus's head jerked up, but his tiny fingers didn't let go of their grip on his mother's reticule, nor did he offer an answer to her question. The elaborately embroidered bag was obviously full of something—its shape suggested it contained a number of oddly shaped items—and it was *heavy*.

The viscountess allowed a smirk to appear, but before she could tell him to put down the reticule, her husband entered the parlor.

"I wouldn't do that if I were you, young man," the

baritone voice of the Viscount Lancaster intoned. Although his manner seemed most serious, his own lips formed a quirk. "Once you get started, it will be like an archeological expedition. You'll find layers upon layers of history, all manner of artifacts going back to the dawn of ..."

"Lancaster!" Mary admonished her husband. "He'll find no such thing," she added as she leaned over and captured the reticule in one hand. "Everything in here is from just this past year," she claimed, her chin rising in defiance of the viscount's words.

"What is archaeol..." Marcus stopped, his brows furrowing in concentration.

"Archaeology is the study of artifacts from prior civilizations," his father explained patiently. "Involves a good deal of digging in the dirt. Or reticules, if a woman ever allowed a man such an endeavor."

This comment had young Marcus turning his attention back to his mother. He was never sure when he was being teased or not. "Will you show me?" he asked in a voice not much louder than a whisper.

Mary allowed a grin to appear. "I'd be delighted," she said, giving her husband an arched eyebrow in the process.

Charles allowed a look of surprise. "What? Why, you would never do me the honor of revealing the contents of your reticule to *me*," he complained, his voice suggesting he was rather hurt.

His wife giggled, a sound that had Marcus widening his eyes. He had never heard such a sound come from his mother before, but the delight she displayed soon had him grinning as well.

"*You* never asked, darling," Mary replied as she moved to give her husband a kiss on his cheek.

Darling.

Marcus always liked it when he heard his mother call his father 'darling.' He knew she adored his father. She teased him, and he allowed it. He teased her, and she feigned offense. But his father would work his magic with the metals he melted in his small foundry out back and every so often present her with all manner of beautiful jewelry and interesting trinkets, including the chatelaine she had pinned to the skirt of the gown she wore.

"I am asking now," Charles stated. "I should like to watch while you reveal the bag's contents to young Marcus."

The viscountess rolled her eyes as she moved to the card table at the back of the parlor. She spread open the gathered end of the reticule until it was as wide as it would go and proceeded to unload the myriad objects onto the table's surface.

A small mirror in a hinged ivory case, a pair of silk gloves, a purse heavy with coins, a pair of opera glasses in an embroidered case. The items continued to collect on the card table, looking as if they would take up far more space than the small bag could contain.

"Good God, Mary, you've barely made a dent," his father had said then, his gaze directed down onto the opening of the reticule.

"May I see?" Marcus asked, rising up on tiptoes.

Mary lowered the bag so he could look inside. His brows furrowed as he tried to determine what was still packed inside. "Go on. Pull out something," she encouraged.

Marcus reached in and snatched out a small metal case with hinges on one side. "Those are my calling cards," she said when he placed the case on the table.

He reached in and pulled out the edge of what appeared to be a scarf. "Oh! My shawl. I've been looking for that," she said as she watched him pull on the thin fabric. Despite how far his arm stretched, the fabric continued to come out of the reticule for another entire arm's length before it finally fluttered onto the table.

Peeking back into the bottom, Marcus wasn't yet sure he could see the bottom. "My ear bobs," his mother breathed as she reached in and pulled out the garnet and gold jewelry.

"I recognize those," Charles said with some pride.

"You made them for my twentieth birthday," she murmured as she studied the stones.

Meanwhile, Marcus had continued the expedition, pulling out a key, a thimble, a needle case, and a spool of silk thread. He couldn't help but notice how his father watched in fascination.

Or perhaps it was disbelief.

"Is there *more* in there?" Charles asked.

Marcus turned the bag over and held it by the bottom. A bracelet, a ring, a hair comb, and a necklace spilled out onto the table top.

"It looks as if you undressed into your reticule," Charles said with some humor. And then his expression darkened.

Mary placed the ear bobs onto the table and was about to chide him for his comment. Then she realized he might think she had engaged in an *affaire*. The evidence was rather damning, given the jewelry and the shawl. "There was that night, after we attended the theatre," she whispered suggestively.

Charles blinked. "Was I there?" he asked with a hint of humor.

Letting out a most unladylike snort, Mary's complexion took on a reddish cast. "It better have been you in our town coach," she countered. Her eyes widened when she saw his narrowed eyes coupled with an expression that suggested whatever she had planned for the afternoon was about to change. And then she giggled when the viscount swooped her into his arms and out of the parlor, leaving her reticule and its contents in the company of their youngest son.

*M*arcus gave a shake of his head, the shelf of reticules coming into focus at the same time Charity said, "Are you well, my lord?" One of her gloved hands had come to rest on his upper arm, apparently to give it a shake.

He blinked and turned his gaze on her, his lips quirked with the memory of his parents' behavior that afternoon. "I am quite well," he replied. "Apologies for having left you for a moment. Your query about my mother's reticule had me remembering an incident from my youth."

"Something pleasant, it seemed," Charity guessed. The viscount had displayed an expression that seemed to youthen him, one that suggested he preferred living in the past.

Nodding, he said, "Indeed. And thanks to my mother, I do believe I know exactly which reticule I shall buy for Analise."

Charity watched in fascination as he reached for a cream-colored reticule adorned with a bit of embroidery. Embellished with a few beads, it was on the larger side compared to the others on display. Given its style, it would be appropriate for a garden party or for shopping. Even for a night at the theatre. "It's beautiful," she said.

"You think she'll like it?" he asked as he pulled the drawstring apart and peered inside, as if he expected to find something in there.

"I would," Charity replied. "If she doesn't, I'll take it," she added with a grin. She sobered when she saw how he gazed at her. "What is it?"

Marcus leaned closer, but then suddenly straightened, as if he just then realized where they were. "I had an over-whelming desire to kiss you just then," he murmured. He winced when he saw her reaction. "Did I just say that out loud?"

Charity blinked and gave a curt nod. "You did." Thinking she should take a step back—they were standing rather close to one another—she found she couldn't make her feet move. "But it's passed now. Hasn't it?" she added, just before she dared a glance in the direction of the shop-keeper. The older gentleman's attention was on a news sheet, though, and she breathed a sigh of relief.

Marcus shook his head. "I... I can't imagine it ever will," he whispered. At her slight inhalation of breath, he added, "I've had that overwhelming desire for twenty years."

Knowing there was only one way to react to such a claim so she wouldn't have to provide an immediate reply, Charity stared at the viscount as her knees buckled beneath her. If she managed to grip his lapel, she might not crumple all the way to the floor below. Surely the viscount would understand she was fainting and see to it she was lifted into his arms and carried out to the curricle.

At least she didn't end up on the floor. Marcus under-stood her distress almost before she did, his arms wrapping around her shoulders so he could pull her against the front of his body. The reticule, still held in one hand, ended up behind one of her shoulders, and her head, adorned with a petite hat, ended up in the small of his shoulder.

"Oh, now I've gone and done it," he murmured, his other arm snaking around her waist to help hold her up. *She probably hasn't eaten anything since breakfast,* he thought, dismayed by how thin she was. He thought of calling out to the shopkeeper, but he found he didn't want to give up his hold on the countess. Her soft body, warm in his arms, seemed to fit perfectly against the front of his own body. Had he wanted to, he could easily lift her into his arms and carry her out to the curricle, but then he would have to give up his hold on her, and he didn't want to do that.

Not yet. Not when he could inhale the floral notes of her perfume, feel her soft breath against his shirt, angle his head and then lean down just so and kiss her.

He thought of the time they had spent in the Attenborough gardens, remembering how she had felt in his arms when she had fainted and he held her on the stone bench.

Except that it hadn't really happened.

And yet, right this moment felt exactly as it did then.

Giving his head a shake, as if to clear it of the memory that was entirely made up in his imagination, Marcus gazed down at the woman he held and saw that her eyes were open. "You have the most beautiful eyes," he whispered.

Charity blinked twice, but didn't move to straighten. She was quite comfortable right where she was, although she had managed to get her feet firmly under her. "Are you aware you said that out loud?"

Marcus furrowed his brows. "Did you take offense?"

"No."

"Then, yes. Yes, I am aware," he murmured, emboldened. He was about to kiss her—he imagined it in vivid detail—if only because she looked as if she wanted to be kissed.

The sound of a throat clearing had Marcus giving up his hold on Charity, as if he'd been caught with his hands in the biscuit jar. The countess immediately stepped back and stared at the shopkeeper, who regarded the two of them with the most curious expression.

"Can't say as I've ever seen the reticules inspire a marriage proposal 'afore," he said, his hands folded together at his waist. "Will that be on your account, sir?"

Marcus realized he still held the reticule for Analise in his hand. "I'll pay in cash," he said, deciding he didn't want the shopkeeper to know his identity. He reached into a waistcoat pocket and extracted his purse, fumbling inside for coins. Handing them over, the shopkeeper studied them a moment before moving back to the counter to wrap the reticule in tissue.

Charity watched the shopkeeper go before she finally turned her attention back to Marcus. She knew her face was flushed with embarrassment, although perhaps it wasn't as red as the viscount's.

"I wasn't going to do that until we got to the park," he murmured. "Kiss you, I mean."

Charity dared a glance around the small shop, relieved to see they were the only customers. It was bad enough the shopkeeper had paid witness to their embrace. At least he didn't seem to recognize her—it had been years since she had made a purchase at the small shop. She turned her attention back to Marcus. "You said that out loud," she whispered, not yet sure she *wanted* to be kissed by the viscount.

"I am well aware of that," Marcus murmured. "I don't live in my imagination all the time."

"But you prefer to," she guessed.

The viscount jerked at hearing the comment, darting a glance in her direction before hurrying up to the counter to complete his purchase of the reticule. When the shopkeeper gave him the box, he allowed a nod. "Much obliged."

"Did she say yes?" the older man asked in a whisper.

Marcus blinked and then realized what the man meant. He dared a glance to where Charity stood near the door. "We were interrupted before I could ask," he whispered, allowing his annoyance to show. "I'll try again in the park."

He wouldn't, of course. He wasn't even sure they would make it to the park.

Chapter 29

A HEROIC ACT COSTS A VISCOUNT

moment later

Depositing the box in the curricle before helping Charity up the step, Marcus watched as she settled into the squabs. She didn't look his way but seemed lost in thought as he took the reins from the boy. The street urchin quickly scampered off to another carriage.

When he took his seat next to Charity, Marcus couldn't help but notice her reticule wasn't between them, but rather on the other side of her body. Perhaps he had misjudged the situation. Perhaps she was still amenable to a ride in the park.

"I don't always live in my imagination," he said, holding the reins in one hand as he turned to regard her. "Or in the past. I don't usually prefer it to the here and now," he continued and then added, "Except during especially boring sessions of Parliament. Or when I've pulled an artifact from the dirt, and I wonder to whom it might have belonged. What they might have used it for."

Charity nodded her understanding. "That doesn't sound like a poor use of your imagination," she replied, her attention suddenly on a carriage that had just passed them, headed in the direction of the park. "I believe that was the Bostwicks," she commented, straightening on the bench. "We should be going, or we'll be the last in line."

Marcus blinked, shocked to hear she still wished to accompany him. "Of course, my lady." He took a quick glance at his chronometer, relieved to discover they still had plenty of time before the five o'clock hour.

He had the horses pulling away from the curb and following the Bostwick carriage before he was aware of Charity's gaze on him. "Is something the matter?"

"You said you don't usually prefer living in your imagination," she replied. "But when you do—when you're attending an especially boring session of Parliament—what is it you think about?"

Marcus cleared his throat, sure his cravat was doing nothing to hide his reddening face. "It depends, I suppose. Sometimes I imagine my children when they were younger. Last week, my daughter was wearing one of her mother's gowns, and I remembered the picnic when Joan first wore it." He almost winced when he realized he had spoken of his late wife, but Charity didn't seem to mind.

"You didn't make up those memories, though," Charity reminded him. "They were about events that really happened."

One of his brows furrowed. "True."

Charity dipped her head. "The day you told me about our talk in the gardens—"

"The talk that never happened," he said with a shake of his head.

"You had me a bit... frightened, if only because you were so convincing. You had me questioning my own memory," she said as one of her hands went to her breast.

"If what you described had happened, I would always wonder how it was I remembered nothing of it."

His expression indicating his regret, Marcus sighed. "I admit, that was entirely my imagination. But in my recalling it...it seemed so *real*."

"Does that happen often?" she asked, her voice barely above a whisper.

Marcus furrowed a brow. "No," he replied with a shake of his head. "No," he repeated more firmly. "In fact, I rarely make things up in my head." He gave his head a shake. "I just relive events that have already happened. Happy events."

Charity pursed her lips and leaned back in the squabs. "Then why that particular scene?" she asked.

Dipping his head, Marcus gave her a quick glance before saying, "Wishful thinking?"

Inhaling slowly, Charity held his gaze for a moment too long, for several horses were about to collide in the intersection just ahead of them.

"Look out!" she shouted, just as the matched pair pulling his curricle reared up and halted. The Bostwick's carriage barely cleared the intersection before a coach-and-four bolted between them. Horses whinnied in protest, the town coach jerked forward and then halted, moved forward again as if its driver couldn't decide if he wanted his team to go straight or to turn into Oxford Street.

Marcus was about to call out to the driver when he saw that there wasn't one. There was, however, a woman inside the coach, her screams and shrieks evident above the sounds of traffic. "Dear God," he said under his breath. He handed the reins to Charity. "Hold onto these, please," he said before he jumped down to the street and rushed to the coach.

He was about to gain a foothold on the step that would take him up to the bench, but the horses, torn between racing ahead or rearing up in protest, jerked the coach forward. Marcus was forced to run alongside the coach until it paused long enough for him to gain a foothold.

Hoisting himself up onto the seat, Marcus discovered the ribbons had come loose from where they should have been tied around a post. He found them dangling below, barely on the footrest. He flattened himself on the bench, reached down, and managed to snag the leather reins just as the horses lurched forward again, the front pair rearing up in protest.

Nearly losing his grip on the edge of the bench, Marcus experienced a moment of terror when he realized he could end up falling on his head to the street below. The next jerking motion worked in his favor, though, giving him the momentum he needed to get back up onto the bench. He pulled hard on the reins, his quick glance taking in the surrounding traffic. He was trying to decide if he should have the team pull over or remain where they were—just beyond the intersection but in the middle of the street.

"Sir!"

Glancing to his right, Marcus found a groom struggling to gain a foothold on the coach. "Where's the driver?" he called out.

"He'll be along in a moment. Can't run as fast as me," the groom said as he got himself up and seated on the bench. "Right daring of you to rescue Lady Pettigrew," he added with a nod. "Much obliged."

"Lady Pettigrew? Marcus repeated. In his haste to get

to the driver's seat, he hadn't given a thought as to who might be *in* the town coach. "What happened?"

"She was having a hissy fit about some shopkeeper and rocked the carriage somethin' awful," the groom said in a hoarse whisper. "Horses got spooked, and took off while the driver was shuttin' the door behind her."

Marcus was about to ask why the groom wasn't the one shutting the door, but thought better of it. If Lady Pettigrew was angry when she took her leave of a store, then it stood to reason the driver might have attempted to console her while the groom stayed on the back of the town coach. "The reins weren't tied to the post," Marcus said as he gladly handed them to the groom.

His eyes widening in alarm, the groom nodded. "What with her ladyship yelling at him, I suppose he forgot."

Once the groom had the reins firmly in hand, Marcus jumped down from the bench and hurried back to his own curricle. He stepped up and into the equipage, took his seat, and calmly took the reins from Charity's gloved hands.

That is, once he was able to peel her fingers from their grip on the ribbons. If she hadn't been wearing gloves, her white knuckles would have been apparent.

"Did that really just happen?" Marcus asked as he turned his attention to Charity. His manner betrayed his excitement. The adrenaline rush had his entire body humming and a grin lighting his face.

She blinked. And blinked again. "If you cannot discern from my wide eyes and pallid complexion that, yes, it did indeed happen, then you, my lord, are *blind* as well as deranged," she whispered hoarsely.

Marcus furrowed a brow, well aware of the anger—or

was that fear?—in her voice. His gaze raked over her entire body—she was shaking, and her lower lip was trembling as if she were about to cry. "I apologize, my lady. I didn't mean to frighten you," he said. He wrapped his free arm around the back of her shoulders and attempted to console her, but her body was unyielding.

"Remove your arm, Lord Lancaster, or I shall scream as loudly as Lady Pettigrew was doing a moment ago."

Marcus pulled his arm away as if he'd been burned. "Forgive me," he murmured. "I only meant to—"

"Take me back to the office, please. Or..." She considered where they were. "Or home," she amended. "Home."

Chapter 30

A MATCHMAKER IS UNDONE

A few minutes before, just ahead in Oxford Street

"Something's happening," Elizabeth said as she glanced over her shoulder. Her eyes widened, and then her gloved hand gripped her husband's arm. "A runaway team!"

George was managing the reins of a newly matched pair of greys. His phaeton, a rather conservative model in that it was black, had provided a comfortable ride until just the moment before, when he sensed more than saw a coach racing toward Oxford Street.

Directly at them.

He made sure his phaeton cleared the intersection with plenty of room to spare, but he knew whoever was behind him might not stop in time.

Lord Lancaster.

George pulled on the reins in an effort to slow down the spirited horses and then dared a glance back over his shoulder. Uttering a curse, he directed the horses to park at the curb. "*Damnation.* They'll collide with something if they don't stop," he claimed, just then noticing that the town coach barreling into the intersection had no driver.

Elizabeth had both her hands covering her mouth, as if to hold in a scream. The older viscount's curricle was directly behind them, although at a bit of a distance.

George wouldn't forgive himself if Lord Lancaster and his passenger were hurt. He had been the one to suggest to Lancaster that he take Lady Wadsworth to the park for a ride. Elizabeth and George had been on the phaeton, waiting until Lord Lancaster emerged from the charity offices—either with the countess or without—so that George might discover if his attempts at matchmaking were proving fruitful or not.

Although it seemed as if events occurred in slow motion, Elizabeth was stunned when she saw Lord Lancaster mount the driver's step of the runaway coach. Within moments, he had the team under control, the town coach coming to a stuttering halt halfway down the intersecting street. With the coach having cleared the intersection, Lancaster's curricle, halted just shy of where the town coach had passed, held only Charity Wadsworth. The countess sat gripping the reins of the matched blacks, an expression of horror on her face.

"That was Lord Pettigrew's coach," George said, his brows furrowed. "But he's not in town this week."

"Which means Lady Pettigrew is in there," Elizabeth murmured, swallowing hard. "Which would explain the screaming. Poor woman." She had never felt sorry for the gossip monger in the past, but no one should have to undergo the terror the old woman had just experienced.

"She'll be fine," George replied, rather proud to have witnessed a fellow viscount stepping up to save the day.

"But what of Charity? She looks as if she's seen a ghost," Elizabeth remarked, her brow furrowed in worry.

George was about to step down from the phaeton, but Elizabeth placed a hand on his shoulder. "Don't you dare think to leave me alone with these horses," she warned.

Hesitating, partly because he expected a young street urchin to hurry up and offer to hold the reins, George straightened on the bench. The spectacle of the runaway coach had everyone in Oxford Street gawking in the direction of where it had come to a stop. Some applauded as a groom raced down the street followed by an older gentleman who had been attempting to run for some distance in an effort to catch up to their equipage.

Another moment, and Lord Lancaster jogged back to his curricle. Elizabeth watched as he seemed to struggle to regain the reins from Charity.

"She'll think him a hero," George announced proudly.

Elizabeth shook her head, noting how Charity's expression hadn't changed with the arrival of her host. "I rather doubt that," she murmured. Even from this distance, she could tell Charity was either angry that she had been left with the ribbons or scared to death.

Probably the latter.

George frowned. "If I had been the one to stop that team?" he started to say.

"I would be sleeping in the mistress suite for the rest of the week. *Alone*," she interrupted.

Blinking, George furrowed both brows. "Do you dislike Lady Pettigrew so much?" he countered. "That you would prefer to see her injured?"

It was Elizabeth's turn to blink. "I am barely acquainted with Lady Pettigrew," she argued. "My reaction would be due to the fact that *you* could have been injured," she explained.

"I hardly think that is likely. Had I been in a position to do so, I could have caught up to the coach and easily—"

"Been killed," Elizabeth interrupted, her gloved hand moving to cover his lips.

George blinked. He thought to argue with her, but then thought better of it. Better he simply agree with her. "I love you," he said, hoping to deflect her anger. When her expression didn't change much, he decided kissing her might be a better tactic. He did so, removing her gloved hand from his face just before he took her mouth with his own.

After a few moments of stunned silence, Elizabeth finally opened her eyes and regarded her husband with a wan smile. "I know why you did that."

"Because I love you," George said, turning his attention to the horses. After a pause, he added, "And because I don't want to end up like him."

Elizabeth followed his line of sight, noting how the Lancaster curricle was pulling into Dean Street, heading south instead of straight towards Hyde Park. "Oh, dear," she murmured. "Follow them, darling. Please."

Chapter 31

A VISCOUNT MAKES A
MISTAKE

Meanwhile, back in the Lancaster curricle

Allowing an audible sigh, Marcus was aware of shouts coming from behind him, shouts filled with expletives. His equipage was blocking the street. He had the horses in motion in an instant and, at the next intersection, made for Westminster. He couldn't help but notice how Charity studied the hand that had held the reins, her glove displaying a tear in the fabric. "I'll have a replacement pair sent to your office on the morrow," he said. "What size do you wear?"

"You will do no such thing," she replied, her words clipped.

"But I am responsible for ruining them," he countered. "It's the least I can do. Besides, it's not as if you can afford to replace them."

The words were out of his mouth before he could sensor them. He, along with nearly every other aristocrat, knew Wadsworth—or apparently his man of business—had left his earldom in a shambles when it came to money.

Charity boggled at his comment. "How dare you?" she hissed. "How? How would you even *know* such a thing?"

Knowing full well he had made a mistake in the eyes of the countess—unintentionally, but a mistake none-the-less—in reining in the runaway horses, Marcus was overcome with sudden spitefulness. "Because Wadsworth was an ass. It's no secret he was an irresponsible rake who spent all his coin on mistresses. Everyone knows, my lady. "

He saw how his words cut her, but he went on. "Damn fool could have been spending his time with you. He could have spent every night of your marriage in your bed. But no. He was off with his mistresses and harlots—"

"Stop it," she whispered.

"When *I* could have had you," he went on, apparently not hearing her plea.

"Stop it."

"He knew I wanted you. He knew from the time we were at university that I loved you. Do you think it made a difference?" he hissed. "Of course, not. It only made him more determined to see to it you would be his countess, just to spite me."

Once again, his words were spoken before he realized he had said them aloud.

Charity's jaw dropped in disbelief. "Spite you?" she whispered. She had a thought she might faint—for real, this time—but she was getting quite enough air.

His tirade having ended, Marcus rolled his eyes and gave his head a shake. "We used to be the best of friends," he murmured. "At Eton. And then, we got into a fight over... over you." This last came out as a mere whisper.

"Your imagination is getting the better of you again," she said, this time her words loud enough for him to hear.

"Is it?" he countered. "He wanted nothing to do with marriage."

"He did his duty. As did I. Now stop and let me out of here," Charity insisted, moving closer to the door. Thoughts of returning to Suffolk immediately came to mind. She would have Thompkins begin packing this evening. They could be on their way by noon on the morrow.

Marcus turned his gaze on her and saw her determination. Resigned to his fate with her, he had the team pull the curricle to the side of the road, but only after he determined that the Bostwick phaeton was directly behind them. It pulled on ahead and then parked in front, its passengers both turning to look at them in confusion.

Moving to get out of the curricle so he could assist her, Marcus was shocked when Charity simply let herself out of the equipage and hurried up to the phaeton. Despite the tight fit, she was soon perched alongside Elizabeth, their arms interlinked.

Meanwhile, George dared a glance back at Marcus, his expression conveying his concern before he turned around. As the phaeton pulled into traffic, Marcus, his elbows on his knees, dropped his head into his hands and allowed a ragged sigh.

The awful memories of his time spent with Wadsworth had come crashing back at the worst possible moment. He hadn't realized just how much anger he felt toward the earl. How much resentment he still felt over what had started as a mean-spirited jest and then spiraled into outright hatred.

All because Edmund, Earl of Wadsworth, had warned him that he would wed whomever Marcus hoped to court.

Why?

Because he could.

Or so he claimed.

Convinced there was nothing to worry about—Charity didn't know Marcus existed, nor did Marcus believe Edmund's claim that he would soon know her in the carnal sense. The girl was barely sixteen at that point, and she hadn't yet had her come-out. Her older sister, Faith, did have hers that year, but Marcus didn't attend the ball since he was still at university.

Before Wadsworth made his ridiculous claim, he hadn't even been aware of Charity Seward. Barely knew her father, the Earl of Eversham, despite the two sharing the same political party, but then they were decades apart in age. He did, however, attend Faith's come-out ball at the Eversham residence.

Making it a point to seek out the younger sister, Edmund ruined the poor girl and then insisted to Eversham that he had to marry her. Eversham agreed, if for no other reason than he could avoid an expensive come-out for her the following year.

Before Marcus knew what was happening, Charity Seward was betrothed to Edmund.

The wedding was the following summer. The heir was born seven months later, and the spare barely two years after that. Then Wadsworth took up with the mistress he had employed before he wed.

The one who gave birth to Marguerite.

Marcus closed his eyes and sighed again, remembering he had a daughter at home who was about to turn eighteen and might suffer the same fate as Charity if he didn't keep her safe.

When his second son was old enough, he'd make sure the boy knew better than to ruin a young woman. He had already had the same discussion with his oldest son and been assured Andrew would never do such a thing.

Now Marcus almost wished *he* had been the one to ruin Charity Seward, for if he had, she would have been spared a loveless marriage.

Don't be a fool, he thought just then. For he was pretty sure she would have despised him as much as she despised her late husband.

Or would she have?

Marcus blinked as he reconsidered the situation. Reconsidered what had happened—or almost happened— in the fripperies shop. He had been about to kiss her. The shopkeeper thought he was going to propose.

And he did neither!

What if Charity *wanted* him to kiss her? She seemed willing—until she fainted. Or pretended to.

Was that supposed to be a warning that she didn't want him to kiss her? Or that she was trying to give him an out when the shopkeeper mentioned the marriage proposal?

He could consider alternatives for the rest of the day and night, but the answer wasn't going to make itself known until he spoke with Charity.

But first, he had to buy her a pair of gloves.

Chapter 32

FAILURE ON ALL ACCOUNTS

*M*eanwhile, in Oxford Street George merged the phaeton into traffic and then did a quick turn around halfway to the next intersection. He took the turn onto Dean Street, surprised to discover the Lancaster curricle was pulled over to the curb. Evidence of a spirited discussion had him cursing under his breath.

"What is it?" Elizabeth asked.

Sighing, George gave his head a shake. "I believe my efforts at matchmaking have failed."

About to put voice to a protest—Elizabeth had no idea her husband engaged in such a past-time—she understood what he meant when Charity approached the phaeton.

"Might I trouble you for a ride to Belton Street?" the countess asked, her light voice at odds with what they had just witnessed.

"Of course," George replied, even before Elizabeth could properly greet the countess. He was about to step down and assist Charity, but she had already bounded up the two tall steps and was seated next to Elizabeth before he could do so.

Despite Elizabeth's curiosity, she didn't ask what might have happened with Lord Lancaster, and Charity didn't offer. She did mention the unfortunate incident with the town coach. "After all that excitement, I hardly thought I would be good company for a ride in the park," she said, putting on a brave face.

"I admit to a bit of surprise that Lady Pettigrew didn't faint," Elizabeth replied. "I think her screams could be heard all the way to Rotten Row." After a pause, she added, "I do hope she thanked Lord Lancaster for his assistance. Why, if he hadn't done what he did, she might have been *killed*."

Feeling less than charitable at that moment, Charity nearly made a comment she would regret, something along the lines of, *Well deserved, don't you agree?*

She had no idea why she thought such a thing. No idea why she felt *jealous* of the old biddy whose gossip did so much damage. Lancaster would have done the same for her, had she been in such a situation.

Wouldn't he?

Her attention dropped to her hands, and she turned the palms up at the same moment Elizabeth glanced in her direction.

"You're bleeding!" Elizabeth exclaimed, her words forcing George to take his eyes off the road for a moment to see what his wife was talking about. He had a handkerchief out of his pocket and into Elizabeth's hand in a moment, and she quickly stripped the torn glove from Charity's hand and wrapped it in the linen. "Whatever happened?"

Charity stared down at her hand as if she were seeing

it for the first time. "It's nothing, really. Lancaster left me with the reins when he went off to stop the coach," she whispered. "I must have... I think I just gripped them too tightly." She was sure the leather hadn't done the damage. Her fingernails had poked through the threadbare fabric of her glove and dug into her palm. "I didn't know what I was doing. I've never handled horses before," she added in a meek voice.

"Oh, my lady, you have been frightened out of your wits," Elizabeth murmured, tying together the corners of the handkerchief to make a bandage.

Charity nodded, remembering how her entire body had begun trembling the moment Lancaster jumped out of the curricle. Left alone in the middle of the street, with a pair of matched horses that had just come down from rearing up after nearly being bowled over, she had thought she would die at any moment. That the horses would bolt in all the excitement and take off at a run, and she would be helpless to stop them. She would be forced to scream like Lady Pettigrew and hope that some derring-do young man would recognize her plight and come to her rescue.

But she didn't want to have to *be* rescued. She didn't want to be put into a position where she would ever have to scream. She never wanted someone to have to come rescue her.

And she certainly didn't want Marcus Batey thinking he loved her. Not when she hadn't done anything to deserve the sentiment. Done nothing to encourage him.

"I'm afraid that's true," Charity admitted just then, to Elizabeth's claim that she must have been frightened out of her wits. "I *was* frightened. Enough so that I never wish to be put in that situation again."

Elizabeth furrowed a brow. "Lord Lancaster only did

what he thought he must," she murmured, but she felt George's slight pinch on her arm. "But it was rather rude of him to leave you alone like that."

The three simply sat in companionable silence for the next half-hour as the phaeton bounded south. When George delivered the widowed countess to her front door, he afforded her a bow. "Might I inquire what it was that had you taking your leave of Lancaster's curricle, my lady?"

Charity regarded him with a combination of sadness and annoyance. "I really couldn't say," she finally responded, her gaze going to her bandaged hand. It wasn't the ruined glove that had her so upset with Lord Lancaster, nor even his insistence at seeing to it a replacement was to be sent. She was sure a pair would be delivered on the morrow.

Perhaps it was because he had told her he loved her, when they were in the shop. Or perhaps it was because he made it clear everyone in the *ton* knew she had been married to a worthless man. An earl who had squandered his living—or allowed his man of business to do so—and his livelihood on whores and mistresses, drink and gambling. "I don't know why it is I defend a rake when it would be so easy to simply agree that he was one," she murmured. At George's look of sudden confusion, she added, "I refer, of course, to my late husband."

As George lifted her gloved hand to his lips, he noted how his handkerchief had been used as a bandage, blood stains dark red against the stark white linen. He knew that she spoke the truth. "Perhaps you defend him for the sake of your sons, my lady," he suggested.

Startled at his simple response, Charity dipped a curtsy and bade him a good night. "I may not be at the office tomorrow morning," she added, at the same moment the door opened.

Her butler appeared in the opening and then stepped back when George said, "Then I'll let Elizabeth know you'll be there in the afternoon."

Before Charity could put voice to a protest—she had thought never to return to the office since she would be on her way to Suffolk—George was already bounding up and onto his phaeton, Elizabeth waving from where she sat next to him.

Dipping a curtsy, Charity entered her townhouse with her chin raised. By the time she made it to her bedchamber, tears were streaming down her cheeks.

Chapter 33

A LAST-MINUTE PLEA FOR CLEMENCY

*L*ater, at Wadsworth Hall, Westminster

As Charity expected, a pair of gloves was delivered to the house, but not the morning after. Instead, they arrived in the hands of Lord Lancaster, and did so only a half-hour after George Bennett-Jones had delivered her to her front door. She was in her bedchamber, dressing for dinner, when Beasely appeared at her door with the news.

"There is a Lord Lancaster paying a call, my lady," the butler said as he held out a calling card. "He says there is something he forgot."

Holding a curling iron, Thompkins eyed her mistress's reflection in the dressing table mirror, noting the woman's look of surprise. "Is he the one that did that to you, my lady?" she asked, her gaze directed at Charity's newly-bandaged hand. The wound—or wounds, rather, three half-moon-shaped splits in her left palm—had stopped bleeding.

"Of course not," Charity replied. "I was merely hanging onto the reins too tightly." She redirected her attention to the butler. She was about to tell Beasley to say she wasn't at home, but then decided she *would* see the viscount. "Could you see him to the parlor, please? I'll be down in a moment."

Her eyes boggling at this bit of news, Thompkins regarded her mistress a moment before saying, "But, my lady, I haven't started repairing your hair."

Charity gave her head a quick shake, noting that although her coiffure was a bit loose, it would do for the short time she would spend in the viscount's company. "It's fine. It's not as if I'm hosting anyone for dinner this evening," she replied. She stood up from the dressing table and moved to the japanned screen in the corner, determined to simply get dressed, meet the man, say to him what she must, and be done with it. Thompkins could have her things packed tonight, and they could be on their way to Suffolk in the morning.

A tremor of guilt passed through her when she thought of Mr. Weatherby, the valet, and his desire for a wife. She had promised she would see to a match for him, and she hadn't yet found a suitable woman. Lancaster's randy maid came to mind, and she remembered thinking Mary Baker might suit a man who wanted someone willing in the marriage bed. Perhaps she could make some arrangements in the morning. And then they would be able to leave for Suffolk.

Thompkins helped with the fastenings on the red satin gown. Trimmed in black lace, it was the only gown Charity still possessed with any black on it. Adding a pair of earrings—gold with garnet stones set in the shape of a flower—had the countess feeling like she had the night of the Attenborough ball—like her life was starting over and anything was possible.

Again.

"Do you like this man?" Thompkins asked, offering Charity a pair of black satin gloves.

The countess furrowed a brow as she considered the question. "I do, actually, but that's not why he's here. Is there a pair of gloves in red?" she asked, hoping to deflect the lady maid's attention from her visitor.

The lady's maid frowned. "You do?"

"He's probably just brought me a pair of gloves. To replace the one that was ruined when I cut my hand," she reasoned as she held up her newly bandaged hand. Thompkins already had Viscount Bostwick's blood-stained handkerchief soaking in cold water. "He offered to replace the torn glove, and of course I said he couldn't, but he is a stubborn man."

Thompkins blinked before turning her gaze back onto the black gloves. "You don't have any red satin gloves, my lady."

Disappointed but not surprised, Charity quickly pulled on the black gloves, wincing when she saw her reflection in the dressing table mirror. Either black was not a good color with her complexion, or she was more sick of it than she thought. She stripped them from her arms and tossed them onto the bed. "I'll go without this evening," she murmured.

"Yes, my lady," Thompkins replied as she watched the widow take her leave of the bedchamber. She glanced down to find the pair of red satin slippers still on the floor, which meant her ladyship was wearing only her stockings. Even before she could race after the widow, though, Charity apparently realized she wasn't done dressing.

The countess reappeared in the doorway and allowed an impatient sigh. "Apparently, I have forgotten my shoes," she said on a sigh, wondering what had her so addled. She was just going to meet Lord Lancaster and accept the pair of gloves he had to offer, because, well, she did need a new pair, and who would know but the two of them that he had purchased a pair on her behalf?

She allowed Thompkins to help with the slippers, gave a quick glance in the cheval mirror in the corner, and once again took her leave of her bedchamber.

As Charity made her way down the stairs from the second floor to the first floor, Beasely was leading Lord Lancaster up the stairs from the ground floor to the first floor. Of course the viscount looked up, his feet stopping on the landing as he stared up at her. From there, he didn't move but rather afforded her a deep bow.

"My lady," he said in a voice filled with awe.

Charity paused, wondering why her belly did a little flip at seeing him appear so awestruck. She had just seen him less than an hour ago! "Lancaster," she acknowledged, when she had only one step to go. She couldn't help but notice Beasely sneaking back down the stairs, and for a moment, she thought to call out for him to join them in the parlor.

But she was a grown woman. A widow. If she hadn't wanted a word with the viscount—and she still wasn't sure she did—she could have told Beasely she wasn't accepting callers.

Marcus reached for her bare hand and kissed the back of it, his lips lingering a bit too long on the tender skin. Then his attention went to her bandaged hand and his shoulders seemed to give way. "Is it bad?" he asked as he took her other hand, his own warm hand where it held her wrist.

About to curl her fingers into a fist, Charity found she

couldn't—the bandage prevented her from doing so. Instead, she watched as he lowered his lips to the linen and left a kiss there.

She couldn't help the frisson that shot up her arm, and she was sure he noticed. "It's but a scratch," she murmured. "I'll be fine."

Marcus stepped back so she could take the last step down, and he offered his arm. "Thank you for agreeing to see me," he said as they passed over the parlor threshold. He shut the door behind them. "I owe you an apology and a pair of gloves." He fished a flat, tissue-wrapped package from the inside of his top coat and offered it to her. "I know it's not proper, but no one need know," he murmured.

Charity gave a start, wondering if he had read her mind, given she had the same thought not five minutes ago. She took the package and placed it on a nearby side-board. Daring a glance at Marcus before she unwrapped the tissue, she wasn't surprised to find it contained a pair of white silk gloves. Almost an exact match for the damaged pair, they featured a small button and loop at the wrist her pair didn't include. "They're beautiful," she said, thinking she could wear them on the trip to Suffolk. "Thank you."

"I got them at the fripperies shop," he replied. "It was there I realized how foolish I had been."

"Foolish?" she repeated.

"Yes. Stupid, really, but we men frequently are," he affirmed. He couldn't help but notice how Charity had to suppress a grin just then. At least she couldn't be too angry with him if she could find humor in what he had admitted. "In going after that runaway coach, I left you in a precarious position. I never even considered the horses might bolt. You could have been injured… far worse than you were," he said as he reached for her bandaged hand. "I… don't even know what possessed me to do such thing. Can you ever forgive me?"

Charity allowed him to hold her hand again as she considered his apology. He seemed so bereft, she thought he might cry.

"Did you do it because Lady Pettigrew was in that coach?" she asked.

Marcus frowned. "Who?" Although he briefly remembered the groom mentioning who was in the runaway coach, he hadn't given it another thought once he rejoined Charity in his curricle. He also remembered hearing screaming, but he knew men could scream just as effectively as women if given the impetus.

Resisting the urge to roll her eyes, Charity made a rather unladylike sound before a hand went to her hip. "Lady Pettigrew."

Shaking his head, Marcus said, "I'm not familiar with the woman. Should I be?"

All the air seemed to go out of Charity just then, and Marcus stepped forward thinking she was about to faint. She held out a staying hand though, as if to keep him away. "She's the very worst gossip."

Marcus blinked. "Oh." After a moment, he said, "Oh!" again, just as he reasoned why his rescue of the elderly lady would be seen by some as wasted effort.

"There are those who would have thought death by runaway coach too good an end for her," Charity murmured, and then, when she realized how uncharitable her words sounded, she added, "Whatever am I saying?"

"That I was a fool to save her," he offered. "But, I didn't know who was in that coach. I just knew someone had to stop it. I was right there. I was close enough." He paused and allowed a wan grin. "For a moment, I thought... I thought I might impress you with my derring-do." He sighed, a long audible sigh that seemed to suggest it was time he give up.

"You did," Charity said as she stepped toward him. "I didn't think so at the time, of course. But... later. After I had a chance to think about it." She stared up at him. "I suppose you've been thinking of nothing else since it happened."

Marcus furrowed a brow and shook his head. "I've only been thinking of you," he countered. "Of what we talked about, and the horrible things I said about Wadsworth—

"Well deserved, actually," she interrupted.

"About our time in the shop, and how I was about to kiss you, and that damned shopkeeper..."

Forced to stop speaking when Charity's lips were suddenly on his, Marcus placed a hand at her waist as if to steady himself.

It was a moment before he could return the kiss. A moment before he was aware that one of her hands had reached around his neck to pull him down while her bandaged one gripped his shoulder. Another before his arm went around her back and pulled her hard against the front of his body. And it was yet another before the two ended the first kiss and then started another.

They might have continued kissing there in the parlor for the rest of the night, but for Beasely's quick knock at the door. He opened it before they could even react and announced dinner was served. Then his eyes widened before he quickly regained control of his facial expression.

His forehead pressed against Charity's, Marcus had a

mind to propose right there and then. She spoke first, though.

"I have to see to a wife for one of my clients."

Marcus blinked. His eyes darted to one side before he said, "Don't you have to do that for all of your clients?"

Charity nodded. "Yes. Except this one has very particular requirements. Ones that include a woman who has long, dark hair and who is willing in bed."

Blinking again, Marcus said, "Oh?"

"I've found a woman who is more than willing, but she has her curls cut short. It's quite the thing now to have short, curly hair," she explained. "And I found a woman who wishes to marry, and she has very long hair, but she's not..." She paused.

"Willing," he finished for her. Then his eyes widened. "I know someone who would be perfect," he said, thinking of the randy housemaid.

Charity grinned. "Your housemaid, Mary Baker, perhaps?"

"The very one," he agreed, remembering that he had told the matchmaker about her the very first time he had visited her at the charity. "She needs a husband. She has long hair. It's nearly black. And she is... willing."

When Charity's expression darkened, Marcus gave his head a shake. "Oh, not with me," he assured her. "With the footmen. But... we've put a stop to it. The housekeeper, I mean. She gave her a warning, and told her she had to find a husband."

"Did she now?" Charity murmured, her gaze dropping as if she were deep in thought. "When is Baker's day off?"

Realizing he had an opportunity to impress the widow, Marcus said, "I can see to it she has whatever day off she needs to have off, if it helps to get her married."

Charity angled her head and regarded him with narrowed eyes. "I'll see what I can do," she said finally. She allowed a sigh.

"Your dinner will be getting cold," Marcus said, allowing a sigh. "And my daughter is expecting me for dinner."

The mention of a daughter had Charity staring at him. He was so devoted to his children. "Of course," she replied, rather surprised by the disappointment she experienced.

"May I see you tomorrow?" Marcus asked. "Collect you at the end of your day at the charity? Take you for that ride I promised you earlier?"

Angling her head, Charity narrowed her eyes. "So you can kiss me behind a hedgerow?" she guessed.

Marcus was about to agree but clamped his lips shut. After a moment, he asked, "Did you have someplace else in mind?"

Charity blinked several times but quickly recovered. "Well, there is a little spot near a park bench that's rather secluded," she replied, rather surprised at how fast she sounded. Besides, if she could get Mr. Weatherby and Mary Baker married by noon, she would be halfway to Suffolk by four o'clock in the afternoon.

Which was just ridiculous to even consider. It would be at least a week before she learned the outcome of any possible match between those two.

"Sounds perfect," Marcus murmured. He leaned over and bussed her on the forehead. "I'll come to the charity at four o'clock," he promised. He lifted her wounded hand to his lips and kissed the bandage. "I'll be thinking healing thoughts," he added before he placed the hand on his arm. He led her out of the parlor and down to the dining room.

"My lady," he said before giving her a bow and taking his leave.

Charity stood staring after him, long after the front door shut, and wondered what she had been thinking to allow him to kiss her.

Then she remembered she had been the one to initiate the kiss.

Oh, what have I done?

Chapter 34

A DAUGHTER KNOWS BEST

ater that night, at Stanton House

Marcus felt as if he were walking on air as he made his way into his townhouse. Harrison met him in the vestibule, greeting him before taking his hat and coat. Marcus held onto the package for Analise, wondering if he should give it to her during dinner or simply wait until tomorrow and bring it to the breakfast parlor.

"Your daughter has a caller, my lord," Harrison said, arching a bushy gray eyebrow. "He is in the parlor."

Not about to allow the butler to bait him when he was in such a good mood, Marcus merely allowed a nod. "Very well." If the caller proved to be Christopher Carlington, Earl of Haddon, he would simply inform the earl he was to steer clear of Analise.

And if it wasn't Haddon, then who could it be?

When he hurried up the steps, Marcus could hear Analise, and he grinned. Then he heard a familiar male voice and he frowned.

"Wessex?" he said as he entered the parlor. He had

forgotten to leave behind the package containing Analise's birthday gift and still held it beneath one elbow.

Luke Merriweather stood up from a chair near the fireplace and gave a quick bow as Analise grinned from the settee. "Father!" she said in greeting. "We've been waiting for you."

Marcus was about to ask what they had been *doing* while they had been waiting for him, but then he noticed Analise's lady's maid. She was sitting in a chair at the back of the parlor, busy sewing. He felt a bit of relief knowing they had a chaperone. "Apologies for my late return."

"How was the park?" Analise asked as she stood up and kissed him on the cheek. She stepped back and regarded him a moment, her eyes narrowing. Her father looked... different. His lips were a bit puffy. And he had a glow about him she hadn't seen before.

"We never got that far," he admitted. "There was a... a runaway coach-and-four, and after I got it under control, Lady Wadsworth asked to be taken home."

Analise blinked. She was about to accuse him of having gone into Lady Wadsworth's home with the countess and enjoying a different kind of ride, but she didn't want to shock him with what she knew of consenting adults and bedchambers. "You...?"

"Yes. I know it seems unlikely of me, but I saved Lady Pettigrew from certain injury. Death, even," he said in an exaggerated manner. "Now... what have we here?"

Analise blinked again, but it was Luke who spoke up. "Well done, old man," he said with a nod. "If ever there was a woman you wanted to impress, Lady Pettigrew is the one. Never want to be on her bad side," he added with a grin.

Marcus sized up the viscount for a moment before

turning his attention back to his daughter. "What have we here?" he asked again.

Inhaling with the intention of replying, Analise didn't have a chance when Luke said, "I would like to request your permission to court your daughter."

A punch in the gut wouldn't have had the impact the younger viscount's words had just then. Marcus stared at Luke for a long time before he gave his head a quick shake. "No," he replied finally.

"No?" Analise repeated. "But—"

"Why ever not?" Luke asked, surprised by the outright denial. "You said you didn't want Haddon courting her."

"I don't want *anyone* courting her," Marcus replied. "She's too young to marry—"

"He's not *proposing*, Father," Analise argued. "And you married Mother when she was only a year older than I am now."

"Two years," Marcus countered.

"My birthday is tomorrow," she reminded him, her gaze going to the box he held under his arm.

Marcus drew in a breath and finally let it out, as if in surrender. "So it is. But I still think you're too young to... for courtship."

Analise sighed. "I promise, Father, that when I do decide to marry, I will do so with someone I love," she assured him. "Not like Mother and you."

A hiss came from Luke before he could cover his mouth with a hand while Marcus furrowed a brow at his daughter. "Now, see here, young lady. I won't have you saying such things about your mother," Marcus said, a hint of warning coloring his words.

"Oh, Father, you were never in love with mother. At

least, not like that," Analise replied with a shake of her head. She had to suppress the grin she nearly allowed at seeing her father's expression of shock.

"But... but I was," he argued.

"As a *friend*, yes. Her very best friend," Analise agreed. "But you two were not *in* love. Not like I think you are with Lady Wadsworth."

Marcus darted a glance at Luke, hoping he might chime in with some useful words. He allowed a grimace when he saw the younger viscount's expression, though. The Viscount Wessex was staring at Analise with eyes that could have belonged to a puppy dog. Luke would probably start drooling at any moment if Marcus didn't redirect his attention. "And what say you, Wessex?"

"She is right," Luke replied. "You are truly, madly, deeply in love with the lady, and it would behoove you to do something about it."

Marcus was about to respond with a less than complimentary comeback, but he couldn't help but notice how his daughter was gazing at Luke—with eyes that looked like they belonged to a puppy dog—and he blinked.

"Oh!" he managed to get out. For just a moment, he understood how it was a woman could faint. For there was that dizzying sensation in his head at the same time he couldn't seem to catch a breath, and stars were darting about in front of his eyes. "How long has this been going on?" he asked in dismay, one of his fingers waving in the air.

"This?" Analise repeated.

Marcus used a hand to form a circle in the space between her and Luke. "Yes. This," he repeated. "You two."

Analise took on the persona of a demure young lady at the same moment Luke straightened and lifted his chin. "Since the night of the Attenborough ball, if you must know."

"The afternoon after it, actually," Analise corrected him. "During the ride in the park."

"So says the woman who couldn't afford me a dance the night before," Luke chided her, although his expression still displayed his desire for her.

"I would have danced with you if my card hadn't already been full," she assured him. "Darling."

Marcus rolled his eyes, about to ask if they were putting on some kind of show as a means of teasing him.

But Luke had stepped forward and taken both of Analise's hands in his. "My sweeting," he murmured.

"What do you think you're doing?" Marcus asked in alarm.

"Saving you from having to purchase another Season of gowns for your daughter," Luke replied, his attention never leaving Analise. "Or from sending her to a nunnery." He managed to pull his gaze from Analise long enough to regard Marcus with a raised brow. "I do have your permission, do I not?"

Marcus blinked again in an effort to clear the odd stars from his eyes. "Oh, dear," he managed to get out, his hand going out to the back of a chair so that he might have something to fall against.

"I'll take that as a yes," Luke said before he turned his attention back to Analise. "Will you do me the honor of becoming my wife?"

Analise dimpled and gave a slight bob before saying, "Yes. Oh, yes."

Luke pulled on her hands until she was standing as

close as she could without touching his body. He leaned down and took her lips with his own in a brief kiss, as if to seal the deal.

All the while Marcus slowly fell to the carpet in a dead faint.

Chapter 35

AFTERMATH

Five minutes later
"I've a mind to challenge you to a duel in Wimbledon Common," Marcus murmured as he stared up at Luke. Although he had ended up in a sitting position, propped up against a chair after his head had begun to spin, he was well aware of just where he was and why he had suffered such a fate. "And I would if I wasn't so damned *hungry*."

Analise stepped forward with a plate of walnuts. "Eat some, Father. You'll feel better," she said as she knelt down in front of him. "I apologize for not having said anything before today. I just wasn't sure how to."

Marcus frowned. "A few words is all it would have taken," he chided her.

"I was going to say something at dinner the other night, but I didn't think it appropriate with Lady Wadsworth in attendance," she countered.

His lips protruding in a pout, Marcus helped himself to a fistful of nuts and ate one. "Do tell me you weren't trying to hide anything from me," he said, an eyebrow arching up as if he were daring his daughter to lie.

"We weren't trying to hide anything from you," she said, just before her lips pressed together. "At least, not intentionally." When she saw his eyes widen, she added, "Every moment I have spent with Luke—"

"*Luke?*"

Analise allowed a prim smile. "He told me today I could call him Luke," she argued. "And in the event you think we have been sneaking about, let me assure you that every moment I have spent with him has been done so in the company of others."

Marcus blinked, just then realizing he hadn't spent much time in *her* company the past week. "Such as?" he prompted, a bit alarmed that he had somehow missed the blossoming relationship.

Had he been so involved with thoughts of Charity that he had ignored his own daughter?

"Lady Morganfield's *soirée*, rides in the park, Lady Torrington's *musicale*, and this afternoon's call," she recited for him. "We were hoping you might make the announcement at the next ball."

Marcus blinked again. "Oh, you were?" he countered, although he couldn't seem to muster the kind of protest he probably should have.

"Just after you announce your engagement to Lady Wadsworth," Analise went on, ignoring his jibe.

Marcus's mouth dropped open. "Well, you've certainly given this a good deal of thought," he accused.

"Well, of course I have," she replied. "Marriage is a serious undertaking. I refuse to marry just anyone, and I certainly didn't want to end up with some old..." She was about to say 'fart' but thought better of it. "Old baron."

Furrowing a brow, Marcus asked, "Were you going to say 'old fogey'?" He wondered if she wouldn't have considered a wounded man simply because he was a cripple.

"Of course not," she replied with a quick shake of her head. "I haven't even been introduced to any officers who were wounded in the war," she argued. She dipped her head and offered him more walnuts. "*Fart*," she whispered. At her father's arched eyebrow, she added, "I was going to say 'old fart'."

Unable to suppress a grin, Marcus gave his head a shake. "I wouldn't have allowed you to marry an old fart," he said on a sigh.

"And you wouldn't have allowed me to wed a man as young as Christopher Carlington, so that just left Wessex," she reasoned. "A rather perfect choice, don't you agree?"

Marcus allowed a sigh and moved to get up. Analise straightened and offered him a hand, grabbing and jerking on his arm as he unfolded himself from the floor and stood up. "He isn't a bad sort," he hedged.

"You count him as a friend," she reminded him, depositing the plate of walnuts on a nearby table.

"Not after this day," Marcus argued. At her look of surprise, he added, "Not if he's to be my son," he said with a shake of his head. He glanced around the parlor, noting the lady's maid had taken her leave as had Luke Merriweather. "Speaking of Wessex, what have you done with him?"

Analise gave a one-shouldered shrug. "I thought it best he take his leave. I didn't want you challenging him to a duel."

"Clever girl."

His attention went to the door, where Harrison stood

with his hands behind his back. "Dinner is served, my lord, my lady."

"Thank the gods," Marcus said as he offered his daughter an arm.

Analise regarded his proffered arm a moment before lifting her head. "Did you really stop a runaway coach-and-four?" she asked, as if she just then remembered what he had said earlier.

Marcus arched a brow at hearing the disbelief in her voice. "I did," he replied. "Something I know better than to do ever again. I'll tell you all about it over dinner."

Frowning, she murmured, "This sounds like your imagination might have gotten the best of you."

Blinking, Marcus shook his head. "Believe me when I say I could not have dreamed up what happened this afternoon. Even my imagination has its limits."

With that, Analise placed her arm on his and they made their way to the dining room.

Chapter 36

A MATCHMAKER MEETS
A MAID

he following morning
When the town coach pulled up to Charity's townhouse at ten o'clock, she was about to tell the driver to take her to 'Finding Wives for the Wounded' when she remembered Mary Baker. Or rather, Mr. Weatherby.

Thinking it likely that both servants would be in residence at their respective places of employment, she told her driver to take her to Viscount Wessex's townhouse in South Audley Street.

Although it wasn't exactly proper for her to be paying a call on a bachelor's townhouse, she figured the viscount would be at Parliament. With any luck, the valet would be there, and she could arrange for him to meet Mary Baker.

Remembering Lancaster's comment that the housemaid could have a day off for something as important as meeting with a potential husband, Charity decided to take him at his word. She amended her instructions to the driver. "Go to Stanton House first," she ordered.

Having passed the white stuccoed townhouse in Park

Lane many a time, Charity realized she had never actually stopped and looked at the fashionable abode. The single door, painted a dark green, sported a brass knocker in the shape of a clam shell. Pairs of Palladian windows, trimmed with black gloss paint, were perfectly positioned on either side of the door, and above, the rows of rectangular windows continued for four stories. The number of chimney pots on top suggested there were at least twelve fireplaces inside.

Remembering the comment about coal buckets, Charity cringed at the thought of having to carry them up even a single flight. And several times.

She was pondering where the two servants might live should they end up married when Harrison opened the door as she was making her way up to the house.

"Good day," she said as the butler assessed her mode of dress and the equipage parked out front. "Mrs. Seward to see Miss Mary Baker," she said, just then wondering if she should have gone to the back door. Charity was about to make her excuses when she noted how the butler was staring at her. She lifted a gloved hand to her face, thinking she must have a spot of dirt on her cheek.

"Lady Wadsworth?" he countered. His gaze once again darted to the coach parked out front. The earldom's seal, emblazoned in gold, clearly showed on the door.

Charity sighed. "Yes," she admitted. "Although I am here on behalf of 'Finding Wives for the Wounded', so I am Mrs. Seward."

Harrison gave a nod as he stepped aside. "Of course. Do come in, my lady," he said, leading her to the upstairs parlor when she declined to give up her pelisse.

The sound of a small child's giggle made its way down

the steps from the floor above, and Charity paused to listen. The giggle sounded again, and she allowed a grin.

Harrison paused a moment, turning to note how she had stopped to listen. "Master John takes great delight in vexing the nurse," he said with a staid expression.

Charity was about to chide the butler, but thought better of it. Perhaps the boy was simply entertained by something his nurse was doing. *Oh, to hear such a sound again*, she thought as she hurried to catch up to Harrison.

"I will have Miss Baker join you momentarily. With tea," he said before bowing and leaving the room.

Her gaze taking in the rose and green decor of the parlor, Charity felt a stab of jealousy. Lady Lancaster had obviously had good taste, the furnishings perfectly suited to a parlor that had probably at one time been two rooms. A quick glance at the four windows facing Park Lane confirmed her suspicion, their placement suggesting a wall had at one time stood between them.

She imagined Lady Lancaster entertaining callers in the parlor, and wondered what it must be like to enjoy the life in Mayfair. Then she remembered that Lady Lancaster hadn't lived long at this house—perhaps not even a year before she died in the childbed.

Perhaps it was the former Lady Lancaster who had seen to the decor. Who had ordered the portraits be painted. Charity gazed up at the one over the fireplace, realizing almost immediately that the family in the painting wasn't Marcus Batey's family, but rather his father's. Two boys who barely looked as if they could be brothers stood with their expressionless mother and a stern-faced father, a hunting dog lying at their feet.

Even when Marcus was at his most serious, he didn't look as severe as the fifth Viscount Lancaster. A frisson passed through her when she remembered how Marcus had looked at her the night of the Attenborough ball, mischief in his eyes. Their waltz had been exhilarating. The perfect means to forget her despair and remind her there might be a life for her in London.

When she was sure she knew which boy in the painting was Marcus, Charity turned her attention to the other evidence of family in the room. She was studying a series of miniatures on the fireplace mantle when a maid appeared at the threshold, a tea tray held in front of her.

Charity waved her in. "I can see to serving," she said, watching as the timid young woman placed the tray on the low table in front of the settee. Instead of taking her leave, the maid stood nervously to one side and dipped a curtsy.

"Harrison said you wished to have a word with me."

All at once, Charity realized the maid was Mary Baker. "Oh, forgive me. I didn't realize you were Miss Baker," she said as she stepped forward. "I am Mrs. Seward. From the charity, 'Finding Wives for the Wounded'." She held out her hand, and Mary finally took it and gave it an uncertain shake.

"Hello, my lady," Mary replied, glancing back toward the hall. "Might you also be Lady Wadsworth? That's the name Harrison said when he told me I had a caller."

Her cover completely blown, Charity angled her head to one side. "Indeed. I am Lady Wadsworth, but not when I am acting in my capacity as a matchmaker," she said, noting how the maid's eyes widened at hearing her profession. She indicated the maid should take a seat and then saw to pouring tea. Asking if Mary took sugar or milk, Charity wasn't surprised by the maid's response.

"Both, if I may," Mary replied, her eyes wide as she

watched the countess prepare a cup of tea for her. "Are you acting in your capacity as a matchmaker now?" she asked, struggling with the words to be sure she repeated them correctly.

"I am," Charity replied. "I understand you are in need of a husband."

Mary nearly choked on the sip of tea she had just managed to take. "I am?" She blinked and then seemed to slump into the rose and green upholstered chair. "Oh, yes. I suppose I am," she agreed with a sigh.

Frowning, Charity wondered at the girl's reaction. "I have a client who is a valet to a viscount. He is interested in taking a wife, and I thought of you."

Mary's eyes widened into saucers. "How can that be, seeing as how I've never met you before?" she asked in alarm.

Charity took a breath and held it for a moment before saying, "Your reputation precedes you, Miss Baker. In this case, it does you credit, however, as you may be exactly the sort of wife Mr. Weatherby is looking for."

Blinking several times, Mary took another sip of tea and angled her head. "Are you saying he wants a wife who..." She paused, and a bright pink blush colored her face.

"Who is willing when it comes to the marriage bed, yes," Charity stated, deciding it best to simply say it. "Is your hair long?" She couldn't tell given the maid wore a mob cap that covered most of her hair.

"Down to my waist," Mary replied, one hand moving to her side to reinforce her words. She frowned. "This Mr. Weatherby. I suppose he's some high and mighty valet who thinks he's too good for those of us in service?" Her words were tinged with scorn, and Charity immediately wondered if Marcus Batey's valet behaved that way in this house.

"Mr. Weatherby is a former soldier who was wounded in one of the wars. He walks with a limp and does not strike me as a particularly proud man," Charity explained.

"Then why does he need a matchmaker?" Mary asked, her posture defensive.

Charity regarded the maid for a moment before she gave a slight shrug. "He wishes to marry. He doesn't know many women of marriageable age, and he trusts me to help him find a suitable wife," she explained, daring the housemaid to counter the statement.

"You said he's wounded. How so?"

Lifting her chin a bit, Charity said, "He walks with a limp. Uses a cane. Other than that, he's perfectly fit. And rather handsome."

This last had Mary's interest, both her hands holding onto her teacup as she was about to take another drink. "More handsome than the footmen who work here?"

Having only seen the one ginger-haired Stanton House footman, Charity couldn't be sure. "You'll have to be the judge of that, Miss Baker," she replied. "Are you interested in meeting Mr. Weatherby?"

Mary seemed to think on the offer for a moment before finally nodding. "It depends, I suppose. When?"

When, indeed? Charity considered schedules and realized she couldn't answer for the valet. "Your employer has assured me I can take you from your duties if necessary." This comment had the maid's eyes widening once again, as if she just then realized her reputation in the household was known even by the viscount.

For a moment, Charity wondered if the maid was on the verge of tears. "I shall pay a call on Mr. Weatherby and determine an appropriate place and time for the two of you to meet. With a chaperone, of course." Charity wondered about the following day. "Tomorrow is Sunday. Perhaps in the afternoon?"

Her face finally relaxing into an expression of acceptance, Mary gave a nod. "I'll wear my very best gown," she replied with a nod.

"I'll send word once I've had a chance to speak with Mr. Weatherby," Charity said. She stood up. "And I will be sure Lord Lancaster knows should I have to take you from your duties."

Mary leaned forward. "Could you inform Mrs. Barstow instead? She's the housekeeper here and will be vexed if I'm not where I'm supposed to be."

"Mrs. Barstow," Charity repeated, pulling a pencil from her reticule and making a note on a pad of small paper. She regarded the young woman a moment before furrowing a brow. "You *do* wish to marry, do you not?" she asked.

The maid gave a slight shrug. "I know I should," she started to say.

"But you don't really wish to?" Charity guessed.

Mary sighed. "Truth be told, I... I really enjoy being tupped," she whispered.

Charity blinked. "Well, there's... there's really nothing wrong with *liking* it," she whispered in reply, daring a glance at the parlor door to be sure no one was eavesdropping on their conversation. "Which is why you might find Mr. Weatherby an agreeable husband."

Although Mary didn't appear convinced, she at least nodded. "I'm willing to meet the man," she said. "But... I ain't agreeing to anything 'afore... Well, that is to say—"

"He's had a chance to prove himself in the marriage

bed?" Charity guessed. As a widow, she just then realized she could demand the same sort of proof of performance from a potential husband. She wasn't a virgin, after all. No one expected a widow to remain chaste.

"Exactly!" Mary replied with a curt nod. Then her face screwed into a grimace. "Makes me sound fast, don't it?"

Charity shook her head and said, "There is something to be said for knowing what you want." Her eyes widened when she realized the words applied to her, too. *I want a daughter*, she thought as she inhaled sharply. *A legitimate daughter.* The only way she could have what she wanted was if she remarried. "And then going after it," she murmured, more to herself than to the young woman who sat across from her.

Shaking herself from her reverie, Charity glanced at Mary's empty teacup. "Would you like more?" she asked as she lifted the teapot.

"May I?" Mary asked, her eyes once again wide in surprise.

"There's enough in here for several more cups," Charity countered, a teasing grin lighting her face.

"Then, yes, please," Mary said as she held out her cup.

Charity poured milk and dropped a couple of lumps of sugar into the maid's cup before refilling it and her own cup.

"I do know what I want," Mary said then.

"Oh?" Charity responded, afraid the maid might say she didn't wish to be married.

"I want a husband who will treat me good."

"All right."

"Not beat me."

"Of course not."

"Tup me when I've a mind to be tupped."

Charity inhaled slowly. "Which is usually... when?"

Mary angled her head. "In the morning. 'Afore the sun has come up. When it's still a bit dark outside. Or..." She paused and seemed to give her answer a good deal of thought. "Maybe at night. 'Afore bed. But long after dinner, though, so my stomach's not too full."

Charity nodded, thinking the young woman was describing her own desires. "I believe Mr. Weatherby could accommodate your... needs." She inhaled again before draining her teacup, wondering just how she was going to make Miss Baker's demands known to the valet. "Is there anything else, Miss Baker?"

The maid shook her head. "I don't think so."

"Tell me, then. Should you end up married to Mr. Weatherby, can you put voice to some assurance you won't continue to tup the footmen here at Stanton House? I am quite sure Mr. Weatherby wants a wife that will be faithful."

Mary straightened in her chair. "Well, that all depends now, doesn't it?"

Charity blinked. "On what?"

"Will Mr. Weatherby put voice to some assurance that he will be faithful to me?"

Jerking in shock at hearing the query, Charity once again realized the maid had a good point. Should she ever agree to marry again, she could demand fidelity of her husband. Never again would she abide someone spending his nights with a mistress or with prostitutes in a brothel.

"That will be between you and Mr. Weatherby, of course," Charity replied. "So I suggest you bring it up with him should the two of you decide to consider matrimony."

Her face screwing into a grimace, Mary asked, "Will you tell Mr. Weatherby? What I said, I mean?"

Charity blinked. "Do you *want* me to tell him your terms?"

The maid nodded. "Oh, would you? I fear I'll be all tongue-tied wif' him and forget everything I told you," she claimed.

Dipping her head, Charity finally allowed a nod. She tried to imagine just what her conversation with Mr. Weatherby was going to entail when an older woman appeared on the threshold.

"There you are!"

Mary stood up and curtsied to Charity. "I have to get back to work," she whispered.

Before Charity could give a reply, the maid hurried out of the parlor, the prune-faced woman watching her quick retreat with a frown. When the woman turned that expression on her, Charity said, "Mrs. Barstow, I presume?"

The housekeeper froze and stared at her for a moment before finally dipping a curtsy. "Pardon me, my lady," she said, obviously at a loss for words. "I didn't realize... that is to say—"

"You are pardoned. But only because Miss Baker and I have completed our business." With that, Charity stood up and walked past the incredulous housekeeper, her only thought that she would probably replace the woman should she ever become the mistress of Stanton House.

Charity was in the town coach and on the way to Lord Wessex's home before she even realized just what she had imagined.

Her, as mistress of Stanton House.

She grinned and rolled her eyes when she murmured, "With Miss Baker as my lady's maid."

She was still grinning when the coach pulled up to the front of Lord Wessex's townhouse.

Chapter 37

A VALET IS CAUTIOUS

*L*uke Merriweather's townhouse

Staring up at the townhouse that loomed before her, Charity checked the address against the note she had made for herself to confirm that the numbers matched. The street name—South Audley—was correct. She was rather surprised Lord Wessex had such a posh address, as well as a townhouse that might have been home to an earl.

Then she remembered he would one day *be* an earl. He was the heir-apparent to the Middleton earldom. Perhaps this was an entailed property.

When the groom opened the door to the coach, Charity eyed the front door and then turned her attention on the young man. "Could you request that Mr. Weatherby join me here in the coach? I hardly think I should pay a call on him in there." She gave him a calling card.

The groom nodded. "I'll see to it, my lady."

She watched as the groom made his way to the front door and gave the brass door knocker a rap. After a wait of several seconds, the door opened to reveal Mr. Weatherby.

Perhaps he was butler as well as valet to the viscount, Charity considered as she watched the young man take the proffered card and then give a glance in the direction of the coach.

Half-expecting him to give a shake of his head and send the groom back with news that he couldn't meet with her just then, Charity was surprised when the valet followed the groom, a slight limp apparent, and then stepped into the coach.

"My lady," he said as he managed a slight bow. He took the seat opposite, leaning his cane against the bench. "This is… a surprise."

And not the only one you'll have today, Charity almost said in reply. "Mr. Weatherby," she acknowledged. "I thought it best we meet in here."

"Of course. I suppose you have come with… news for me?"

"I have just come from Stanton House," she said.

The valet regarded her a moment. "Viscount Lancaster's home?"

"Indeed," Charity replied. "There is a maid there who is… well, she is everything you described wanting in a wife."

The young man's eyes widened. "Everything?" he repeated.

"She has dark hair down to her waist," she said with a nod. "And she is comely and willing," she added, remembering the maid's large brown eyes and flawless complexion. Charity paused before she added, "She has conditions, however."

Mr. Weatherby allowed a shrug. "I expect she does."

"You do?" Charity replied in surprise. She gave her head a quick shake. "Of course. Forgive my… my next comments, but I am merely relaying Miss Baker's... her *requirements* for a husband."

When Weatherby appeared to wait to hear said requirements, Charity struggled not to blush too terribly much. "If she is expected to be faithful in the marriage, then she requires fidelity on the part of her husband."

"Agreed," Weatherby stated.

Charity blinked. "Oh. Well, then. As for marital relations, she... well, first, she is not a virgin—"

"I wouldn't expect her to be," Weatherby stated. "Otherwise, how would she know to make conditions?"

Resisting the urge to blink again, Charity allowed a nod. "Quite right. She wants them in the mornings. Before it's too light. Or at night. But not too soon after dinner."

"Agreed. Perhaps other times might be negotiable?" he half-asked.

This time, Charity did blink. "She seems ever so reasonable, so I suppose so."

"When can I meet her?"

Well. This wasn't so hard. Why, she probably wasn't even blushing too badly. "What about tomorrow afternoon? A walk..." She took a quick glance at the cane. "Or a ride in the park?"

"I am capable of walking," he replied. "Although I will be limping."

"She's aware of your limp," Charity put in, hoping she wasn't offending the man. "I can introduce the two of you—"

"I'll pay a call at Stanton House on the morrow. At three o'clock," he stated.

"Three o'clock," Charity repeated, briefly wondering if she could arrange for Miss Baker to be available. Lord

Lancaster had said he could see to it she had time off to court. "Very well." Before she could say anything else, the valet retrieved his cane, gave a slight bow, and stepped out of the coach.

"Good day, Mrs. Seward. Or should I call you Lady Wadsworth?"

Charity dipped her head. "I will answer to either."

Weatherby nodded. "Very good, my lady. And thank you."

With that, the coach door closed and Charity Seward Wadsworth settled herself into the velvet squabs with a single thought on her mind.

She really needed to make these sorts of calls in an unmarked town coach.

A few minutes earlier...

Atop his phaeton, Marcus directed his horse to head onto South Audley Street. He was on his way to Park Lane from Bond Street, where he had paid a call on his daughter's modiste. Barely paying any mind to the traffic he passed, he did a double-take when he recognized the crest on the door of a town coach parked in front of Lord Wessex's townhouse.

Wadsworth?

He halted the horse pulling his phaeton, annoying the beast as well as the driver of the dray cart directly behind him. His gaze went to the gold-painted crest of the Wadsworth coach, and then to the townhouse.

A rock seemed to drop into his stomach, and breathing was suddenly difficult.

Charity?

With Luke Merriweather?

A shout from the man behind him had Marcus putting his horse in motion. An attempt at simply pulling over was quickly thwarted when another coach came from the other direction. "Dammit," he murmured, realizing his only option was to continue to the end of the street and take the turn into Curzon Street.

With one last glance at the Wadsworth coach, Marcus fought his own growing despair with seething anger— anger directed at the man who had just proposed to his daughter.

How could he? How could Wessex court his daughter and claim to love her whilst carrying on an *affaire* with Charity Wadsworth?

He remembered the night of the Attenborough ball. Remembered how he had been referring to his daughter when he spoke of a gorgeous lady. Luke's gaze wasn't on Analise at the time, though, but on Charity.

How did I miss the obvious? Marcus wondered, his despair so consuming, he was nearly in tears.

A pain in his chest had him clutching it with a gloved hand. Charity had tried to put him off. *Had* put him off. Over and over. And yet, like a fool, he pursued her, sure he could change her mind. Convince her to marry him.

No wonder she wasn't in the market for a husband.

She had a younger man as a lover.

Chapter 38

ANGER AND ACCUSATIONS

few minutes later
Marcus stormed into Stanton House, his hurt
having turned once again to anger.

"My lord?" Harrison breathed, his eyes wide. He had
never before seen his master display such an expression of
angst.

"Where is my daughter?"

Harrison blinked. "The parlor, sir."

Marcus took the stairs two at a time, mentally
preparing himself for what was about to come.

There would be wailing, he was sure. He would be
doing some of it—how could he not, given how he felt
about Charity?—but he thought Analise would also shed
tears. Perhaps they could cry on each others' shoulders.

There would be gnashing of teeth. He had already
been doing some of that, in between curses and hoarse
whispers of hate directed at his best friend of late. Once
Analise learned the truth, she would no doubt join him,
their shared dislike of Luke Merriweather, Viscount

Wessex, giving them the energy they would require to get through the next few weeks of despair.

There would be questions. Some without answers. Like, how the hell had this happened? How had he missed all the obvious signs? The obvious cues?

Love is blind, he reminded himself. *And deaf and dumb.*

There would be despair. Endless nights spent alone, wishing things could be different. Analise would find another, better suitor, of course. She was young. Well-liked. Made friends easily. And there was that gorgeous Simpson boy.

But there would be no other woman for him. Charity had always been that woman. The one he had wanted his whole life, it seemed. Without her, he may as well resign himself to nights at his club. Nights spent alone in his study. Reading tomes on domestic farming techniques or how to master chess without a playing partner.

By the time Marcus walked into the parlor, his anger had been replaced by a dull ache that had filled his chest and left him nearly breathless.

"Hello, Father," Analise said as she bounded up from the settee and hurried over to him. She kissed him on his cheek and said, "Luke has come to take me for a ride on his phaeton."

The mention of her fiancé brought up a sudden volcano of anger, and Marcus was about to erupt and spew it all over the younger viscount when he saw how Luke was regarding him.

"What happened?" Luke asked as he jumped up from the chair in which he was seated. "Were you robbed?"

Marcus blinked and gave his head a shake. He glanced at his daughter, then at her maid who sat sewing by the window. Then he turned his attention back to Luke. "How... how long have you been here?"

The young viscount dared a glance at the clock on the mantle and said, "About half-an-hour. We were waiting for your return to let you know we were heading to the park."

Half-an-hour?

"You're not with Lady Wadsworth." Marcus couldn't help how the words spilled out, nor how they must have sounded.

Analise and Luke exchanged worried glances. "I am *never* with Lady Wadsworth," Luke replied. "I've never even been introduced to the countess."

Another thought—nearly as awful—crossed Marcus's mind just then. If Luke Merriweather wasn't the one having an *affaire* with Charity Wadsworth, then that meant...

"Your valet."

Luke scratched the side of his eye. "Well, he admitted he is one of her clients, although I can't imagine how Lady Wadsworth is going to find a woman who meets his criteria."

All of his energy having been spent on the myriad of emotions he had experienced this past fifteen minutes, Marcus fell into the nearest chair and allowed a long sigh. "Let me guess. She has to have long, dark hair and be willing."

His eyes widening in surprise, Luke asked, "How did you know?"

And then, because he didn't know what else to do, Marcus chuckled. His chuckling soon turned to laughter, an infectious laughter that eventually had Analise grinning and Luke wondering if his father-in-law-to-be had become a candidate for Bedlam.

Chapter 39

A VISCOUNT AND A
VALET PLOT

L ater that night

Luke Merriweather stepped down from his phaeton and handed the reins to the stableboy, pleased the urchin was so quick to meet him. Although he could have parked out front, he preferred to drive his equipage to the mews, especially with how spirited his horse could be.

He fished a coin from his waistcoat pocket and held it out. "I'll give you another if you have this shined up for tomorrow at four, o'clock," he said by way of a bribe.

The stableboy regarded the coin, his eyes wide. "You'll see your reflection, guv'nor," he replied, displaying a mostly toothless grin as he took the money.

Making his way into his townhouse by way of the back door, Luke met his valet at the bottom of the stairs.

"My lord. I apologize. I didn't hear the knocker," Roger said as he glanced toward the front door.

"I sneaked in by way of the back," Luke said, his eyes narrowing on his servant. He was about to make his way up the stairs but paused. "Are you... ?" He stopped, thinking how ridiculous his query would sound. Roger Weatherby wouldn't be in the market for a wife if he already had a lover, would he? The idea of his valet with Charity Wadsworth seemed far-fetched at first, but stranger couplings had happened. "Never mind."

Furrowing a brow, Roger asked, "What is it, my lord?"

Luke was several steps up the stairs when he turned and regarded his valet. "Did Lady Wadsworth pay a call here today?"

Roger nodded. "She did, my lord."

Luke blinked, one of his hands moving to clutch the bannister. "Does she... does she do so on a regular basis?"

His valet angled his head to one side. "Not that I'm aware. I'm quite sure I would know if she did."

Immense relief settled over the viscount just then. "Was she... looking for me?"

Roger shook his head. "She was here to see me, sir. She believes she might have found a young woman for me to court." He took a deep breath. "I've... I've made arrangements to pay a call on the young lady—a maid—on the morrow. At three o'clock, if that's acceptable."

Luke's eyes widened before a grin erupted. "Good on you," he teased. "Someone close by?"

The valet shook his head. "In Park Lane. At Stanton House. I wondered if perhaps I could borrow your horse— ?"

"Stanton House?" Luke repeated, immediately recognizing the name. He had just come from there! Oh, this was rich, indeed.

"My lord, is something... amiss?"

Luke rolled his eyes. "I think I was about to be beaten to a bloody pulp by my betrothed's father because he thought I was having an *affaire* with Wadsworth's widow," he replied.

Roger dipped his head. "Well, her coach was parked directly in front of this house," he replied with a nod. "My apologies. She came seeking me. She didn't even come into the house. I went out to speak with her in the coach."

"Clever of you to do that, although it apparently didn't help," Luke replied. "Whatever you do, steer clear of Lord Lancaster when you're under his roof tomorrow. As for the horse..." He stopped, remembering he would be taking the phaeton at four o'clock to pick up Analise for their ride in the park. "You're welcome to take the phaeton if you have it back by four. Doesn't give you much time there, though."

The valet regarded his master with awe. "That's very generous of you, sir," he said. "Since I've only plans to meet the maid, I rather doubt there will be time for a ride. Besides, if we don't suit, I will have the best of excuses to take my leave after ten minutes or so."

Luke nodded. "So, long dark hair and willing?" he teased.

Roger's eyes widened, and his cheeks displayed a sudden bloom of color. "My lord, may I ask that you afford her a bit of respect? You could be speaking of my future wife."

Blinking, Luke sobered and allowed a nod. "I apologize. But you have made your wishes known," he countered. "Given your requirements for a wife, do you have plans to—?"

"I do not, my lord," Roger interrupted. In truth, he had wondered how they might go about getting to know one another, at least in an intimate sense. How would they know if they would enjoy one another in bed if they didn't at least give it a try?

"And what about when you're not in bed? I should think there might be other considerations you should be... considering," Luke murmured. "Such as how you two might suit one another."

Roger inhaled and dipped his head. "May I remind you I am a servant? I spend my days in service to you and to this household," Roger explained. "Meanwhile, Miss Baker is a housemaid, and is in service to the Lancaster household until such time as she's dismissed for the evening. I rather doubt the two of us will have waking time to spend in one another's company. So it probably matters not if we suit in any other regard besides a bed."

Luke frowned, suddenly feeling sorry for the servant. "You'll both have Sundays off," he argued.

The valet looked as if he'd been punched in the gut. "True," he hedged. He allowed a sigh. "Well, I suppose that's the reason I shall spend what little time we have together learning what we might have in common."

Nodding, Luke regarded his valet another moment before one of his eyebrows arched up. "I do have some influence over Lord Lancaster," he hinted. "He'll be my father-in-law before long. Should you require some time together, I'm sure I can arrange for you and her to have time off. At the same time. During the day."

Roger dipped his head. "Very good, sir. But only if Miss Baker and I suit. I haven't married her yet." He paused before his eyes widened. "I haven't even met her yet."

Luke allowed a chuckle. Although he had memory of seeing the happy maid—servants always just seemed to blend into the background—he figured his valet would be pleased when he finally met her on the morrow. "I am so relieved I'm already betrothed," he breathed. "I can't imagine having to go through it all over again."

Furrowing a brow, Roger stared at his master. "I wasn't aware you suffered, sir," he murmured. Indeed, Lord Wessex had seemed in the very best of moods since Lord Attenborough's ball.

The viscount considered his valet's words a moment. "*Suffered* might be too strong a word," he admitted, even if there had been that punch in the gut he had endured by the fist of Lord Haddon. He deserved that one, though. He had been an ass to think the young earl was pursuing any young lady with an idea of ruining her. "Prolonged uncertainty does weigh on a man's mind, however."

Roger nodded his understanding. Even though his wait to meet Miss Baker might only be a day, he felt as if he'd been waiting to meet her far longer. Like half his life. If she wasn't what he was hoping for in a wife, then he would simply have to wait longer.

He didn't want to have to wait for the rest of his life, though.

Living in quiet desperation had him struggling to get out of bed in the morning, knowing every day would simply be exactly like those that had come before. "May I ask... do you feel as if you have something to look forward to now that you will have a bride?"

Luke angled his head to one side and wondered about his servant. Despite the older man having worked for him as his butler and valet since his departure from the Middleton country estate in Surrey to take up residence in London, the two of them hadn't ever engaged in such a serious discussion before. "Are you feeling old?" he asked in concern.

Wincing, Roger finally allowed a nod. "Perhaps I am," he admitted.

"Well, stop it. You're no where near Death's door, and I shouldn't want you getting there before me."

Roger's brows went up in surprise. "Very good, sir." He paused a moment. "Speaking of... doors, may I enquire as to if you and your betrothed will live here? Or will you be looking to find a larger townhouse?"

Luke's good mood disappeared in an instant. "Larger townhouse?" he repeated. His eyes darted to one side. At some point, he would inherit the Middleton earldom. But his father didn't live in a lavish house in the capital. He, too, only inhabited a townhouse suitable for a bachelor since his countess preferred the country and spent her days in Surrey. "Do you think this too small? There is a mistress suite." He knew this because he had ended up in that bedchamber after a particularly long night of imbibing brandy at a public house. When he awoke, Luke thought he was in the wrong house, not recognizing the pink and gold decor that surrounded his pounding head. "Is there a nursery, do you know?"

Suppressing the urge to grin, Roger said, "There is a room suitable for a nursery, as well as one for a nursemaid," he replied. "And a room for a lady's maid in the servants' hall." There would be another if he married and moved to the larger quarters at the end of the hall.

Luke sighed. "Then I shall not be on the hunt for a house," he replied. "At least until Miss Analise is a countess. Then we shall search for something appropriate to the station."

"Very good, my lord," Roger replied. "Your mail is in the study. Are you in need of my services at the moment?"

Not having paid a visit to his study in a few days, Luke

dared a glance in that direction. "I am not. Take some time if you'd like. Shopping or... paying calls. I will see to business and then head to my club for dinner."

With that, Luke moved back down the stairs and into his study.

Roger heaved a sigh of relief as he felt for his purse in his waistcoat pocket. If he intended to make the very best impression on a potential wife, he thought he could benefit from a new suit of clothes and perhaps a new cane.

Taking his leave of the townhouse, Roger made his way down to the corner where he could hail a hackney. A half-hour later, and he found himself among the throngs of shoppers in Bond Street. Two hours after that, and he was headed back to the townhouse armed with boxes of fine clothes and a brass-topped walking cane.

Miss Baker would hardly guess he was a servant.

Chapter 40

A MATCH MADE IN BED

The following day at 3:00 o'clock in the afternoon

"I don't know why I'm so nervous," Mary murmured, her fingers pleating the fabric of her skirt. "It's not as if I've never met a man before."

Rodney, the ginger-haired footman, dipped his head and glanced down the hall, just to be sure there weren't any other servants watching them. "Are you sure about this? This... courting, I mean," he added.

Mary frowned as she regarded the tall footman. "Mrs. Barstow says I haf' to get married. If I don't, and she catches me with the likes of you, with my skirts up past my bum, she'll be forced to let me go," she argued.

"What if I marry you?" Rodney replied, his chin lifting in defiance.

Recoiling, as if the footman had punched her in the stomach, Mary stared at Rodney for several seconds before she suddenly burst out laughing. When she saw how seriously he stared at her, though, she sobered. "You funnin' me?" she whispered.

"No," Rodney replied, his head shaking from side to

side. "I like you, Mary Baker. I already know I like tuppin' you. Marry me, and we can do it every night and whenever we can sneak away," he reasoned.

Mary's eyes widened. "And where would we live?"

Rodney shrugged. "Upstairs. You can move into my room—"

"It's smaller than mine!"

"Perhaps Harrison will let us move into a larger room," he countered. "There's one at the end of the hall."

Mary furrowed a brow, wondering if she could abide being married to Rodney. "You would have to give up tuppin' Jones," she warned, referring to the second floor housemaid.

The footman's gaze darted to the left. "I would?"

Angling her head to one side and pinning him with a glare, Mary allowed an audible sigh. "There are vows to say when you marry someone, you dolt," she replied.

Rodney winced at her rebuke and simply shrugged. "If it don't happen with this... just who is supposed to come meet you?" he asked.

"A valet. Butler, too, I think," Mary replied, deciding she wouldn't share the man's name. Should Rodney learn of it, he might spread the gossip with the neighboring footmen. Within two days, every household in Park Lane would know she had a caller.

The sound of heavy footfalls on the stairs had Rodney disappearing into the nearest bedchamber. Mary rolled her eyes as she smoothed her skirts and faced Harrison when he made it to the top of the stairs.

"You have a caller, Baker. I've ordered tea be brought to the salon on the ground floor."

Mary blinked. "You have?" She blinked again. "Why?

Giving his very best expression of infinite patience,

Harrison said, "His lordship said I should afford Mr. Weatherby all the courtesies of any caller at Stanton House."

His lordship? How did Lord Lancaster know she was going to have a caller? "He came to the front door?" she asked, still incredulous.

The butler inhaled slowly. "He did. And I rather imagine he'll be taking his leave by that same door should you keep him waiting much longer, Baker."

"Is he... is he in there?"

The butler's eyes rolled heavenward. "He is."

Mary Baker dipped a quick curtsy and hurried down the stairs. She almost ran to the small salon at the front of the house, pausing just before the opening so she could catch her breath and paste a pleasant expression on her face.

A few seconds later, and she stepped beyond the threshold to find Mr. Weatherby regarding the painting above the fireplace. "Good afternoon," she said as she dipped a curtsy.

Roger Weatherby turned his gaze onto the younger woman and remembered to give a bow. Being a butler in a bachelor's townhouse rarely afforded him an opportunity to practice the courtesy with a woman. "Good afternoon," he replied. Then his faced screwed into a frown. "Mary?"

"Roger?" she countered. "What are you doing here?"

The valet rolled his eyes before he practically fell into the nearest chair. "I thought I was paying a call on a housemaid named Mary Baker," he replied. "What are *you* doing here?"

Mary sighed and moved to join him, settling herself into the chair opposite his. "I work here. I thought I was meeting Mr. Weatherby. It is three o'clock, is it not?"

Roger dipped his head, his eyes closing as if he could erase what was happening. "I *am* Mr. Weatherby."

Blinking several times, Mary regarded him in shock. "Since when?"

"Since I started my employment with Lord Wessex. And who are you to call yourself *Mary Baker*?" he added in dismay.

Mary glowered at her old brother. "Since there were already two Joneses in Stanton House," she replied. "And what about *Weatherby*?" The name came out tinged with spite. She let out a squeal of annoyance that made it sound as if she had just been frightened by a mouse.

Looking suitably chagrined, Roger allowed his shoulders to slump. "Jones is a rather common name for a butler," he replied. He sighed and rolled his eyes. "Here I thought I was going to meet my perfect match, and she turns out to be my baby sister."

"What about *me?*" Mary countered. "I thought I was going to meet a man that was goin' to like tuppin' me every night."

Roger winced before his eyes widened. "Me? I was told you wanted to be tupped morning and night!" he countered. He was about to chide her for her fast reputation, but the sound of someone approaching had him holding his tongue.

The two of them stared at one another until it was apparent someone had stopped at the door.

Miss Parker stood on the threshold with the tea tray. She moved to set it on the low table positioned between the two servants and asked, "Would you like me to serve?"

Mary said, "Would you please? My brother, Mr. *Weatherby*, has paid a call," she said, with particular emphasis on the 'Weatherby'.

"Oh, it's vera nice to meet you, Mr. Weatherby," Jane Parker said as she turned her attention on Roger. "I'm Parker."

The valet stared at the blonde-haired maid, his mouth dropping open in awe. "Hullo," he managed to get out before coming to his feet.

The maid blushed. "Oh, you needn't stand up on my account," she murmured as she shook her head. The blonde curls surrounding her face bobbed about with her words. Her gaze had already gone to the brass-topped cane, its intricate carving suggesting its owner was a man of some means. As did his clothes.

Jane dared a quick glance at Mary before she turned back to Roger and found that he had taken her hand in his to kiss the back of it.

"'Tis very good to meet you, my lady," he said when he straightened.

The comely maid who stood before him dimpled. "Oh, I'm not a lady," she replied, her slight smile accompanied by vibrant eyes and a perfect nose. "You can call me Jane," she offered.

"Roger," he countered. He dared a glance over at his sister, whose mouth had dropped open at the same time her brow furrowed. "I was here to pay a call on my sister, but we're all caught up now. Might you join us?" he asked.

Jane blinked. "I'd like that," she said, her own gaze darting to Mary, as if she were seeking permission.

"That would be splendid. Then the two of you can be the first to know that Rodney..." She paused and turned her attention on her brother. "One of the footmen here at Stanton House... has proposed marriage. I was just about to ask for my brother's blessing."

Her eyes wide at hearing this bit of *on-dit*, Jane said, "Why, it's about time."

Mary's jaw dropped, and she stared at her brother as if she expected him to scold her. But Roger was still staring at Jane as if he'd been struck by lightning.

Her lightning.

"You have my blessing," Roger said, his attention entirely on the delectable housemaid. "Tell me, Miss Parker. Are you... married?" He offered his arm and indicated the chair adjacent to his.

Jane sat down and angled her head. "I am not. Nor am I courting anyone," she replied, oblivious to the fact that Mary had stood up and was making her way to the door.

"Are you... *interested* in marriage?"

"Isn't every young woman?"

Roger blinked. "I can't say I was aware they all were, but I am heartened to hear you are. Tell me, might I be allowed to call on you? Take you for a ride in the park, perhaps? Or if you're able to step away from your duties for a few minutes, perhaps we could walk in the park?"

*M*eanwhile...

Mary hurried up to the first floor and ducked into several bedchambers before finally finding Rodney in a guest bedchamber overlooking the side garden. "There you are," she murmured, moving to join him at the window.

"Is it done then? Are you going to marry the valet?"

Mary screwed up her face as she lifted a finger to his cheek, forcing him to turn in her direction. "Now why would I go off and marry a valet from a household in

South Audley Street when I could marry you and live right here?" she asked with a teasing grin.

Rodney inhaled and slowly let out the breath. "Why, indeed?" He gave a nod. "I promise, I'll only tup you," he added, straightening to his full six-foot, two-inch height.

"Good. Because I think Mr. Weatherby is about to propose to Jane, and he won't abide an unfaithful wife."

A brow furrowing in confusion, Rodney finally gave his head a shake. "Ain't never tupped her," he claimed. "She's a virgin." This last was said in a hoarse whisper.

Mary considered what the matchmaker had said about her brother. He was in search of a wife who had long, dark hair and was willing. Perhaps Jane would be, but she had short curly hair. And she was blonde.

Giggling, Mary stood up on tip-toe and kissed Rodney on the cheek. "Then I promise I'll only let you tup me," she said.

Rodney lowered his face and kissed her on the forehead. "Then I'll carry the coal buckets for you."

Her eyes rounding in delight, Mary said, "I think I may be falling in love wif'—" Her words were cut off when Rodney's lips lowered to hers and captured them in an awkward kiss.

They might have continued to discover how to correct their clumsy attempt at kissing, but footfalls on the stairs had them separating and hurrying off to their respective positions.

Chapter 41

AT LAST, AN
UNDERSTANDING

ater that afternoon, outside of Stanton House

"Hello, Charity," Marcus said, a grin lighting his face as he opened the door to the Wadsworth town coach. "Would you like to come in for tea?"

Charity regarded the viscount with a sigh. Despite how she had treated him only a few nights ago, he was still eager to please her. "I would," she agreed.

He offered a hand, and she took it, stepping out of the coach into the bright sunlight.

"I suppose I have you to thank for the young man who called on Baker a few minutes ago?" he half-asked, offering her is arm.

"Only if they agree to marry one another," she replied. She placed her hand on his arm.

"Having been in my study when Miss Baker met her would-be suitor in the salon, I have no doubt she will be amenable to a match," he said as he led them across Park Lane.

"Oh?" Charity replied. "Whatever did she say?"

Marcus allowed a grin filled with mischief. "I didn't hear a word *per se*, but rather a squeal."

Dipping her head, Charity felt a moment of pride.

"He looked familiar," Marcus hinted, knowing full well the identity of Mary Baker's caller.

"Mr. Weatherby is Lord Wessex's valet. And butler, I think," Charity replied.

Rolling his eyes, Marcus allowed a chuckle. "Then this will be interesting," he replied. "Wessex thinks his valet expects too much in a wife."

Alarmed, Charity nearly paused mid-step. "In what way?" she asked.

Marcus inhaled as if he were about to respond and then seemed to think better of what he was about to say.

"Because he wants a willing wife?" Charity asked gently.

His eyes widening with her query, Marcus finally gave a nod. "Exactly."

"Well, she is. They both want fidelity. So perhaps this will work."

"She told you that? Miss Baker?"

Charity nodded. "She did. She knows what she wants, and she's unwilling to accept anything less," she explained.

They walked in companionable silence for a time before Charity realized they were in the park. Up ahead, she could make out Mr. Weatherby and a young woman strolling side-by-side, the valet's slight limp not so noticeable from this distance.

"Much like you," Marcus said after a time.

Furrowing a brow, Charity turned her head to regard him, his profile silhouetted against the bright blue sky. She thought of what it would be like to wake up to see that profile every morning, rather startled when a frisson passed through her lower body. "I won't apologize for knowing what I want," she said, not sure how he meant his comment to be construed.

"Neither will I," he replied, pausing so he could turn to regard her.

Charity inhaled and then swallowed. "What is it you think I want?"

"A daughter. A legitimate daughter," he clarified. "But you also want a husband who will love you. A faithful husband who will treat you well. Kiss you in the mornings before breakfast and at night when you come to bed. A lover, who will hold you close and pleasure you until you beg him to stop and then do it all over again until you're pleasantly exhausted," he murmured, thinking of the Stanton House footmen and feeling a bit of jealousy. "Did I miss anything?"

For a moment, Charity wished she was standing closer to the viscount, for she felt a bit light-headed and may have listed a bit as she regarded him. "No," she replied. "That is to say, I don't think so." She allowed a sigh. "So... what is it *you* want? That you'll not apologize for?"

Marcus allowed a wan grin. "You."

Charity gripped his arm a bit harder, as if she had to steady herself. "Me?" she repeated in a whisper.

"Will you marry me, Charity?" he asked. "Please say you will before you faint," he added in a whisper, an arm going around her shoulders to pull her closer. He felt relief when she simply gave into his hold and ended up pressed against the front of his body.

"I will," Charity finally replied. "But first..." She paused and glanced around the park, as if she worried that others might see them in the inappropriate embrace. "You have to get a child on me."

Marcus blinked, and then his immediate frown was soon replaced with a mischievous grin. "I accept your challenge, my lady," he said as he continued to hold onto her but turned around. He started to lead them back toward Stanton House.

"Where are we going?" she asked, struggling to keep up with his quick pace.

"Your future bedchamber," he replied, thinking of the mistress suite that was accessible from his bedchamber by way of the dressing room. "I was thinking I might don a mask and black leather gloves and pay a call on you. Not to steal your jewels, of course, but instead to ravish you before I take my leave at dawn."

What jewels? she almost challenged, but Charity blinked several times, realizing he had conjured this particular scenario sometime in the past. "Ravish me?" she repeated. "And just how do you intend to do that?"

A sly grin touched Marcus's lips. "Why, I plan to worship your body with my lips and tongue. Use my leather-clad fingers to draw little circles all over your heated skin and incite a million darts of pleasure beneath the surface."

Charity swallowed. "A million darts of pleasure?" she repeated, wondering what might have become of meek, mild Marcus Lancaster.

He took great delight in seeing excitement spark in her eyes. "And then I'm going to make love to you—"

"As if you haven't already been doing—"

"Bring you pleasures you haven't ever experienced before—"

"You do realize you're setting rather high expectations?"

"Until you beg me to stop."

A shiver shot down her spine as she stared at him. "You're not teasing, are you?"

Marcus sobered and wrapped an arm around the back of her shoulders. "If I do that, will I be welcome to join you in your bedchamber again?"

Dipping her head in an attempt to hide the blush that colored her face, Charity said, "Possibly."

"And again? It may take more than one try to get a child on you. Maybe a hundred tries."

"Marcus!" she scolded. But she grinned and allowed him his fun, even when he kissed her in broad daylight.

He was going to give her what she wanted, it seemed. The least she could do was let him.

Chapter 42

A CHANGE OF PLANS

The following day

Charity regarded the front of Stanton House a moment before finally stepping out of her town coach. The groom held the door for her and then offered to escort her.

Having just been here just yesterday—and having agreed to one day be this house's mistress—Charity declined the offer. "I am not paying a call on Lord Lancaster," she said with a shake of her head.

The memory of what he had done with her—to her—the afternoon prior had her entire body shivering in delight. Never would she have agreed to such an assignation except that at the moment he accepted her challenge, she found she wanted him to prove himself. Wanted him to have his way with her. Prove his ability between the sheets or fail in the attempt.

He certainly hadn't failed.

Perhaps he might have decided she wasn't what he truly wanted. If that had happened, they could have simply parted on good terms, and she would return to Suffolk.

She wouldn't be returning to Suffolk.

Marcus was at that moment on his way to secure a license so they might wed in a week. She had been about to remind him of his promise to get a child on her first, but she remembered how after their third round of love-making—slow and quiet and ever so satisfying—he had placed a warm hand on her bare belly and held it there before leaning over to place a kiss in the same spot. He did it as if he were blessing her body for the child he was sure had been conceived moments earlier.

She placed a gloved hand there now, remembering how desire for him had bloomed. How her sense of him had changed. How she had come to realize he truly cared for her and would have been satisfied even if she hadn't provided anything in return.

Well, his love for her wasn't about to go unrequited. She would be a fool not to love him in return. A fool not to accept his generous soul without giving him hers.

There was a thought that this was moving entirely too fast—perhaps they should court for a time—but her gaze darted to the note she held in a gloved hand, and she knew that time would be better spent as his viscountess. As his wife. As his lover.

The missive, written in a neat script, had been delivered earlier that morning by a footman from Lord Wessex's townhouse.

> *Dear Lady Wadsworth,*
> *I am writing with the express purpose to thank you for your efforts on my behalf vis-a-vis a wife. I wish to share*

with you the happy news of my betrothal to a housemaid in Stanton House.

However, I will not be marrying Miss Baker.

The words had Charity's good mood turning to sadness for Miss Baker. The young housemaid seemed eager to meet the valet, even though there was an under-current of caution in her manner. Almost as if she had resigned herself to having to marry and had decided to simply accept whoever was offered.

When Charity continued reading the missive, she was glad she was alone, for her mouth dropped open and she let out a sound of surprise not usually associated with a countess.

Miss Baker is, in fact, my sister. For reasons I will not expand upon in this letter, neither Miss Baker nor I use our true family name, Jones, so of course I do not blame you for attempting to make an unholy match.

Our meeting was a fortuitous one, though, for Miss Parker, a lady's maid in Lord Lancaster's employ, served tea. From the moment she stepped into the room, the young lady had my complete and undivided attention. After only a few minutes in her company, she had my respect and admiration. Another ten minutes, and she had my heart.

Never mind that her hair is not dark, but blonde. That she has it cut short to allow the natural curls to frame her beautiful face. That she is nothing as I described to you when you asked what I sought in a wife. I will be marrying a virtuous woman who is not the least bit bothered by my infirmity, and so I am blessed. As to that other trait I sought, I realize it falls onto me to ensure my wife is willing. A challenge I look forward to with utmost happiness.

In fact, yesterday would have been a perfect day except that I left my poor sister in a state of stunned disappointment. Perhaps you have another client to whom you can introduce her? One who can overlook her apparently fast reputation?

I thank you again for your assistance.

Yours in service,

Mr. Roger Weatherby

The door to Stanton House opened even before Charity could lift the brass knocker. Harrison appeared and stepped aside.

"I wondered if I might have a moment with Miss Baker?" she asked as she held out the calling card for 'Finding Wives for the Wounded'. "I don't wish to take her from her duties, though."

Harrison angled his head and gave it a shake. "I am quite sure Mrs. Barstow will not mind," he said, his normally staid expression suggesting a hint of amusement. He led her to the adjacent salon and said he would see to tea. Before she could put voice to a protest—she didn't intend to stay more than a few minutes—the butler disappeared, leaving her in the salon.

Allowing a sigh, she took a seat in one of the chairs, glanced around, and gave a start of surprise. Such a pleasant little parlor, populated with a few upholstered chairs in a floral pattern, a low tea table, a fireplace, and a half-round table beneath the room's only window. And in the chair she'd had her back to when she entered the room was Marcus.

"Don't blame Harrison," he said with a grin. He

moved to place a kiss on her cheek before taking the chair opposite. "I saw your coach pull up and asked him to bring you here."

"It's a beautiful salon," she said, dimpling when she noticed how he gazed at her.

"Only because you're in it," he replied. "Have you come to... see me?" he asked, his uncertainty apparent.

Charity shook her head. "I thought you would be at the bishop's seeing to a license."

He pulled a paper from his topcoat pocket. "All done," he said, referring to the marriage license he held. "We just have to... set a date. That is... if you still—?"

"How soon can we wed?"

Marcus blinked. He had half-expected she might claim to have changed her mind. "We have to wait a week," he replied, just then regretting not having purchased a special license instead of the standard marriage license.

"A week, then," she said on a sigh. "But I have a favor to ask—"

"Anything. It's yours," he replied.

Charity's eyes darted to one side. She supposed she shouldn't be surprised he would pretend to be so accommodating. Why, she was sure he had assumed she had changed her mind and was there to beg off. "I would really hate to leave my position at the charity, especially since Lady Bostwick has had so many leave before me, all because they wed," she explained.

"You wish to keep matchmaking?" The query came out sounding not the least bit judgmental. Nor did he sound surprised.

"I do. Although I've had a bit of a setback with one couple, I've had good success with others... and I'd like to continue."

Marcus lifted a shoulder, as if to shrug. "If it's what you want, I certainly have no objections."

Charity blinked. "You don't?"

He shook his head. "I want you to be happy," he replied. "I will want to have a groom stay close while you're at the office, of course. See you home safely."

Dipping her head, Charity took a breath. "I'm going to fall in love with you, aren't I?"

Mischief appeared in Marcus's eyes. "Aren't you already?" he countered with a grin. "If not, I'd like to invite you to join me for the day. Maybe in the same bedchamber we were in yesterday, so that I might convince you."

A frisson shot through Charity, and she was sorely tempted to accept the offer. "Perhaps... later," she replied.

"You're welcome to move in now," Marcus said, his face brightening with the thought she would spend some time with him on this day. "Stay the night, if you'd like," he added, even though he knew she wouldn't do such a thing.

Charity's eyes widened before she let out a giggle. "Perhaps I'll have a few things brought over," she replied.

Marcus was about to say something else—his gaze had gone to the note she held—but Miss Baker appeared at the door with a tea tray, and he stood up. "I'll leave you to it, then," he murmured, just then realizing he didn't know *why* Charity was there. Or why Miss Baker was delivering tea. He had thought their business was concluded now that the housemaid was marrying.

"I hope that you don't mind, but I'm taking one of your housemaids away from her duties for a time."

He gave a private smile. "She'll be one of *your* house-maids soon enough, so what does it matter?" he said in a hoarse whisper. His gaze fell on the necklace she wore, one with purple stones, and he remembered the necklace he had given his wife when Analise was born. "I'll be upstairs. I am reminded of something I need to give to my daughter," he murmured, giving her a kiss on the cheek.

Charity watched her future husband leave the room as Mary dipped a curtsy and then stepped in. "Do take a seat, Miss Baker," she said. She waited until Mary had placed the tea tray on the low table and settled herself into the chair across from her. "Hullo, Mrs. Seward."

"First, I wish to apologize," Charity stated.

"But why?" Mary asked. She was in the middle of pouring a cup of tea and stopped.

Charity held up the letter. "I heard from your brother, Mr. Weatherby, this morning."

Visibly relaxing, Mary allowed a wan grin. "Oh, that," she said. "You couldn't have known we were related," she added with a shake of her head.

"True, and at least it seems your brother has a potential wife in Miss Parker."

"Oh, she's over the moon about it," Mary agreed, a grin splitting her face. "But then, so am I." She offered the tea to the matchmaker.

Taking the cup and saucer, Charity furrowed a brow. "You're happy for your brother, no doubt, and gaining a sister, but you must feel as if you've been... cheated."

Mary took a sip of tea and regarded the matchmaker for a moment. "Not at all. One of the footmen here —Rodney—"

"The one with the red hair?"

"Him, yes. He was so jealous when he discovered I was going to meet with Mr. Weatherby that he proposed marriage."

Charity blinked. "Just... just like that?"

Mary nodded, helping herself to a biscuit. "I accepted his offer yesterday, 'specially when he said he would carry my coal buckets for me."

At first thinking to say 'best wishes' to the housemaid, Charity allowed a frown. "But not *just* because he's going to carry the coal buckets for you?" she half-asked, remembering what Mary had said she did in exchange for the services of the tall footman.

Mary twinkled. "No. We're learning how to kiss," she whispered.

Charity was sure she blushed, even though she was expecting the housemaid to say something completely inappropriate. "We shall have to see to it you're given larger quarters," she commented. "Since I must meet the housekeeper on other matters, I can bring it up with her."

Her eyes widening in question, Mary said, "That's very kind of you, my lady."

"Yes, well, it means the room you move out of will be available for my lady's maid, Thompkins."

Charity had thought to let Marcus inform his household he would be taking a wife, but if the staff heard the news from a fellow servant, it would save him from having to make the announcement. "I agreed to marry Lord Lancaster yesterday." She watched Mary carefully, wondering how the housemaid would react to the news.

"Then best wishes are in order," Mary replied, although the joy she had exhibited only moments earlier seemed to have disappeared.

"Thank you." Noting the change in the housemaid's demeanor, Charity asked, "What is it?"

Mary set down her cup and saucer. "I suppose you'll

be letting me go then, given what you know about me an' all." She struggled to breathe, as if tears were about to fall.

"On the contrary," Charity replied, leaning forward to add, "I rather appreciate already having met one of my maids."

"Even knowing what you do about me?" Mary challenged.

Charity knew to what she referred, but said, "That you've a mind of your own, and you know what you want? What you like?"

Mary's eyes darted to one side. "I suppose I do," she hedged. "What about my reputation? For... for being willing?"

Charity sighed. "Since you're about to be married, I should hope you willingness will only extend to your husband."

"I told him I would only let him tup me," Mary agreed.

Hoping her face wasn't as pink as she thought it might be, Charity gave a slight shrug. "Then I shouldn't think your willingness will a problem for your position."

"It won't, ma'am," Mary assured her. She took in a stuttering breath. "Is there anything else, ma'am?"

Charity shook her head. "Best wishes to you, Miss Baker." She watched as the housemaid stood, dipped a curtsy, and hurried from the salon. About to stand up to go, Charity decided instead to enjoy another cup of tea and a biscuit.

And she might have finished both, except a certain viscount had other ideas just then.

Chapter 43

WAITING FOR AN ARRIVAL
OR TWO

*S*tanton House, nine months later

"I cannot believe I allowed this to happen," Marcus said as he paced in his study.

Luke passed him, pacing the other direction. "Allowed?" he repeated. "This isn't something you could have allowed or disallowed, or unallowed, or whatever the word is," he argued. "This... just happens. It's supposed to happen." He reached the end of the study, turned on his heel, and headed the other direction at the same moment his father-in-law did the same at the other end of the room.

"Besides, you made a promise to her."

"Did you make one to my daughter?"

"Of course. Or she made one to me."

"I should never have let you marry her."

"I would have just taken her to Scotland," Luke countered.

"Gentlemen, your arguments are fruitless," George Bennett-Jones said from where he sat in one of the leather chairs, one ankle resting on the other knee. Unlike the two viscounts pacing in front of him, he was completely relaxed, as was Teddy Streater, who sat on the nearby divan. "They'll come when they're good and ready. Teddy's did, finally," he commented, remembering how panicked Theodore Streater had been that afternoon a few months ago when Daisy had given birth to a boy. George feared his best friend would suffer a coronary before Elizabeth appeared carrying the swaddled babe. At least he hadn't hurt himself when he fainted upon seeing the newborn for the first time. The boy wasn't that ugly. A bit wrinkled looking, but his face had smoothed out and was now usually home to a rather pleasant expression, especially when someone was giving him attention.

As Teddy was doing at the moment.

"Oh, I suppose you know all about this?" Luke replied, his manner suggesting he was about to punch something.

"As a matter of fact, I do," George replied, straightening in the chair. "I have three of them now, and I played midwife for the first."

This bit of news had Marcus and Luke halting their steps so they stood directly in front of George. "Midwife?" Marcus repeated as he turned to regard the younger viscount.

"Indeed. David was quite insistent he wanted out, and Elizabeth was helpless to stop him," George replied. "So, I did what I had to." He allowed a wan grin. "I wouldn't have missed it for the world," he whispered. "Although it was a messy business."

"You must have been panicked," Luke said, his own state of unease apparent in how beads of perspiration dripped from his temples.

"I couldn't afford to be, actually," George said with a

shrug, remembering how he had to remain calm—at least on the outside—for Elizabeth's sake. "That's not to say I wasn't feeling exactly as you two are this very moment when the last two were born," he added, daring a glance in the adjacent chair. His newest son was sound asleep. "You especially," he added with a nod to Marcus. "A child and a grandchild on the same day? I can't imagine it happens very often." He pointed to the carpet. "By the way, my study's carpet looks much the same."

The other two viscounts glanced down at their feet, immediately understanding George's comment. There was a well-worn path in the Aubusson carpeting.

A knock at the open door had all four of them turning their attention to Elizabeth, Viscountess Bostwick. She stood holding a swaddled baby in one arm, a huge grin on her face. She turned her attention to the baby. "Miss Batey, may I have the honor of introducing you to your father?" she asked. Then she offered the bundle to Marcus, who stood with his mouth hanging open. "You do remember how to do this?" she asked when she noted how he hesitated.

"Miss Batey?" he repeated. A huge grin appeared, and he stepped forward to take the babe. "How is she? Charity, I mean?" The other two viscounts dared a glance at the sleeping baby, not surprised Marcus seemed to know exactly how to hold it. He had three other children, after all.

Elizabeth gave a nod. "She's sleeping at the moment, but I'm sure she'll be awake soon, if you'd like to go up."

Marcus nodded to the other men and hurried out of the study, about to take the stairs two at time in his haste to get to his wife.

"What about Analise?" Luke asked, worry etched in

his face. He appeared at least ten years older than he usually did. A sleepless night contributed to his weariness.

"When I left her..." Elizabeth paused and angled her head as if she were listening. A faint baby's cry reached her ears. "I'll know in a moment." She hurried back up the stairs as Luke moved to stand at the bottom of the staircase.

George and Teddy followed him out of the study and stood next to him. "You've been massaging your wife's feet?" George asked in a whisper.

"Every night," Luke replied with a nod.

"And doing the other things we discussed?"

Luke gave him a quelling glance. "That would be none of your business," he replied before he finally allowed a wan grin. "Whenever I had a chance," he whispered. "Or she asked me to."

George gave his fellow viscount a knowing grin. "Ah, the demands of impending fatherhood," he said on a sigh. A giggle came from the study, and he went back in to retrieve his spare heir. "Ah, you've discovered your toes," he said before lifting the four-month-old into his arms "And you've gained another stone. How *do* you manage that?"

Luke gave him a glance from where he stood rooted at the base of the stairs. "He looks the same to me," he commented. His brows furrowed and he turned his gaze onto George. "I am nervous."

"As you should be."

"Frightened, actually," he whispered.

"No need to be," Teddy chimed in.

"What if she...?"

"She'll be fine," George said in a quiet voice, hefting his son onto his shoulder, one hand beneath the babe's bottom.

"How can you be so sure?"

George dipped his head and considered how to respond. He didn't really know if Analise would survive the childbed, but he didn't want the younger viscount panicked any more than he was already. "Because I have faith in the midwife and in my wife," George replied, his face breaking into a huge smile when Elizabeth appeared at the top of the stairs.

"A bit anxious, are you?" she chided.

Elizabeth didn't have a chance to take a step down, for Luke bounded up the stairs, two steps at a time. "Is she all right?" he asked, ignoring the bundle Elizabeth held.

"She's tired, but she's awake," she replied, about to offer him the babe she held. Elizabeth furrowed a brow as she watched the young viscount hurry off toward his wife's bedchamber.

"First time father," George said as he climbed the steps. "I know exactly how he feels, poor man. More concerned for his viscountess than for his heir. Or his daughter," he commented, lifting a brow in question.

"An heir," Elizabeth said, holding the babe out so he and Teddy could take a look. Her gaze went to her own son, who showed a toothless grin and giggled when he caught sight of her. "And you're just flirting because it's nearly your dinnertime," she scolded.

"I would do the same if my sustenance came from your breast," George whispered, leaning over to kiss his wife.

"And here I thought it did," she teased.

He arched a brow and said, "Touché," before daring a glance in the direction Luke had taken. "How long before Wessex realizes he was supposed to take the babe from you?" George asked.

"Oh, any moment, I should think," she replied, following his line of sight. "I suppose you four enjoyed some brandy whilst you waited?" she half-asked.

Teddy frowned. "Not a drop," he said with a shake of his head. "Lancaster didn't offer, and I was afraid they would be too foxed if I suggested opening the brandy." He gave his son a kiss on the forehead, noting how the boy seemed to hang on his every word. "A couple of nervous viscounts, those two."

Elizabeth grinned, and then allowed a titter when Luke appeared from his wife's bedchamber and hurried towards her.

"I forgot something," he said, standing before her with an expression of uncertainty.

"Some*one*, don't you mean?" Elizabeth chided. "What will you name him?" She held out the swaddled babe and helped position it in his arms, although he already seemed to know what to do. She raised an eyebrow. "You've done this before," she murmured with appreciation.

"Younger nieces and nephews," he acknowledged. He stared at the babe he held, all bald and wrinkly, and then he hefted the bundle, as if he were determining the babe's weight. "He's quite solid," he said before he finally allowed a grin of relief. "I was thinking of naming him Mark, but now I'm wondering if I should consider Abraham," he murmured.

George frowned and shook his head. "Mark," George said firmly. "For your grandfather and brother, and for her father. It's perfect."

Luke gave a nod, then a bow. "I must take my leave of you. Thank you all for your help." He seemed uncertain of what else to say and disappeared into his wife's bedchamber.

"Well, I think that's our cue to take our leave," George said before kissing his son's forehead again.

Elizabeth gave him a nod. "I'd like to look in on Charity just one more time," she said, as if she'd just then remembered something. "Let her know about one of her clients."

"Oh? Which one?"

"Mr. Weatherby. He's valet to Wessex, in fact," she said, which explained the reason she was reminded to mention something to Charity. "He married one of the lady's maids in Lancaster's household last year," she explained.

"And?" he prompted.

"My lady's maid said that a footman from this house told her that Charity's lady's maid said that a housemaid from Wessex's house told her that Mr. Weatherby's wife, who used to work as a lady's maid in Stanton House, gave birth to a baby boy last week."

George blinked and glanced around. "We're *in* Stanton House, my love," he said.

A brilliant smile appeared on Elizabeth's face before she sobered. "Oh, that's capital. Then Charity must already know of her success," she murmured.

"I would think so," Teddy agreed, although from his expression, it seemed he was still trying to sort all the relationships. "Wouldn't that be Lady Wessex's lady's maid?"

Elizabeth allowed a giggle, which had both baby boys reacting in delight.

"Come. Let's take our boys home," George said as he offered his arm. "After spending so much time with these nervous viscounts, I need a drink."

"Me as well," Teddy said.

"As do I," Elizabeth agreed. She glanced at her son,

still in her husband's arms. "As will he in a moment or two." She placed a hand on his arm and they descended the steps, happy to be taking their leave of Stanton House.

"I cannot believe you forgot our son," Analise chided her husband, when Luke returned to her childhood bedchamber carrying their first baby.

"I was worried about you," he replied as he took a seat on the edge of the bed. "Are you going to recover?"

Analise nodded. "I'll be fine," she insisted. "A good night's sleep, and I'll be ready for the next ball." The babe began to fuss, and she rolled her eyes. "In a few months," she added as she took the bundle from Luke and placed the babe at her breast. "I suppose you'll want to be going to your club this evening?" she half-asked, her voice light despite her comment.

"I will not," Luke replied, watching in wonder as his son latched onto his wife's breast and took his first meal. "I really don't care how much money I made from the betting books on him," he added.

Analise blinked. "Betting books?" she repeated in surprise.

Luke shook his head. "Happens with every babe born in the *ton*. Bets are placed on if it will be a boy or a girl."

"And how did you bet?" she asked with an arched brow.

Taken aback by the question, he said, "Why, a boy, of course!" He reached into a pocket and pulled out a small box. "This is for you."

Her eyes widened. "What is it?" she asked.

He lifted the lid and showed her a pair of amethyst earrings.

"Luke! They'll go perfect with my mother's necklace and bracelet," she breathed. Her father had given her the amethyst necklace the day he announced he would be marrying Charity. The day after Luke had proposed to her.

"I hope so. That was the plan, anyway. Perhaps you can wear them to the next ball we go to," he suggested.

"I will," she agreed, thinking of one of the ballgowns Madame Suzanne had created for her as part of her wedding clothes. The purple stones would look stunning with the green and purple satin gown. She took a deep breath. "How did you know I was going to give you an heir?"

Luke allowed a shrug. "I didn't know for sure. But you were carrying high, and my aunt always had boys when she was carrying high," he said as he held the flat of his hand up against his chest.

Analise blinked at hearing this. He hadn't said a thing to her about how high she was carrying the newborn. "Did my stepmother have a girl?" she asked then, moving her son to her other breast.

"She did," Luke replied with a nod. "Ugly little thing. All wrinkly and red."

"Luke!" she scolded. "What a horrible thing to say about my one and only sister!" But she grinned as she held her boy.

"I apologize," he replied in a quiet voice. "I'm a bit bitter about that one."

Analise furrowed a brow. "But, why? Father and Charity both wanted a girl."

Luke sighed. "Yes, but I bet your father she would have a boy."

Her mouth dropping open in disbelief at this bit of

news, Analise gave a very unladylike snort. "Serves you right," she replied.

"Does, doesn't it?" he replied with a grin. Then a bit of mischief had his eyes twinkling. "There's always next time."

"*S*he's beautiful," Marcus said as he stared down at the sleeping babe he held. The fingers of one of her hands had gripped his index finger, their tiny fingernails white against his tanned fingers. "You're beautiful," he added before leaning down to kiss his wife.

"I must look like a drowned rat," Charity replied, her eyelids heavy. Despite having given birth to two boys in the past, she had done it so long ago, she had forgotten what it was like.

Deliberately, she sorted.

"Not at all," he countered, his voice sounding as if he were scolding her. He sat on the edge of the bed, heartened to see his new daughter opening her eyes. "Are you well?" he asked as he used his free hand to take one of Charity's hands to his lips. He kissed the back of it but didn't let go.

Charity nodded, deciding she shouldn't be surprised at how attentive he was just then. He had stayed home every night for the past few weeks, determined to remain at her side in the event she went into labor. "I am well. Just tired," she assured him. "Now that you've had a chance to hold her, do you still like the name we chose for a girl?"

Marcus stared at the infant for a moment, mesmerized by her tiny hands and nose, the curly lashes and rosebud lips. He was reminded of how Analise looked when she was first born. "Hope," he murmured as he stared at his newest daughter. "It certainly fits the situation. Were you having second thoughts?"

Angling here head in a pillow, Charity said, "Perhaps we should name her Faith," she suggested.

"For your sister?" he asked.

She shook her head. "Because you had so much of it." Although Marcus had been assuring Charity all along she would give birth to a girl—he had promised her he would give her a daughter—Charity had secretly expected to deliver another boy.

"Faith Hope Batey," he said as he regarded the sleeping baby. "Agreed. Now what do you suppose they're going to name her nephew?"

But Charity's eyes were closed, sleep having taken her for a moment. Alone with his daughter, Marcus was about to ask her some questions, but she, too, nodded off.

"Well," he murmured, settling himself into the room's only chair. "Let's see what my imagination can come up with," he said to no one in particular.

AFTERWORD

Thank you for taking the time to read The Charity of a Viscount. *If you enjoyed it, please consider telling your friends or posting a short review. Word of mouth is an author's best friend.*

Thank you,
Linda Rae Sande

ABOUT THE AUTHOR

A self-described nerd and lover of science, Linda Rae spent many years as a published technical writer specializing in 3D graphics workstations, software and 3D animation (her movie credits include SHREK and SHREK 2). Mythology, immortality, and ancient Greece have been lifelong interests.

A fan of action-adventure movies, she can frequently be found at the local cinema. Although she no longer has any tropical fish, she does follow the San Jose Sharks. She makes her home in Cody, Wyoming.

For more information:
www.lindaraesande.com
Sign up for Linda Rae's newsletter:
Regency Romance with a Twist

* 9 7 8 1 9 4 6 2 7 1 1 9 8 *